With the Slightest Touch

A woman with hair the shade of a full moon and eyes the color of violets captured his gaze. She stepped toward him. "Let me see your hands."

"I beg your pardon?"

She grabbed his wrist, turned up his hand, and placed her palm against his. He was unprepared for the jolt of warmth her touch sent through him. There was nothing in her caress to entice a man, and yet, he experienced a keen sense of loss when she released her hold on him. He closed his hand as though by doing so, he could recapture her touch.

"It's the characters that make a romance meaningful, and Ms. Heath has created some gems."
Romantic Times

LORRAINE HEATH

A Rogue in Texas

AVON BOOKS ◆ NEW YORK

AVON BOOKS, INC.
1350 Avenue of the Americas
New York, New York 10019

Copyright © 1999 by Jan Nowasky
Excerpt from *The Last True Cowboy* copyright © 1998 by Kathleen Eagle
Excerpt from *The Runaway Princess* copyright © 1999 by Christina Dodd
Excerpt from *The Sweetest Thing* copyright © 1999 by Barbara Freethy
Excerpt from *A Rogue in Texas* copyright © 1999 by Jan Nowasky
Excerpt from *Someone to Watch Over Me* copyright © 1999 by Lisa Kleypas
Inside cover author photo by Work of Art Studio Portraits
Published by arrangement with the author
Library of Congress Catalog Card Number: 98-93887
ISBN: 0-380-80329-1
www.avonbooks.com/romance

First Avon Books Printing: April 1999
First Avon Books Special Printing: January 1999

AVON TRADEMARK REG. U.S. PAT. OFF. AND IN OTHER COUNTRIES, MARCA REGISTRADA, HECHO EN U.S.A.

Printed in the U.S.A.

WCD   10 9 8 7 6 5 4 3 2 1

For Nana,
with love

1

July, 1865

Grayson Rhodes' father had always warned him that he would burn in hell, but he had never expected to arrive at the damnable place while he was still alive.

Sitting in the rear of the wagon, Grayson suffered through the sweltering heat that clung to his body. Flies and gnats joyfully buzzed around his ears as the vehicle bounced over the rough road. He would have thought the seven men crowded into the abominable mode of transportation would have kept the damn thing on an even keel. How the man to his left—Christian Montgomery—could sleep through the incessant jostling was beyond Grayson's comprehension, but he had to admire Kit's ability to do so.

Unlike his traveling companions, Grayson had long ago given up any pretense at being a gentleman. He'd tossed his cravat aside, removed his jacket, loosened the top buttons on his white linen shirt, and

1

rolled his starched cuffs past his elbows. But none of his efforts diminished the suffocating heat.

With his sleeve, he wiped the sweat from his brow. He could do nothing to prevent the beads trickling down his back.

He sliced his narrowed gaze to Benjamin P. Winslow, who sat on the bench seat beside the driver. The rotund man had convinced the fathers of every man in the wagon into paying him five hundred pounds to bring their wayward sons to Texas and make men of them.

Grayson shifted his weight, wincing as a splinter jabbed his backside. If he ever had occasion to travel by coach again, he would not take its comforts for granted.

And although he was beginning to have doubts that fortune truly awaited him here, after this excursion into hell, he knew he now had a chance to gain with hard work what his father could not bequeath him—respect.

"What do you make of that?" a deep voice grumbled.

Grayson cut a quick glance to Harrison Bainbridge, second son of the Earl of Lambourne, before gazing in the distance. Heat rose from the earth, creating walls of shimmering white flames. Beyond them, shadows of two or three buildings hovered.

"Satan's throne, perhaps?" Grayson suggested drolly.

Harry flashed the easy grin for which he was famous. "I'll wager five pounds that it's an inn, and we'll finally have beds in which to sleep."

"I would take you up on it, but you've already managed to swindle me out of the two shillings I had jingling within my pockets."

"I'll be glad to mark you down for it. I know you're good for it—or you will be, once we've reached our destination."

"How can you be so certain?" Kit asked.

Grayson snapped his attention to the man sitting beside him. "I thought you were asleep."

Kit gave him a laconic smile, his pale blue eyes effectively shielding the windows to his soul. More than one woman had referred to them as eyes of the devil after she'd succumbed to his infamous charms. "I've merely been pondering our situation and trying to remember what possessed us to climb into this wagon once we'd docked at Galveston."

"Winslow's promise of fortune had us eagerly clambering aboard," Grayson reminded him. "The notion of becoming men of means in our own right and rubbing our fathers' noses into it appealed to us."

"An appeal that lessens as each day progresses. Perhaps we should consider jumping ship, as it were, and heading back to Galveston. I'm certain we could find a gaming hall or two." He smiled in anticipation. "Along with some feminine entertainment."

"And abandon fortune?" Grayson asked. "I think not."

The driver guided the wagon onto a narrower, rougher dirt road than the one upon which they'd been traveling. On one side of the road, dark green cotton stalks reached toward the sun. Grayson had seen the crops growing in a few fields along the route. The abundance of growth in Texas surprised him.

As the wagon continued on, he was able to distinguish the shapes of women and children toiling between the neatly planted rows. They ceased their labors and began walking through the fields toward the road, toward the wagon, falling into step behind it.

"Winslow, shouldn't we offer them a ride?" Kit called out.

"It's not much farther," Winslow assured him.

When they neared what Grayson had taken for Satan's throne, he realized it was nothing more than a barn. A simple clapboard house stood nearby, blue gingham curtains fluttering through the open windows. He doubted extra beds awaited them here. He cursed himself for not taking Harry up on his wager.

The driver drew the team of horses to a halt. The wagon rocked as Winslow lifted his portly body from the bench seat and turned, tottering as though he were a child's toy until he gained his balance. His smile broad, his black eyes gleaming beneath his black top hat, he folded his fingers around the lapels of his brown wool tailcoat. "Gentlemen, we have arrived!"

Grayson felt as though he'd just stepped into the middle of a boxing ring with his eyes closed. Apparently, he was not the only one. His traveling companions' mouths went agape and their eyes bulged. Harry struggled to his knees. "Exactly where have we arrived?"

"To the fields where you'll work."

"Are you telling us that all this time when you assured us that fortune awaited us, you were talking about our working in bloody fields?"

"Indeed I am, lad."

"Bloody hell, who would have thought he meant for us to become common field laborers?" Harry demanded.

"Obviously, none of us," Kit said. "Or we wouldn't be here."

"Come on, lads, hoist yourselves out of the wagon. The ladies are waiting!" Winslow exclaimed.

Against his better judgment, Grayson climbed out, his booted feet hitting the ground and creating a cloud of dust. His aching body protested the movement. He longed for a soft bed and an even softer woman. Unfortunately, he doubted either was in supply at this rut in the road.

An awkward silence descended as the women gathered before them, many as barefoot as the children peering around their threadbare skirts. Some women attempted hesitant smiles, but their wary gazes revealed their emotions more clearly. Grayson was beginning to understand how a fox felt near the end of the hunt.

A woman with hair the shade of a full moon captured his attention. She looked worn, as though whatever dreams she might have once held had been turned under the soil and never bloomed.

She stepped toward him, so close that he was forced to look down to meet her gaze. He saw her body twitch as though she suddenly realized she stood closer than she'd intended, but to step back now would reveal her mistake. She angled her chin in defiance, and he somehow knew she was the kind of woman who would stand her ground rather than hop back out of harm's way. Her violet eyes challenged him.

"Let me see your hands," she demanded.

"I beg your pardon?"

She grabbed his wrist, turned his hand up, and placed her palm against his. Her roughened hand was callused, dry, and cracked, leaving him completely astonished by the jolt of warmth her touch sent spiraling through him. He jerked his gaze from her work-worn hand to her provocative eyes and saw bewilderment swirling within the violet depths.

She parted her lips slightly, almost breathlessly, and he was hit with the realization that he had not drawn a breath since she'd touched him. What was it about her—

She dropped his hand and stepped back as though she couldn't remember why she'd grabbed it to begin with. Her caress possessed nothing to entice a man, and yet he experienced a keen sense of loss now that their contact had been severed. He closed his hand as though by doing so, he could recapture her touch.

She gave her head an almost imperceptible shake. The bewilderment retreated and the challenge returned in full force, more intriguing than before. She spun on her heel and faced Winslow. "What in the hell did you think you were doing, bringing these men here?"

"I brought them so they might have the opportunity to learn a trade, to put in an honest day's labor—"

"His hand feels like satin. It'll be bleeding before noon—"

"We don't have any choice, Abbie," another young woman said. Her hair was the same flaxen shade, but her blue eyes contained none of the other's fury. She placed her hand on Abbie's shoulder, a comforting gesture that spoke of more than friendship. Grayson had often seen Kit do the same thing with his brother. More than their similar features, the strong bond that vibrated between them told him they were sisters.

"We've got a little over a month before that cotton is ready to be harvested," the other woman continued softly. "We all agreed to let Mr. Winslow bring men to work the fields."

Abbie flung her hand out in a circle. "But look at them, Elizabeth. They've never worked in fields from dawn until dusk—"

"Neither did I before the war. They can learn. Their hands will toughen up," Elizabeth assured her.

"Maybe. If they stay long enough."

"Perhaps if we gave them a Texas welcome instead of acting like a belligerent Yankee—"

"I wasn't acting like a belligerent Yankee," Abbie retorted.

Grayson found her blush fascinating. He'd never known a woman's cheeks to burn so brightly, but then the women he'd known had blushed becomingly on demand in order to entice a man, never to reveal their anger or absolute embarrassment.

"You weren't welcoming either."

"You can't honestly tell me they are what you were expecting," Abbie said.

"No, but from the look on their faces, we weren't exactly what they were expecting either."

Turning her attention toward the fields, Abbie folded her arms beneath her breasts. Small breasts. Not at all what Grayson favored, yet he found his gaze lingering where it shouldn't, grateful it had when she heaved a deep sigh.

"Now that they're here, I don't know that John would want foreigners working his land," Abbie said.

"I don't see that we've got a choice," Elizabeth replied. "We lost too many men during the war, and no telling when those that survived will make it home."

Grayson saw the muscles in Abbie's jaw tighten before she gave a brusque nod. Obviously, she begrudgingly accepted that the battle was lost. He found it oddly appealing that she did not accept defeat easily.

"We agreed to room and board one apiece. The sun will be setting soon so we might as well take them home and let them get settled. Which one do you want?" Elizabeth asked.

Abbie shook her head. "I'll just take whatever's left." Turning, she ambled toward the house. Three children—two boys and a girl—rushed to catch up with her.

With an overly bright smile, Elizabeth faced Grayson and his companions. "Gentlemen, I'm Elizabeth

Fairfield. We're happy you're here to work. I suppose we could put everyone's name in a hat and draw to see who stays where."

"Excellent idea," Winslow said. "I'm certain once everyone gets to know each other that all will work out splendidly."

"Johnny!" Elizabeth yelled, and the taller boy following Abbie stopped and glanced over his shoulder. "Bring me some paper and a pencil."

The boy gave a quick nod and raced ahead to the house.

Grayson shoved his hands into his trouser pockets and sauntered to the fields. For as far as he could see, the crops blanketed the earth. Crouching, he scooped up a handful of the rich, black soil. He allowed it to sift through his fingers. It carried the weight of permanence, the promise of wealth.

In England, immense deference was given to a landowner, even if he held no title. Grayson knew he would never inherit a title. But here land burst forth with abundance, stretching for miles, disappearing beyond the horizon. He simply had to determine the easiest, most profitable way to obtain the land. Then, perhaps, he would be able to put his painful shortcomings behind him.

He paid no attention to the droning of Elizabeth Fairchild's voice as she called out each of his companion's names. The fate of others held no interest for him. But the land was another matter. It fascinated him. He heard the tread of heavy footsteps and slowly unfolded his body.

"Bad luck, Gray. You got the shrew," Harry announced heartily.

"I'll trade with you," Kit offered.

"I've no desire to trade."

"Why in the bloody hell not?" Kit asked. "The woman took an obvious dislike to you."

"She took a dislike to all of us, but I was left with the distinct impression that this land belongs to her."

"What difference does that make?" Harry asked.

"Probably none, but I'm simply contemplating possibilities."

"I don't suppose you'd care to share those possibilities?" Kit asked.

Grayson met his gaze directly. "No."

Kit nodded, and Grayson knew he had taken no offense at his desire to hold his own counsel. In the distance, the sun began to sink beyond the horizon.

"I must confess that I find the sunsets here spectacular," Kit murmured.

Grayson agreed, but he didn't possess Kit's penchant for the artistic so he kept his appreciation safely locked away with all the other aspects of himself that might render him vulnerable.

Harry nudged his shoulder. "Do you honestly believe our fathers had any idea what Winslow had in store for us?"

Grayson watched the fiery flames of the retreating sun send streamers of brilliant oranges and reds across the darkening azure sky. "I have no doubt that they knew exactly what he had in mind—enticing us straight into the bowels of hell."

*   *   *

Grayson stood within the doorway, taking in his new residence. The house was small, more like a cottage. The children sat at an oaken table: the two boys on one side, the girl across from them. He assumed the three doors on the other side of this room led into bedrooms. Rugs that looked more like rags were spread about the rough-hewn floor. Two wing-backed chairs of worn material rested near the hearth. A roll-top desk was pressed against one wall.

Simplicity in everything. A sturdiness. A permanence. Above all else a cleanliness, and an atmosphere of warmth that had nothing to do with the hot Texas weather.

Against his will, his gaze came to rest on the woman kneeling before the lazy fire burning within the hearth. Even from this angle, she intrigued him.

Abigail Westland stared at the stew as the thick broth bubbled and burst. Why had she agreed to this insane scheme to bring Englishmen here to work the fields?

The men who had clambered from the wagon could not replace the husbands who had toiled from dawn until dusk. Their skin wasn't leathery from years of fighting nature. They weren't broad in the chest, with arms that stretched the seams on their shirts. Half of them had faces that would no doubt blister by the end of a day working in the field.

More often than not, she was exhausted by nightfall. Tending to a man and his needs was one burden she had no desire to carry.

The soft knock on the wall gave her a start. She twisted around. A tall man stood in the doorway, his hair the color of wheat. Her heart sped up with the realization that he was the one whose hand she had held, the one whose hand had made her wonder what it would feel like to be caressed with something that held as much strength as softness. The strength had surprised her. The silkiness had unsettled her as much as her wayward thoughts, thoughts she'd never entertained with her husband.

She rubbed her hand briskly on her apron, trying to erase the memory. Dear Lord, she should have made her selection when Elizabeth gave her the chance—anyone but him.

A corner of his mouth lifted and his eyes, the deep blue of a sky retreating before a storm, reflected acceptance. "I'm what was left," he said evenly, but his words carried a lilting cadence, the a's spoken as though with a sigh.

Abigail felt the heat of embarrassment scald her face, and rose to her feet. She didn't want to view her home or herself through the eyes of a man who knew nothing of what it was to do without. And she knew by his well-tailored clothes that he'd never been without. What in God's name was he doing here? A lark? A dare? An adventure?

She gave a brusque nod. "You can set your bag by the door for now. You'll be sleeping in the barn, but you don't have to move out there until after supper." She cursed the slight tremble in her voice. "I'm Abigail Westland."

He bowed slightly from the waist and his smile increased. It was a nice smile, an easy smile. She couldn't remember the last time she'd smiled.

"Grayson Rhodes."

She nodded curtly. "Johnny, Micah, and Lydia are my children." Turning slightly, she basked in the glory of the three reasons she worked her fingers to the bone, the reasons she'd agreed to this harebrained idea of bringing men here. "Just take a seat at the table."

The Englishman's footsteps echoed over the planked flooring as he walked confidently to the table. He didn't slouch from years of carrying burdens too heavy for his shoulders.

She noticed her older son glowering at the man. His jaw tightened when the man reached for the chair.

"That's my pa's chair," Johnny ground out.

The man froze, the only movement the slight arching of a brow. "Where is your father?" he asked quietly.

She'd never known a man could speak in such a hushed tone, the deep timbre of his voice calm, comforting. She saw Johnny's bottom lip quiver.

"Damn Yankees killed him!"

"Johnny!" she scolded. "No swearing."

"You call 'em damn Yankees!" her son insisted, his chin quivering.

"Well, I shouldn't," she told him, hating to reprimand him in front of a stranger. She'd discuss manners and swearing with him later. She nearly jumped out of her skin when Grayson Rhodes cleared his throat.

"It seems to me then that circumstance makes you the man of the house. If your mother has no objection, perhaps you could sit in your father's chair, and I might sit in yours,'' the Englishman suggested.

Johnny snapped his head around so fast to catch her opinion on the idea that she was surprised he hadn't grown dizzy and toppled out of his chair. Hope flared within his brown eyes. At eight, he was a strapping boy who very much resembled his father, working hard to make up for his father's absence. Until this moment, she hadn't realized he wanted to take his father's place at the head of the table.

Swallowing past the knot of regret, she gave him a nod of approval before turning back to the hearth. She heard the scraping of chairs across the floor, the shuffling of feet.

''How come you talk funny?'' Lydia asked. A little over six, she was curious about everything.

''Actually, it's you who sound funny to me,'' the Englishman answered.

''How come Ma called you a foreigner?'' Johnny asked.

''Because I *am* a foreigner. I come from a land on the other side of the ocean.''

''How did you get here?'' Lydia asked.

''I traveled on a big ship to Galveston and then I rode in the wagon.''

''What was it like on the ship?'' Johnny asked.

''Children, stop pestering the man,'' Abbie scolded as she wrapped a thick cloth around the handle of the cast-iron pot and lifted it from the hook over the fire. She wanted to know as little about the new worker as possible.

Dipping the ladle into the thick brew, she walked to the table.

Her son sat erect, shoulders back, pride etched into his young face. Tears burned the back of her eyes. Maybe she had never before suggested he sit in his father's chair because she loathed the idea of him becoming a man.

She was grateful that the war had ended before he'd grown any older. A year ago, he and three friends had run away to join the Confederate army, hoping to become drummers. Abigail and her sister, Elizabeth, had found the boys camped beside the Brazos River. Their goal had been to reach Hempstead, a prominent Confederate supply center. Abigail shuddered to think what might have happened if they'd tried to cross the river.

She ladled the stew into the Englishman's bowl first, noticing his hands once again. They rested easily on either side of his bowl, the nails neatly clipped. They didn't carry the stain of dirt or the scars of hard work. Yet they looked more powerful than she'd first thought—capable even—although she wasn't certain what they were capable of.

She strolled around the table, filling bowls, wishing she couldn't feel the Englishman's steady gaze. She resisted the urge to tuck a stray strand of hair back into the netting that held her hair at the nape of her neck. What did she care what he thought of her?

She dropped into her chair and gave the children permission to begin. They dove into their stew with relish. The Englishman skimmed his spoon across the top as though he wasn't quite sure what it was.

"Are there accommodations available in town?" he asked after a time.

"What's accommodations?" Johnny asked from his new position as head of the household.

"A place to stay," Abigail explained before meeting the Englishman's gaze. "The saloon has a few rooms, but it's a two-hour ride by wagon into Fortune."

His brow furrowed as deeply as any freshly plowed field. "Fortune?"

"It's the nearest town."

"Fortune awaits," he mumbled, as though testing the words on his tongue. Then he smiled broadly, tipped his head back, and laughed heartily, the sound causing her heart to twist tightly. Years had passed since she'd last heard such carefree laughter.

Her children stared at the Englishman as though he'd gone mad. Perhaps he had.

"Mr. Rhodes?" she began, wondering at the wisdom of letting a man she did not know into her house.

With seemingly great difficulty, he stifled his laughter. "Old Winslow kept telling us that fortune awaited. All the while, he was talking about a bloody town."

"I suppose that's why you all looked like a good wind would knock you over."

"Yes, we were expecting a bit more—"

"Our home is humble—"

"I wasn't referring to your home. I was referring to our expectations."

Beneath the table, she fisted her hand around her

apron. She didn't know why she had to take offense at every word he said. "The lodgings in town aren't any better than you'll get here. Besides, the time you'd use traveling could be better spent working the fields. That's why we agreed to give you a place to hang your hat."

"I appreciate the consideration."

She watched as he ate his stew in silence. He removed a handkerchief from a pocket inside his jacket and periodically wiped at the corners of his mouth. She felt poor and pitiful next to his refinement.

"I know it's not fancy, but the barn is clean. We put fresh hay up in the loft—"

"I spent much of my youth sleeping in the stable so I have no objection to sleeping in the barn. But I am left with the distinct impression that you don't want me here—"

"What I want and what I need are usually two different things, Mr. Rhodes. The needs of my children come first. I need the cotton picked and I need willing hands to do that."

"Even if the hands are soft?"

She clutched her own hands in her lap. She would be a fool to insult the man further or give him cause to leave. A child could pick a hundred pounds of cotton in a day. An Englishman—even one who had never before worked the fields—should be able to match the efforts of a child.

She remembered how often her own hands had bled when she first began working the fields. Now, they were tougher than cowhide.

"If you work my fields, your hands will bleed and

ache and grow callused. I can promise you that. At the end of the season, you'll receive your share of the profits. But only you'll know if what you gain will be worth what you lose.''

Abigail gazed down at her bowl. The stew had grown cold. She could tell without tasting it, and just as the warmth had left, so had her appetite. She didn't like the thought of being responsible for his care or having a man about the place, but it was necessary. Her entire life consisted of doing what was necessary. Sometimes, alone at night, she found herself longing for the unnecessary—

''I appreciate the meal.''

The words, spoken with a musical lilt, jarred her from her reverie.

''I'll show you to the barn, then,'' she said as she brought herself to her feet.

He did the same with a causal grace that she imagined had accompanied him into the finest dining rooms in England.

She snatched a lantern off the mantel and used the dying embers in the hearth to light it.

''Johnny, get your brother and sister ready for bed,'' she instructed as she walked to the door where the Englishman waited, bag in hand.

''This way,'' she said, stepping onto the porch, into the darkness.

The moon was little more than a whimsical smile in the night sky. The stars glittered like diamonds. As a child she'd once longed to have one of the sparkling gems. Funny how a child could wish for such useless things.

"I put pillows and blankets in the loft," she said to the silent man treading along beside her.

She stopped inside the spacious doorway and held the lantern out to him. "You should be able to find your way from here."

"How is it that Winslow brought us here?"

"My sister Elizabeth told us about him. He said he knew some fathers in England who were looking for a place where their second-born sons could make a go of it, but he needed financing, so we gathered what we had and gave it to him."

"How much?"

She lifted her chin defiantly. "Three hundred dollars, but we'll make more than that if we get the crops in."

"Did he mention that the sons were disreputable?"

She felt her heart tighten as though someone had just thrown a noose around it. The last thing she needed was a man she couldn't trust. "No. He simply said it was unlikely they would inherit so they needed a means to support themselves. Are you disreputable?"

"Very much so."

He smiled warmly, his eyes glinting with amusement. She cursed her fluttering stomach. She wasn't an innocent woman easily swayed by the attentions of an attractive man. She was a widow who understood that a man's needs seldom matched a woman's wants.

Still she had expected him to deny the allegation. She angled her head, trying to determine why a man of questionable reputation would have bothered to give her son his rightful place at the head of her table. "I want to thank you for letting my son sit in his father's chair."

His careless shrug was almost lost in the shadows. "In England, all privileges are bestowed upon the firstborn son. I assumed the same held true here. I'm glad you didn't feel I was overstepping my bounds by suggesting he sit in his father's place."

"No, I'm glad you did. I didn't realize it would mean so much to him. We've just kept the chair empty for so long—waiting for John to come back."

"I'm sorry he didn't."

She nodded briskly, not wishing to discuss her husband. "Since you're here, I assume you're a second son."

Within the lantern's pale golden glow, she saw a profound sadness touch his eyes.

"No, Mrs. Westland. I'm the Duke of Harrington's eldest son." He took the lantern from her and turned away as though he feared bringing the light closer to himself would reveal more than he wished her to know. He stepped into the barn and held the lantern higher, illuminating the cavernous wooden building. "You're quite right. I'll be able to find my way. Good night."

With only the moonlight to guide her, she ambled back toward the house, wondering why a man of privilege would be willing to work in her fields . . . and why he was here if he was the firstborn son.

Hell grew no cooler when night arrived. Instead, the darkness brought with it a heaviness that settled over the land.

Grayson pressed his shoulder against the side of the barn and stared at the moon, the stars. The sky had never seemed so vast or his loneliness so great.

This woman—this Abbie—had deemed him worthless. No surprise there. His father had pointed out his flaws often enough, his illegitimacy being the greatest flaw of all.

His mother had been one of the finest actresses in London. Her final melodramatic performance was to die in childbirth. It was said that the duke had truly loved his mistress, but Grayson often doubted those rumors. For if they were true, would not some of that love have filtered down to their son?

He considered himself fortunate that the Duke had acknowledged his existence. Had even, to his wife's embarrassment, brought the by-blow home and raised him, giving him the finest of clothes and education. But he had never given Grayson the one thing he craved most: love.

Resenting the gifts his father bestowed upon him out of obligation instead of desire, Grayson had decided to become the worthless son his father had always expected him to be. He had gambled away a fortune, drunk enough whiskey to fill the Thames, and bedded every married woman who had a come-hither look. At least if he got a married woman pregnant, she could pass the child off as her husband's—and a child of his would never know what it was to bear the label of bastard. Although to his knowledge, the precautions he'd always excrcised had left no children in his wake.

And being worthless had suited him fine . . . until

today when a woman with violet eyes had touched her palm to his, and he had felt the difference between victory and defeat.

For no matter how worn the woman had appeared, how drab the surroundings, within her eyes, he'd seen the determination to survive—at any cost.

2

*T*he awful din started before dawn greeted the day—the irritating sound of someone pissing on a tin roof.

Grayson's eyes flew open. The loft was still encased in darkness, but beyond it, he saw a dim halo of light. Bits of straw poked into his side as he rolled over.

He crawled across the narrow expanse and peered over the ledge. With a lantern casting a pale glow around him, the older boy sat on a short three-legged stool, his face pressed against the cow's side, his eyes closed. Grayson would have thought the boy was asleep if his hands weren't working to fill the pail with milk.

"Do this every morning, do you?" Grayson asked.

The boy squinted through one eye and nodded. "Yes, sir."

"Always at this time?"

"No, sir. This morning I'm running late."

"Wonderful," Grayson muttered as he dug his

23

hand into his pocket and pulled out his watch. He flipped back the intricately engraved gold cover that bore the Duke of Harrington's crest and turned the face of the watch toward the pale light. Eight minutes after five.

He shoved his watch into his pocket, jerked on his boots, and made his way down the ladder. The odor of the few horses and the couple of cows that shared his dwelling grew stronger.

Leaning against the stall, he watched the boy work. "Is everyone else awake?" he asked.

"Yes, sir," the boy answered, his hands not halting. "Lydia's gatherin' the eggs and Micah's gatherin' the kindling."

"And your mother?"

"Fixin' breakfast. Reckon she'll be expectin' you to sit down with us."

He rather imagined that she would. He wondered what she would serve. Something designed to lay heavy on a man's stomach no doubt—something that would give him the strength he needed to manage a farm. He supposed if he stayed that he, too, would receive morning chores. He could only hope that his would begin at a decent hour—preferably *after* the sun came up. "Do you pick cotton?" he asked.

"Yes, sir. Started pickin' when I was six. Figure I'm big enough that I ought to be able to pick a hundred pounds a day this season."

Grayson searched the recesses of his mind for one moment in his life when his voice and eyes might have reflected the pride he saw mirrored in the boy's.

He couldn't find the spark of a memory. "Is picking cotton hard work?"

The boy scrunched up his face. "It ain't hard. But it's hot and tiring. You ache by the end of the day and you sleep like a dead man." The lad picked up the bucket and set the stool in a corner. "See ya at breakfast."

He ambled out of the barn whistling a melancholy tune that Grayson had heard someone singing on the wharves at Galveston. The words had something to do with wanting to be in the land of cotton. Although based on his first impressions of farm life, he honestly couldn't understand why anyone would want that.

With a heavy sigh, Grayson acknowledged that he'd get no more sleep this morning and decided he needed to locate some warm water. He strode through the barn door and nearly stumbled over his feet at the sight that greeted him.

He wasn't certain what he'd expected. He only knew that he hadn't anticipated seeing the woman standing on the front porch, a cup pressed to her lips, staring into the distance. Without taking her gaze from the far horizon, she ruffled the boy's dark hair as he passed by her on his way into the house. A corner of her mouth tilted up and carried a smile into the violet depths of her eyes. She seemed much younger than she had yesterday, so much younger.

Grayson had no recollection of anyone ruffling his hair as a child: no mother, no servant. He was not the heir apparent, not the one upon whom favors were to be bestowed. He was simply a reminder of his father's youthful folly, a blight upon his father's good name.

The woman shifted her gaze toward him. "Mr. Rhodes, I didn't expect to see you up and about so early."

He didn't want to admit that he wouldn't have been if it weren't for her son milking the cow so instead he walked toward her, rubbing his bristly jaw. "I was wondering where I might find some warm water."

Even in the grayness of dawn, he thought he detected a pink tinge creeping into her cheeks. "My husband used the shaving stand on the back porch. You're welcome to it. I can warm some water and take it back there for you."

"I'd appreciate it." He hesitated a moment before confiding, "Your son tells me that he thinks he'll be able to pick a hundred pounds of cotton a day. Is that likely?"

She smiled softly, her eyes reflecting as much pride as the lad's had earlier. "If my Johnny says he'll pick a hundred pounds, then he'll pick a hundred pounds. He ain't one to fall short of expectations."

Something which could not be said of him. Falling short of expectations was something at which he excelled.

"How much does a man usually pick?"

"My husband could pick well over three hundred pounds a day, but he had years of experience on him."

He felt her gaze travel from the top of his head to

the bottom of his boots, and he knew beyond a doubt that he didn't measure up.

"Are those your only clothes?" she asked.

"I have others, but they look much the same. Most of what I have is in need of a good washing."

"I could loan you a pair of my husband's trousers and an old flannel shirt. He was a sight bigger than you are so they'll probably swallow you, but at least you won't ruin your fancy clothes. You can leave your dirty laundry on the back porch and I'll see to washing it."

"I don't want to impose—"

"It's no imposition. It's part of the deal. You work my fields and I'll see to your needs."

There was no mistaking the blush that suddenly flamed her cheeks.

"Within reason, of course," she stammered before scurrying into the house.

He supposed a woman with three children knew all about a man's needs. But Grayson had never been a man driven by needs. Wants and desires had led him astray more than once, but never needs.

By the time he returned from the barn with his personal belongings, warm water was waiting in a basin on the back porch. A small mirror dangled from a nail on the wall. Luxury took on a whole new meaning.

He'd removed the lather from half his face when he heard the horses. With razor in hand, he turned, unable to stop the smile from spreading across his face as Harry and Kit brought their horses to a halt and dismounted.

"Where did you get those?" Grayson asked as he stepped off the porch and ran his hand along one horse's shoulder.

"The woman who drew my name has several fine horses," Kit said. He raised a brow. "She also allowed me the luxury of shaving indoors."

Reaching out, Harry plucked a piece of straw from Grayson's hair. "What's this?"

Grayson shrugged. "I slept in the barn. Didn't you?"

"No," Harry and Kit said at the same time.

"Had a room and a bed," Harry added.

"The barn wasn't so bad," Grayson said as he stepped on the porch and stared into the mirror. He angled his head and scraped the razor along his cheek. Within the reflection, he saw Kit fold his arms over the porch railing.

"Harry and I have decided to return to Galveston," Kit said. "Did you want to come with us?"

Wiping the remaining lather from his face, Grayson wondered why "Yes!" hadn't exploded from his mouth. "We agreed to come here—to seek our fortunes."

Harry chuckled. "Look, Gray, our fathers paid Winslow to bring us here. As obedient sons, we bowed to their wishes and we came. But now we've seen what awaits us: hard work and tired women. Neither appeals to me. Contrary to what our fathers believe of us, we have sharp minds and a good head on our shoulders. This country was divided by war. Now the war is over, and opportunity awaits any man with the foresight to take advantage of it. But not *here*. There's nothing of value here.''

Except fertile land that needed to be worked.

''These women paid Winslow three hundred dollars to bring us here,'' Grayson said. ''To work their fields.''

''Harry is richer than Midas,'' Kit said. ''He can repay the money if that's what's bothering you.''

''Who'll harvest their crops?''

''I have no desire to watch my hands bleed,'' Harry said. ''As Kit has pointed out, I have the means to set us up in any venture we choose. So we go to Galveston, explore the possibilities, and decide where we want to go and what we want to do.''

Grayson didn't understand why he wasn't packing up his belongings that moment. ''I'm staying.''

''For God's sake why?'' Kit asked.

''A man can pick three hundred pounds of cotton a day. If the three of us leave, that's almost a thousand pounds a day that won't get picked.''

''But it's not our worry,'' Harry pointed out.

''Why?'' Grayson asked, his voice laced with anger and frustration. ''Because we don't need the money despite what our fathers think? Because we didn't pay Winslow? Because we don't want to be here?'' He plowed his fingers through his hair, dislodging more bits of straw. ''I'll catch up with you once the fields are harvested.''

''Fine,'' Harry said with a wave of his hand. ''We'll send word if we leave Galveston and head elsewhere.''

"Do that because I will catch up with you," he promised.

He watched as Harry mounted and urged the horse into a slow lope. Kit hadn't moved from his position at the railing. "What's your true reason for staying?" he asked quietly.

Grayson's gaze fell on the clothes Abbie had laid out for him. He rubbed the homespun cloth between his fingers. Coarse fabric, like the people of Fortune. Yet the material contained a strength that he could not help but admire.

"Have you ever set a goal?" Grayson asked, then grimaced. "I mean other than luring a particular woman into your bed."

Kit grinned. "Does aggravating my father count?"

Grayson gave his head a small shake. "The eldest lad here . . . He can't be much older than eight . . . He was up before the sun, milking a cow."

Kit shrugged. "Because they don't have servants—"

"It's more than that. He did it because it needed to be done. He plans to pick a hundred pounds of cotton a day and he'll take joy in it. I looked in his eyes and saw something I've never before seen. Pride. Not the kind of satisfaction I see in Harry's eyes when he wins a game of chance or what I see on your face when you've seduced a woman. It was a pure kind of self-respect." He shook his head in frustration. "I can't explain it. I only know that I want to experience it."

"And if you don't experience it?"

Grayson snorted. "What will I have lost? A couple

of months of my life when I sometimes feel as though I've lost twenty-eight years?''

Kit rubbed the puckered flesh that lay just below the right side of his jaw and gave a slow nod. ''All right. We'll give it a go, but once the crops are in, we leave for Galveston.''

''You don't have to stay. Besides, I don't think Harry would approve of your decision.''

''I just have to convince Harry that there is something to be gained in staying.''

Grayson had always thought it was a shame that Kit had emerged into the world two minutes after his brother. The Earl of Ravenleigh had applied the tip of a red-hot poker to his second son's jaw moments after he was born in order to permanently mark him so he could never be mistaken for the heir apparent.

''You'll no doubt do it. They say you could talk an angel into sinning,'' Grayson said.

Kit laughed heartily. ''We both know Harry is no angel.''

Clothes made the man—or so Abigail had always heard. But the Englishman looked just as regal in her husband's clothes as he had in his own. Even her husband's tattered straw hat didn't make him look any less worldly.

Strolling along the furrows, Johnny stepping on his heels more often than not, he examined the crops and asked questions as though he cared. Two other Englishmen flanked him on either side. The one with hair the burnished shade of amber seemed equally interested in the fields. The one whose hair shone as black as midnight appeared bored, every so often bestowing upon his friends an indulgent smile. Abigail had little doubt the third man's skin would darken under the sun while his friends' would blister.

Seven Englishmen had arrived. While these three wandered, four were already using hoes to chop at the weeds.

"What do you make of those three?" Elizabeth asked.

Abigail shook her head. "I'm not sure, but Mr. Rhodes isn't going to get any supper if he doesn't lift a hoe before sunset." She cast a glance at her older sister. "Who did you end up boarding?"

"That youngest fella hacking at the weeds there." Elizabeth pointed toward a slender young man whose face was bathed in sweat and scrunched from his efforts. "Jerome Black. He's actually very excited that his father sent him here. But then he's all of nineteen and everyone is excited at nineteen. How were things with Mr. Rhodes last night?"

Abigail shrugged her narrow shoulders. "He didn't put up a protest about sleeping in the barn. And told me he was disreputable."

Elizabeth smiled broadly. "I'll bet he is. He has that look about him."

"What look?" Abigail asked. She had married at sixteen and hadn't dared give even the most casual attention to another man once John had made her his wife.

"Like a man who takes nothing in life seriously."

"Last night he was smiling and laughing like he

didn't have a care in the world. Thought Winslow had played some prank on him.''

"Winslow told me he was going back to England. Asked me if we wanted him to bring any more men. I told him no.''

Abigail cast her gaze over the land that she had kept going by sheer determination alone. "Good. I'm still not sure how John would have felt about strangers working his land.''

"You can't keep worrying over what John would want. He's dead,'' Elizabeth said. "You've got to think about what you want.''

Guilt assailed Abigail with the reminder of John's death. Always the guilt—never the grief—accompanied thoughts of her husband's death.

Leaving his wife, his family, and his fields, he'd gone to fight in battles half a continent away. He'd boasted that he'd be away only a short time. He'd promised to return home.

Abigail had quickly learned that unkept promises left behind bitter memories.

Elizabeth placed her hand on Abigail's shoulder. "I know it's hard. Not a day goes by that I don't look up the road, hoping to see Daniel again. But he's not coming home, and I have three girls to raise. We had to either bring other men here or move elsewhere. We voted to bring men here. I don't think our husbands would begrudge our desire to stay on the land they once farmed. Think of it as a new start, Abbie, with men who are untouched by the war.''

Untouched by the war. God, she couldn't imagine what it would feel like to be untouched by a war.

How had the women survived where the war had actually raged? Here there had been nothing but deprivation, hard work, and loneliness.

"Why couldn't they have sent their bodies home?" she asked, the question always hovering in the back of her mind. "Maybe I could believe it then."

"That's just not the way it was done. They buried them where they died."

"John would have hated not being buried in Texas."

"Don't think about it—"

"How can I not think about it when he was my husband? I have three of his children to raise and his farm to maintain."

"Which is the reason we brought these Englishmen here. You're not going to marry any of them," Elizabeth said quietly. "You're just gonna have them toil in your fields."

Abigail wiped her roughened hands on her threadbare apron. "It was strange having a man about the place this morning."

"Abbie, not all men are like John."

"I know. I saw the way Daniel treated you."

Elizabeth gnawed on her lower lip and swiped the wisps of blonde hair from her eyes. "I could make room at my place for your Englishman—"

"No, if he's gonna work my land then I need to provide for him."

Elizabeth smiled. "That's a girl. And who knows? With Mr. Rhodes helping out around here, maybe you'll have time to take care of yourself."

Abigail was always amazed that in spite of the hardships, Elizabeth managed to turn her sights toward the positive. With a shake of her head, she returned her sister's smile. "Soon as the hard work begins, they'll be hightailing it back to wherever they came from."

"I don't know, Abbie. Your Mr. Rhodes seems to have decided he wants supper this evening."

Abigail snapped her head around to gaze at the fields. She saw Grayson Rhodes listening intently as Johnny gave him instructions on the proper way to cut at the weeds. She narrowed her eyes. "What in the world is he wearing on his hands?"

"Looks like gloves," Elizabeth said.

"What kind of working gloves come in white?"

Elizabeth furrowed her brow. "I don't know. Maybe that's what English working gloves look like."

"They're a strange lot, Elizabeth, but since we're stuck with them, reckon we'd best get the noon meal set out."

The farmers in the area had never had the means to purchase slaves so they had rotated the fields, working as a community on a different farm each year. That put the responsibility of feeding her neighbors on Abigail's shoulders this season. But she didn't mind. She'd rather cook than work the fields any day.

Sitting on the back porch, Grayson gingerly peeled the glove from his hand, wincing as the cloth pulled at bits of his flesh. He didn't imagine he'd be attending any formal balls while he was in the area so using the gloves to protect his hands had seemed like a good idea—even when Kit and Harry had laughed. But now the gloves were ruined—as were his hands.

He studied his ravaged palms. At least they weren't bleeding. They had blistered and a few of the blisters had ruptured, coating his palm in a sticky substance, but they would heal. And the lad was right. Tonight he would sleep like a dead man. With any luck, perhaps he would actually die before morning.

Dangling his hands over his thighs, he shifted his gaze to the sunset. Despite the blisters, "chopping weeds," as the boy called it, had brought Grayson a measure of satisfaction that he'd never before experienced. His actions served a purpose: to keep the area clear so the roots could breathe and workers could walk along the furrows come harvest time.

The sun was unmerciful as it constantly sent its heat to beat down on a man. Now it was quietly fading away as though content with its day's work.

Grayson heard the squeaking of the back door and glanced over his shoulder. Carrying a large bucket, Abigail Westland slipped through the opening. Grayson slowly brought himself to his feet, his tired body protesting each inch of the journey.

"I warmed some water for you. Thought you might want to wash up." She set the bucket near the basin and wiped her hands on her apron.

He forced himself to smile. "I appreciate it. I imagine I'm rather rank."

Reaching down, she picked up one of the gloves

he'd discarded. She wrinkled her nose at the filthy, stained object. "These aren't working gloves," she murmured.

"No, but they were all I had. I thought they would be better than nothing."

She snapped her head up, a fire burning brilliantly within her violet eyes. "Let me see your hands."

Grayson took a step back. "My hands are fine."

"I don't see how they could be—the way you were chopping at the ground—"

"Was I doing it improperly, then?" he asked, hating the thought that he might have expended his energies fruitlessly.

"No, I didn't expect you to do it at all." The smallest of smiles touched her lips, and he was suddenly seized with the irrational desire to have her ruffle her slender fingers through his hair.

"It needs to be done, does it not?"

"Yep, it needs to be done."

"Well then, I shall endeavor to see that it's done."

Her smile grew a little wider. "You use the fanciest words."

"You people seem to cut everything short. Since we arrived in Galveston, I seldom hear the sound of 'g' on the end of a word."

Her smile flew into hiding, leaving her mouth shaped into a hard line. "With all the work we gotta do, we ain't got time to get all cultured."

"I meant no offense," he said hastily.

"I'll get some salve for your hands and some linen strips for you to wrap around them. You want to keep them clean. You get an infection out here, you're likely to lose a hand.''

He watched her disappear into the house. He had most definitely offended her. He wondered if she were embarrassed that she could not offer him better accommodations than the barn. If perhaps he had come across as haughty and arrogant. God knew he was both.

Self-preservation had caused him to build a wall around himself, brick by brick, until his true self was safely hidden inside, away from prying eyes.

Remembering the woman's smile, he feared she might possess the means to destroy the mortar that held the bricks securely in place.

He was dead tired. He should have fallen asleep as soon as his head sank into the pillow. He should have been unable to feel the straw sticking up through the quilt or the heat surrounding him.

But he was acutely aware of everything, especially the constant burning in his hands. He wished he'd thought to bring the salve to the loft with him. Instead, he'd left it by the basin on the back porch.

He had tossed and turned for hours, but sleep was as elusive as his dreams. Perhaps coating more salve on his palms would lure him into slumber.

With only the moon to guide him, he made his way from the barn. Strolling along the side of the house, he removed the linen from one hand and began to unwrap it from the other. Head down, he rounded the corner and slammed his thigh into something hard. One hand grabbed a wooden edge, but before he could catch his balance, the other hand fell into steaming water and molded itself around a very nice mound of flesh, so silky and smooth that it was more comforting than any salve he could have spread across his aching palms.

The breath knocked out of him, frozen in place, he stared at the woman, her face shadowed by the night. He heard a tiny screech, a loud splash, and felt a small foot kick him hard in the stomach. He staggered back, wrapping an arm around his middle, fighting to draw in air.

"Why aren't you in the barn sleeping?" she demanded.

"I'm . . . terribly sorry," he gasped. "I . . . I couldn't sleep. "My hands . . . I thought if I applied more salve—"

"Get outta here!" she whispered harshly.

"I'd sell my soul for a hot bath." He grinned. "Tell you what. I'll wash your back in exchange for a bath."

"No!"

He heard the horror reflected in her voice, saw her silhouette reaching for the towel hanging over the porch railing. Before she could grab it, he snatched it away.

She sank farther down in the water. "What are you doing?"

Her voice sounded timid, afraid, not at all like that of a woman who had survived years of a war without her husband by her side.

"I won't hurt you, Abbie."

"It's Mrs. Westland to you."

"I'm afraid I know you much too well now for such formality."

"Give me the towel."

"No. I don't want you to cut your bath short because I discovered you."

"I wouldn't have come out here, but I thought you'd be dead to the world," she confessed in a tiny voice.

He knew he had her at a disadvantage and if he were a gentleman, he would hand her the towel and be on his way. Instead he tossed the soft linen onto his shoulder. "As well I should have been."

He strolled around the tub, hearing the water splash as she twisted her body to follow his movements.

"What are you doing?" she asked.

He sat on the top step and stretched out his legs. "Watching you," he said in a low voice.

"You can't!"

"Ah, but I can."

Abigail stared at the man who had just made himself at home on her back porch. "It's scandalous for you to be out here while I'm bathing."

"Who's going to see? If you honestly believed anyone would happen by, you wouldn't be out here."

She suddenly despised logical men. "You're . . . you're . . ." She couldn't think of a word bad enough to describe him or his behavior. In the moonlight, she saw him flash a grin.

"Disreputable?"

"You're no gentleman!" she blurted.

"I never claimed to be. I've always fancied myself

a rogue. A bit of a loner, a little mischievous, but harmless."

She thrust out her hand. "Give me the towel."

"Finish your bath and I'll dry you off."

"No!" She cursed the tremble in her voice.

"What are you afraid of?" he asked quietly. "I won't ravish you—at least not without your permission."

"You touched me!"

"That was an accident. Probably one of the most pleasurable accidents I've ever experienced."

Beneath the water, she clenched her hands. She knew she'd been a fool to come out here for her bath, but she'd always found it peaceful, and she'd been certain he'd sleep hard after working the fields most of the afternoon. Now she was naked and vulnerable, and she could feel his gaze latched onto her, watching her, studying her.

"I never would have thought to take a bath outside, but it must be rather relaxing to have the hot water caressing your skin while the stars look down."

She jerked her head up to look at the night sky. She'd always enjoyed having the stars to count while she bathed. She'd never considered they were watching her. She didn't like the thought one bit.

"It'd be a sight more relaxing if you weren't here," she snapped.

He had the gall to laugh, loudly, joyfully.

"Shhh!" she chastised. "You're gonna wake the children."

She heard him swallow his laughter.

"Sorry," he said, but she didn't believe for one minute that he was sorry at all.

"If you were really sorry, you'd leave so I can wash up."

"I'm not stopping you from washing. You're only a shadow in the night, Abbie."

Lord, she hated the way her name rolled off his tongue, soft and lyrical like a song.

She felt along the bottom of the tub until she found the soap that she'd dropped when his hand had accidentally carressed her breast. The memory caused the heat of embarrassment to scald her cheeks. Her fingers closing around the soap, she brought it up, rubbing it back and forth across her breast, but she seemed unable to wash away the feel of his palm cradling her flesh . . .

"Tell me about your husband," he said quietly.

His voice startled her and the soap slipped through her fingers. "He's dead."

"Yes, I know that. What was he like?"

She eased her shoulders back against the tub, sought out the soap, and began to wash her arms. "He was like the cotton, sturdy and strong."

"How old are you, Abbie?"

Her stomach did that little flutter again as he spoke her name. "Twenty-five."

"The eldest lad, Johnny, is he your son?"

"Of course he is. What kind of question is that?"

"You must have been a child when you gave birth to him."

"I was seventeen. Married John when I was sixteen." She said the last to make certain he understood she wasn't a woman of loose morals who would let a man bed her without the benefit of marriage. She couldn't say the same for her sister. Elizabeth's first child had come into the world barely eight months after her parents were married. But then Elizabeth had loved Daniel something fierce, and to hear Elizabeth tell it, loving a man made all the difference in the world.

"Your children look like little stair steps. There can't be many years separating them."

"Ten months. My husband wasn't a ... patient man." She felt the heat flame her entire body with that confession. She held out her hand. "Please give me the towel."

"I'm not like him." His voice, warm as the embers of a fire stirring to life, sent shivers racing along her spine.

"Who?" she asked.

"Your husband. Unlike him, I have all the patience in the world." He stood and draped the towel over the railing, close enough for her to reach, far enough away that she would have to bare a portion of her body to him to retrieve it. "Some night, Abbie, I will dry you off."

She watched him disappear in the darkness, the velvet threat lingering on the breeze.

3

The next morning Grayson awoke when the first stream of milk hit the galvanized pail. He would not have thought a man could ache in so many places and still be alive.

A smile touched his lips at a memory of Abigail Westland bathing in the moonlight. She had not been attempting to be a seductress, but he had been well and thoroughly seduced. That a man of his reputation had kept his backside planted on the porch step when he'd really wanted to strip out of his clothes and dive into the tub with her was incomprehensible.

Neither Kit nor Harry would believe he had not undertaken the challenge of luring Mrs. Westland out of the water and into his arms. Unexpectedly, he realized he had no plans to tell them of the meeting. Not because he was disappointed that the encounter had not ended as it should have—with the woman screaming his name in ecstasy. He wouldn't tell them because quite simply he didn't want those peaceful, tender moments to become sordid.

He struggled to sit up, grimacing as his raw hands pressed against the quilt. He painstakingly made his way to the end of the loft and slowly eased down the ladder. He hadn't even bothered to remove his boots the night before.

With his hands gently squeezing the cow's teats, the lad jerked his head around and stared at him. "You all right?"

"I think I'm beginning to know how my grandfather feels."

"You got a grandpa?" the lad asked, obviously in awe.

Grayson hobbled to the stall. As a bastard, he was considered no one's son, no one's relation. But his mother's father had been as unconventional as she was, and on rare occasions, he allowed Grayson to visit. "Yes, haven't you?"

"Nope. They all died. What's it like having a grandpa?"

"Well, I suppose it depends on the grandfather. I wasn't very close to mine."

"Ezra Jones has a grandpa. He gave him a rifle when he was only six." The lad's eyes widened. "And a knife!"

"Indeed," Grayson murmured, thinking six was a bit young to be loading a child down with weapons.

The lad nodded with so much enthusiasm that his dark hair flopped against his forehead. "His ma said he couldn't have the rifle but his grandpa just winked and gave it to him anyway. Did your grandpa give you a rifle?"

"No, but he gave me a slap on the backside a time or two."

"What did you do to deserve a lickin'?" Johnny asked.

Grayson gave him a rueful smile. "I'm not certain."

Johnny scrunched up his face. "I was gonna fix you a fishin' pole so you could go fishin' with me and Micah, but Ma said you were gonna go live with Aunt 'Lizbeth."

Stunned, Grayson stared at the boy. "When did she say that?" he asked with deadly calm.

"This mornin'."

"Where is she now?"

"Out back, washin' clothes."

"Fix me a pole," he said before spinning on his heel and stalking from the barn. He heard a whoop echo through the building as he strode into the predawn gray. He stormed around the side of the house and saw Abbie scraping his shirt up and down a washboard. The cloth would be threadbare by the time she finished.

"What did I do?" he demanded as he came near enough to smell the rose water that had scented her bath the night before.

She spun around, her cheeks burning brightly. "Nothing," she stammered.

"Then why are you sending me away?"

She shook her head. "I'm not *sending* you away exactly." She dipped the shirt back into the water before wringing it out.

"Johnny was under the impression I'm going to stay with your sister."

She gave a brisk nod and draped his shirt over a rope strung between two trees.

"Why?" he asked.

"Elizabeth has more rooms in her house. You'll have a bed to sleep in."

He touched her shoulder, and she jerked around to face him, her eyes wide, her breath coming in short gasps.

"Have I complained about sleeping in the barn?" he asked.

"No."

"Then why?" he asked again.

"I don't want you!"

"My father didn't, either. If I'd spent my life where people wanted me, I would have rotted in a gutter. I'm not leaving."

"But I want you to leave."

"Have I hurt you since I've been here?"

"Yes! Last night. You shamed me, sitting there watching..." Tears welled in her eyes. "I just needed some time to myself, a few moments to dream, and you ruined it. No matter how much I scrub, I can't get the feel of you off me—" She slapped her hand over her mouth.

He thought he'd grown accustomed to women not wanting his touch, the marriageable maidens fearful that his illegitimacy might rub off on them. The sudden sting he felt in the center of his chest surprised him.

Reaching out, he snatched his trousers from the

pile. "Thank you for washing my clothing. You're quite right that I'll want to take clean clothes with me to your sister's, but I'll finish up."

"I'll iron them this afternoon—"

"That won't be necessary." He dipped his trousers in the hot water, clenching his teeth against the scalding pain gripping his palms.

"I'll get you some hot water so you can shave—"

"Again, not necessary. This water should suffice."

"You'll be happier at Elizabeth's."

"Yes, I'm quite sure I will be." He wrung the water from his trousers and slapped them over the rope.

She took a step back. "I need to see about breakfast."

She scurried away, the rose water fragrance trailing after her. He dunked another shirt into the water and bowed his head. He of all people knew that pain could be inflicted without blows being struck.

He simply hadn't realized that his wanting to spend a few moments with Abbie in the moonlight would have hurt her.

Abbie pulled the pan of biscuits off the shelf within the hearth. They were cooked to a golden brown, just the way John liked them. She had done everything in her life just the way John liked it.

And even then, it had seldom been enough.

She had grown accustomed to not having a man around, to doing things the way she wanted to do them. To prepare the foods she enjoyed eating, to keep the house the way she wanted it kept.

To soak in a hot tub with nothing but midnight for company.

If only the Englishman had left when she'd told him to, if only he hadn't made her feel incredibly vulnerable, if only her stomach didn't flutter like a fledging bird trying out its wings in the spring—

"Micah! Watch where you're goin'!" Lydia cried.

Abbie turned in time to see Lydia shove her youngest brother away from her.

"Lydia, don't push your brother," she scolded.

"But he ran into me! He never looks where he's goin' and he's clumsier than a three-legged calf."

She saw tears gather in Micah's eyes. She reached for him, but he darted through the door before she could comfort him. She gazed at her daughter. "He can't help that he has two left feet."

"He did it on purpose." Lydia stuck out her bottom lip in a pout.

"I'm sure he didn't," Abbie assured her.

"You always take his side 'cuz he's the baby, and you take Johnny's side 'cuz he's the oldest—"

Abbie wrapped her arms around Lydia and held her close. "I take your side because you're my only daughter." She tucked her finger beneath Lydia's chin and tilted her face up. "I love you all the same, but for different reasons. Now finish setting the table while I find Micah."

Grayson saw the youngest boy barrel around the corner of the house and slam into the porch post. He almost laughed at the startled expression that crossed the boy's face before he flopped back onto the ground. Grayson leapt off the porch and knelt beside him. "You all right, lad?"

The boy scrambled to his feet. "Yep. Just didn't see it," he croaked.

Grayson stared at the child. He'd never before heard the boy speak. His voice sounded as though a bullfrog had taken up residence within his throat. He came to his feet. "I'm not surprised you didn't see it, running as fast you were."

"Didn't see Lydia neither." Tears welled in the boy's eyes, and he wiped his nose with the back of his hand.

"Bad morning?" Gray asked.

The boy nodded.

"Am having one myself. A brisk shave usually makes me feel more human. What do you think? Would you like a shave?"

"Ain't got no whiskers."

"Oh, but I see one or two. Come on." He led the boy to the porch and grabbed a rickety chair that someone had set in the corner. He placed it in front of the mirror, then set the boy on top of it. His hair was dark, probably like his father's. But his eyes were his mother's.

"Well, Micah, should we leave you with a mustache?"

The lad squinted his violet eyes and stared hard into the mirror before giving a brusque nod.

"Very good." Grayson stirred his shaving lather before handing the cup to the boy. "You want to put a little on your jaw."

He bit back his smile as the lad gingerly touched

the brush to his cheek, leaving a ball of lather to slide down his face. He took the cup from the boy and picked up his razor. "Until you get the hang of it, I'd best do the actual shaving."

Using the dull side, he skimmed the razor over the lad's face. Micah's eyes grew bigger and rounder as Grayson gathered up the lather. When he was finished, Grayson met the boy's gaze in the mirror. "What do you think?"

The boy twisted his body around. "Ma, I shave-ed."

Grayson snapped his head to the side. Abbie stood beside the porch, tears shimmering in her eyes. "I see that."

The boy hopped off the chair, fell to his knees, and scrambled back up. "Gotta tell Johnny."

His legs churning, he hurried around the corner of the house and out of sight.

"Wonder what he'll run into next," Grayson murmured.

"All children are clumsy at first. He'll grow out of it." She gnawed on her lower lip. "Thank you for giving him a few minutes of your time."

Grayson shrugged and turned to put his shaving equipment away.

"I found you a pole!" Johnny cried.

Grayson spun around. Johnny sauntered toward him, waving a long thin branch through the air.

"What's that for?" Abbie asked.

Johnny nodded enthusiastically in Grayson's direction. "He said he was stayin' and for me to fix him a pole."

Abbie snapped her attention to Grayson. He held her gaze as he spoke. "Actually, I only told you to fix me a pole. I won't be staying, but I'm certain we can fish together sometime. I don't have to live here to do that, do I?"

Johnny furrowed his brow. "I reckon not. We could go Sunday morning."

"I look forward to it."

"I'll get you a line and a hook fixed on here," Johnny said before walking away.

"You told him you were going to stay?" Abbie asked.

"I may have indicated that but it was before you and I had our conversation. You needn't worry, Mrs. Westland. I won't be staying. You'll have all the private moments you could wish for."

Grayson chopped at the ground with a vengeance, ignoring the pain in his hands and his body. Tomorrow, he would begin preparations to leave for Galveston. He had been a fool to think he could make a difference here, to think he might have found a place where he was needed. He had spent his whole life being neither needed nor wanted.

When his father had told him about his plans to send him to Texas, Grayson had pounced on the idea like a dog that had just been tossed a bone. Here, he hoped to find opportunities that weren't tainted by the prejudices of his birth.

But without truly knowing him, Abigail Westland had deemed him unworthy of touching her, was casting him aside like so much rotting fruit. Before he left, perhaps he would enlighten her as to the nature of his birth so she could be truly horrified by the fact that he'd touched her.

"You're going to kill those plants," Harry said.

Grayson spun around, his temper tethered on a short cord. "How the bloody hell would you know?"

"Because of the three of us, I am the most observant—"

"You're the most idle, strolling up and down the furrows like the lord of the manor when there's work that needs to be done."

Harry's green eyes blazed. "I agreed to stay. I did not agree to work."

"So you've got a roof over your head, a bed to sleep in, and food for your stomach while you do nothing to deserve it," Grayson taunted.

Harry drew back his shoulders. "I am not a complete scoundrel. I pay the lovely young Widow Denby a dollar a day for my keep."

Grayson snorted. "What do you pay the lovely Widow Westland for the noon meal she prepares for you?"

"I never considered the Widow Westland lovely," Kit interjected as he ceased his labors and casually folded his arm over the top of his hoe.

Grayson glared at him. "What?"

"I rather thought she more closely resembled a piece of worn cloth," Kit explained.

"You'd look worn, too, if you were up before the sun cooking food and washing clothes and tending to the needs of three children and a man—"

"Is she the reason we're leaving so abruptly? You always were one to fall in love quickly."

"I've never fallen in love. Fallen into infatuation, fallen into lust—but never *fallen in love*. And no, she is not the reason we are leaving," he lied. "Harry is."

Harry jerked his head back. "Me? What did I do?"

"Nothing! That's the whole point. You never do anything."

"She must have scorned you," Kit said quietly. "Being scorned pricks your temper more than anything else."

He despised the way Kit looked at him as though he could reach right into his soul and know everything he felt, everything he feared. "She did not scorn me. It's working in this damnable heat that pricks my temper. I'd just like to see Harry work up a sweat before we go."

"I *am* sweating," Harry said. "I haven't stopped sweating since we set foot in Galveston."

"If you want Harry to work, you'll have to wager him into it," Kit said.

Harry's face broke into a wide grin. "I haven't had a decent wager in days." He slipped his hand into his pocket and withdrew a deck of cards. "If you cut to the high card, I'll spend the rest of the day chopping at the ground. If I cut to the high card, you will serve as my valet on the journey to Galveston."

Grayson smiled. He had an abundance of pent-up anger and frustration, and he knew just how to release it and gain the advantage. "I'm not a fool, Harry. I'd never trust a deck of cards in your hands, but I'm willing to accept your wager if you're willing to go at something a bit more sporting.''

"I welcome the challenge," Harry announced grandly.

"And I look forward to handing my hoe over to you," Grayson taunted.

Abbie chopped at the weeds, cursing her eyes that repeatedly betrayed her by looking for Grayson Rhodes. She couldn't forget the image of her youngest son, standing on a chair on the back porch, leaning into Grayson's shoulder as he gingerly swiped the shaving lather from her son's soft cheek. She tried to imagine John giving his sons the same care, and the image simply wouldn't take hold.

The farm had always come first with John. Not that she held that against him. He was considerably older than she was, had devoted his youth to the farm. She had married him to become his helpmate. It was a silly girl of sixteen who had dreamed his devotion would swerve away from the farm and settle on her.

He had fed her body, but never her heart, never her soul. Guilt gnawed at her because try as she might, she had never come to love him. She had admired his dedication to the soil, but admiration without love made for the loneliest of nights.

She glanced up from her work and looked in the direction where she'd last seen Grayson Rhodes hacking at the ground, but he was nowhere to be seen. She didn't like the way disappointment had her craning her neck to see where he'd gone.

"Looking for someone?" Elizabeth asked beside her.

She scowled at her sister. "I was just looking the crops over."

"They haven't changed since you looked 'em over five minutes ago."

She wanted to slap that little knowing smirk right off her sister's face. Instead she beat her hoe at the ground.

"I wish you'd tell me what he did that made you decide to send him to my place," Elizabeth said.

Abbie clenched her teeth and buried her hoe in the soil, only willing to admit to the most insignificant of reasons. "He calls me Abbie."

"Abbie? Where's the harm in that? It's your name."

"It implies an . . . an intimacy . . . a friendship—"

"Fight!"

Abbie jerked her head around. Johnny was running away from the house, running toward the field, waving his arms wildly.

"They're fighting!" he yelled. "Hurry! They're fighting!"

Abbie glanced at her sister. "It's probably Madeline Mercer's boys. I swear they are as prone to fight as sparks are to fly upward."

Elizabeth gave a brief nod before hiking up her skirts and running toward the house. Grateful Johnny wasn't engaged in the fighting, Abbie followed her. She simply could not understand what possessed boys to hit one another.

A crowd had gathered at the back of her house.

She heard the sickening slap of flesh against flesh, followed by a grunt and groan.

"Why isn't someone stopping those boys?" she asked as she shouldered her way to the front. Her mouth opened so wide that her chin nearly touched her knees. It wasn't boys fighting at all—but men. Grown men.

"Care to make a wager?"

She snapped her head around and stared into the laughing blue eyes of one of Grayson's friends. "What?"

He brushed his hair out of his eyes. "Care to make a wager on who'll win? My money's going on Gray. He's in a foul mood—"

"You should stop them!" she demanded.

He chuckled softly. "I think not. It's a gentleman's sport. No one will get hurt."

"A gentleman's sport? Hitting each other?"

She glanced back at Grayson and the other man. What was his name? Harry something or other. They'd both discarded their shirts. While it was true that Grayson didn't test the seams on her husband's shirt, she was surprised to discover that he was more solid than she'd given him credit for. Sweat glistened over his back and had dampened the light coating of hair on his chest. His fists were raised and he danced around the other man as though familiar with the moves he would make.

The other man made a quick jab. Grayson ducked swiftly and skittered back before beginning to bounce on the balls of his feet. Abbie hadn't expected him to be so surefooted, so graceful. She hadn't expected his muscles to bunch and flex and appear as powerful as they did.

"Breathe, Abbie," Elizabeth whispered near her ear.

"I *am* breathing," Abbie snapped, taking her first breath in what she was certain had been several minutes.

The other man took another jab which Grayson easily sidestepped.

"Why doesn't he strike back?" she asked.

"Patience is Grayson's strong suit. He'll wait until the time is right," the man beside her explained.

She saw the women gawking, heard the boys yelling and cheering. What sort of example was this to set for the children?

"I won't put up with fighting on my property," she stated flatly. She took a step toward the two men dancing around each other. Then everything happened at once.

She felt fingers dig into her arm and pull her back.

"Don't get close—" the man began.

"Get your hands off her—" Grayson yelled as he took a step toward her, just before the other man hit him.

Grayson felt the jarring pain as Harry's fist made contact with his jaw. His head snapped back. He staggered backward before his knees buckled, and he felt the hard ground beneath him. Harry knelt beside him.

"You all right?" Harry asked.

Grayson rubbed his jaw. "You wounded my pride more than my jaw. You always had a poor punch."

"Poor or not, I won," Harry gloated.

Grayson saw Abbie break away from Kit and rush across the small expanse separating them. She fell to her knees. "What did you think you were doing?" she demanded.

"Trying to get Harry to work in the fields."

She released a very unladylike snort and grabbed one of his hands. "You fool! Your palms were already blistered and now you've broken the skin on the top—"

"What do you care, Mrs. Westland?" He winced as Harry grabbed his hand and pulled him to his feet.

She rose slowly, as though she wanted to say something but couldn't find the words. "I'll get some salve—"

"It isn't necessary—"

"It *is* necessary, damn it!" Fire burned within her eyes, and damn him, he wondered if the fire had been there last night while she bathed.

"Mama?"

He glanced down and watched Lydia tug on her mother's skirts.

"Just a minute, Lydia," Abbie said firmly but gently. "I need to see to Mr. Rhodes' hands."

"But Mama—"

"Just a minute—"

"Who's that man?" Lydia demanded in a way that very much reminded Grayson of the manner in which Abbie asked to look at his hands.

He heard Abbie's frustrated sigh. "Which man?"

Lydia pointed her small finger toward the road. "That one."

Grayson followed the direction of Abbie's gaze. A

man trudged up the road. His hat shadowed his face and Grayson could tell little about him except that his dingy gray clothing had obviously seen better days. He slid his gaze to Abbie. "Who is it?"

She shook her head slightly. "I don't know. He's too skinny to be from around here."

"Is it my pa?" Lydia asked, bouncing up and down.

"Your pa's dead," Abbie said absently, her gaze trained on the man marching up the road. Then as though realizing the callousness of her statement, she knelt in front of Lydia and placed her hands on her shoulders. "Remember that I told you your pa won't be coming home?"

" 'Cuz he's with the angels?"

"That's right."

"Then who's that?"

Abbie turned her attention back to the man. He had quickened his step, left the road, and was walking toward the house. Grayson saw recognition and wonder dawn on Abbie's face. She slowly rose and pressed her hand to her lips. "Oh my God," she said on a whispery breath.

"Who is it, Mama?"

"Your Uncle James." She snapped her gaze to Grayson, tears brimming in her eyes. "It's my brother."

He'd never in his life heard such happiness. He was ashamed of the relief that washed over him because it wasn't her husband. What did he care if her husband suddenly rose from the dead and came home?

A small woman released a tiny screech and began

running toward the man. Then Elizabeth hiked up her skirts and followed.

"You should welcome him home," Gray said quietly.

Abbie's gaze shifted between his eyes and his hands. "Your hands—"

"I can take care of my hands."

She gave a brusque nod and rushed toward the man who was now holding the small woman close and twirling her in a circle. Every woman and child hurried to join them.

Grayson took the shirt that Kit offered him and shrugged into it.

"Do you think," Kit began solemnly, "that there is a single person in all of England who would be that glad to see one of us walking down a road?"

It was a question that demanded the answer not be spoken aloud.

Out of the corner of his eye, Grayson saw Harry pick up his hoe and begin walking toward the fields. "Where are you going with my hoe?" Grayson asked as he loped across the yard and caught up to him.

"To work the fields."

"Why? You won."

A sadness briefly touched Harry's eyes before he turned away. "Then why the bloody hell do I feel as though we all just lost?"

His arms crossed over his chest, Grayson stood within the doorway, watching what he'd never before witnessed: the outpouring of love that a family showered on one of its own.

No one had returned to the fields. James Morgan had been fed and hugged and fed some more. His clothes were as tattered as his spirits had been when he'd first walked into the house.

But after a while, his smiles came more easily. Grayson quickly learned that James' wife's name was Amy. She wept softly more than once and constantly touched her husband's shoulder as though afraid he'd disappear. Grayson couldn't imagine anyone rejoicing should he return home.

"I'm sorry about John," James said quietly.

Grayson saw Abbie blush before averting her gaze. "We lost a lot of good men," she said softly.

"We did that," James said. He looked at Elizabeth. "I'm sorry about Daniel as well."

Tears flooded Elizabeth's eyes. "I keep thinking I'll see him coming up the road just like we saw you." Her chin quivered. "But he's not going to come home, is he?"

James wrapped his arms around her, holding her tightly. "No."

Grayson wondered if the morning he'd seen Abbie on the front porch gazing at the horizon, she'd been looking for her husband, if she missed him, if she longed to have him home.

Elizabeth made her way out of her brother's hold and dabbed at her eyes with the hem of her apron. James looked over her head at Grayson.

"Mr. Rhodes, I can't tell you how much I appreciate you and your friends comin' to help with our crops. I passed too many fallow fields on my way home. I was afraid we'd be in for a hard winter."

Uncomfortable with the man's appreciation, Grayson shifted his stance. "I'm glad we could help out," he murmured, wondering if they would be as grateful in the morning when they learned three of them had plans to leave.

"Abbie's never liked being alone," James said.

"James!" Abbie snapped, her gaze darting quickly to Grayson, then back to her brother, her cheeks flaming red.

"It's true, Abbie. There's no shame in not wanting to be alone."

She slapped his shoulder. "Shush up."

Elizabeth glanced toward the door. "Lord, look how late it's getting. We'd best head home."

Grayson shoved away from the doorjamb. "If you'll give me a moment, I'll retrieve my belongings."

He walked out of the house not caring if she'd give him a moment or not. He should probably just gather his possessions, walk to town, and take a room in the saloon. Kit and Harry could find him there easily enough.

His gaze fell on the fields. He'd only worked in them for two days, but he already felt as though a portion belonged to him. He had no doubt that cotton would come from the area where he'd sweated and labored. One day he'd purchase a shirt woven from cotton he'd nourished. Strange, how he found comfort in the thought—that something he'd done might have made a small difference.

He strolled into the barn. His fishing pole was leaning against the ladder that led to the loft. He'd see to it that they didn't leave until he'd gone fishing with the lad as he'd promised. He hoped the boy knew all there was to know about fishing because Grayson had never dropped a hook into a river.

He climbed the ladder into the loft and made his way to the corner where he slept. He began to place his few possessions into his solitary bag. He'd forgotten about his clothes, but it would be easy enough to snatch them off the rope where they hung and stuff them into his bag.

He heard the creak and moan of wood as someone climbed the ladder. His hands froze.

"Mr. Rhodes?" Abbie said quietly.

Grayson shoved his favorite book into his satchel. "Tell your sister I'll be there in a moment."

"You don't have to go."

Grayson twisted his body slightly and gazed at her. Her face was barely visible over the loft platform. "I beg your pardon?"

He saw her hands tighten their hold on the ladder rung just below her chin.

"Well, I . . . I've been thinking about it, and maybe I was a bit hasty in blaming you for last night. I shouldn't have been out there—like I was—knowing there was a man in the barn even if I thought he'd be asleep. And the boys, well, I was thinking it's nice for them to have a man around, even though I know you won't be staying past harvest, at least for a while . . . It's good for them to have someone who can show them things like shaving and fishing—"

"I know nothing at all about fishing."

"Johnny does—"

"Then he doesn't need me, does he?" he asked, wondering why he was arguing with her when he wanted desperately to stay.

"He doesn't know how to fight," she offered.

He rubbed his bruised jaw. "It seems neither do I."

"I think you do. You would have beat Mr. Bainbridge if you hadn't taken your eyes off him when you came to my rescue."

A corner of his mouth lifted. *Some rescue.*

"Of course, you'd have a bed at Elizabeth's—"

"Have I ever complained about sleeping on the straw?"

She shook her head. "That's why I thought maybe you'd stay."

"On one condition. That you don't stop taking baths in the moonlight," he said quietly.

Her cheeks flamed red, and her mouth worked to shape silent words.

"I won't leave the barn at night, but neither do I want you giving up something that brings you pleasure."

"You won't come watch me?" she asked hesitantly.

He gave her a wicked grin. "Not unless I'm invited."

"I'd never . . ." She shook her head. "I'll let Elizabeth know you're staying."

She disappeared from his sight.

"Oh, yes, you will, Mrs. Westland," he whispered softly. "Some night, you'll not only invite me to watch you, but you'll invite me to join you. The rogue in me will insist."

4

Bloody damned hell!

Grayson stared through the wide opening in the loft at the stars that blanketed the night sky. He'd tried counting sheep, the number of places where the straw pricked him, and now the stars. None of his efforts worked to lull him to sleep. He must have been insane to think he preferred sleeping in a smelly loft to sleeping in a soft bed. It was this damned irrational need of his to be wanted.

He jerked upright and tugged on his boots. He'd promised he wouldn't leave the barn. Well, what the lovely Widow Westland didn't know wouldn't harm her. He climbed down the ladder and strode outside. If counting a thousand stars couldn't put him to sleep, perhaps walking a thousand paces would.

He glanced quickly toward the house and considered, only briefly, sneaking over and peering around the corner to catch a glimpse of the woman bathing in the night shadows, but the possibility of having his broken promise discovered stopped him. Instead he slowed his pace and listened contentedly to the night sounds.

He heard no nightingales, no birds at all, but a barrage of insects, creating a low humming cadence. Nearing the edge of the field, he saw a shadow emerge from the rows of cotton. He came to an abrupt halt and held his breath, waiting. He felt Abbie's gaze touch him and cursed the moon that wasn't strong enough to clearly light her face.

"Thought you promised not to leave the barn at night," she said, her voice low.

He took a hesitant step toward her. "I also confessed to being disreputable."

He could make out the faintest hint of a smile in the moonlight.

"If you were truly disreputable, you'd be at the back of the house trying to see me bathing."

"Perhaps I already checked the back of the house—"

"I saw you walk out of the barn. You headed straight for the fields."

"But I was tempted to see if you were bathing. I'm a man who usually gives into temptation. I'm not certain why I didn't tonight."

"Maybe because you know you'll have a soft bed waiting for you at my sister's house if I catch you."

He laughed. "Yes, that must be it. The threat of a soft bed would make the worst of rogues behave."

He watched her smile fade and was reminded of a star falling from the heavens, its brilliance lost.

"I started sewing a pallet tonight. When I'm done,

I'll stuff it with goose feathers. Should give you some protection from the prickly straw.''

He considered telling her not to worry about him, but some padding between his body and the loft would indeed be welcome. "Where would you find goose feathers?"

"Elizabeth raises geese. She always saves the feathers.''

"A wise woman. I welcome the addition of furnishings to my humble abode.''

She shook her head and looked toward the fields. "You talk so fancy. Makes me feel like a chipped pitcher of buttermilk sitting next to a silver goblet of cream.''

"I'm sorry. Comes from years of striving to make certain no one mistook me for what I was.''

She shifted her gaze slightly. "A rogue?''

He swallowed hard. "A bastard.''

He expected horror to wash over her face. Instead, she simply gazed at him. A heavy silence stretched between them. He shoved his hands into his trousers pockets and turned his attention to the fields, wishing he'd kept his mouth shut or better yet, never left the sanctuary of the barn.

"Your parents weren't married then?'' she asked, her voice a soft caress.

He laughed mirthlessly. "My mother was a flamboyant actress. Not suitable marriage material for a man destined to become a duke.''

"Is that why your father sent you here?''

He gazed at the stars. He had once heard that some people had the trivial habit of wishing upon them. He had the distinct impression that Abigail Westland would. "Yes. He thought I could overcome the unfortunate circumstance of my birth, that it wouldn't matter here."

"It doesn't."

He looked at her directly and raised a brow, even though he doubted she could see the gesture. "You aren't more offended that I touched you now that you know the truth?"

"No, and if your birth brings you shame, you don't have to tell people. A lot of people who come to Texas leave unsavory things about their past at the border."

"What possible unsavory thing could you have left at the border?"

She gave him a tentative smile that made him want to see more.

"I was born here. I've never been to the border to leave anything."

"It's just as well. I can't imagine that there is anything about you that you would not want to acknowledge."

She wrapped her arms around her middle and turned her attention back to the fields. "When we go into town for supplies on Saturday, we'll purchase you a proper pair of working gloves."

She sauntered away, a shadowy wraith in the night, and he fought the urge to trail after her. Perhaps his bastardy didn't matter to her, but it did matter a great deal to him—had shaped him into the man he was instead of the man he wished to be.

*   *   *

"It is moments like this that make life worth living," Harry murmured.

Grayson agreed wholeheartedly as he sank his aching body farther down into the huge wooden tub and enjoyed the steam rising to tickle his face.

It seemed everyone came into Fortune on Saturday, and when he'd crossed paths with Kit and Harry, he hadn't hesitated to join them on a tour of the town, a tour that had begun with a detour by the bathing house.

He heard a shy giggle and opened his eyes slightly. A young woman stood in the doorway holding an armload of towels.

"Hello, sweetheart," Kit said, removing the slender cigar from his mouth.

She giggled again and raised her shoulders until they touched her ears. "I shore do like the way you talk."

"I like the way you smile," Kit replied.

Grayson closed his eyes so she couldn't see that he was rolling them. He heard a few steps and a soft thump so he assumed the woman had set down the towels.

"You fellas holler if you need anything else."

He heard her giggle and the echo of her rapidly retreating footsteps.

"Lovely lass," Kit murmured.

"She's a child," Grayson pointed out, snapping his eyes open.

"Hardly. I put her at seventeen. What do you think, Harry?"

"At least."

"Still too young for you," Grayson said.

Kit shrugged. "Doesn't mean I can't appreciate the beauty she'll become." He angled his head thoughtfully. "Are you still being scorned?"

"I am not being scorned. I just don't understand why you have to go after everything that wears a skirt."

"Good God, you've gotten self-righteous of late," Harry said. "It's beginning to wear thin. He made an innocent comment—"

"His eyes held no innocence as he looked at the girl," Grayson said.

"There hasn't been any innocence about me since I was a lad." Kit dropped his head back against the tub. "It's my understanding that tomorrow is a complete day of rest. Thank God. What say, when we're finished here, we take a stroll to the saloon. I could use a stiff drink."

Grayson thought of Abbie. He felt guilty enough indulging in the warm bath while she was shopping for supplies. She'd told him to run along and have fun with his friends—but the fun had yet to arrive.

"I'm all for it," Harry said. "Perhaps we'll find a little gaming as well."

"I don't imagine the pockets of the men of this town contain much more than lint," Grayson said.

"They have other things of value," Harry said.

Grayson narrowed his gaze and studied his friend. "Such as?"

"Good horseflesh for one thing." A gleam of anticipation came into his eyes. "A sturdy wagon. A new roof on the barn—"

Grayson sat up and the water splashed around him. "A roof on the barn?"

Harry suddenly looked as though he'd been caught pilfering pockets. He waved a hand dismissively in the air. "The Widow Denby could do with a new roof on her barn, and that thing she calls a wagon is a monstrosity—all rusted and rotting." He gave Grayson a harsh glare. "Don't worry. I won't take from someone who can't afford to be taken from."

Kit chuckled. "So Robin Hood comes to Fortune, Texas."

"Hardly," Harry said. "What we need to concentrate on is finding a venture that will make us wealthy without all the toil associated with cotton. It's little wonder the South fought to keep the slaves."

"From what I've seen of this state so far," Grayson said, "I don't think anything comes without hard work." He stood, the warm water running in rivulets along his body.

"Ready to visit the saloon?" Kit asked.

"No, I'm afraid I'll have to decline the invitation. I need to help Mrs. Westland load the supplies onto her wagon."

"She loaded them just fine before you arrived," Kit pointed out.

Grayson grabbed a towel and rubbed briskly. "Yes, well, as you say, that was before I arrived."

Abbie ran her fingers over the calico. At ten cents a yard, it was an extravagance she couldn't afford or justify for herself, but for the children . . .

Thoughtfully, she gnawed on her thumbnail. If she

bought a few yards, she could sew a dress for Lydia; a few more and she could make shirts for the boys; a lot more and she could sew a shirt for Mr. Rhodes. She slammed her eyes closed. Where had that last thought come from? With his fancy linen shirts, he probably wouldn't be caught dead in homespun. He wore John's shirt easily enough when he worked in the fields, but he always wore his own clothes when he came to supper in the evening. She couldn't imagine him wearing a shirt she'd sewn for him.

She heard the door to the general store open and glanced over her shoulder. Grayson Rhodes strode in. He bestowed a warm smile upon her, and her stomach furled like the petals of a flower tucking away for the night.

"I didn't mean to stay away so long, but the temptation of a hot bath was more than I could resist. I hope I'm not too late to help you load the wagon."

She could see the ends of his golden hair curling where they were still damp. She supposed she really needed to make arrangements for him to bathe at the house. With the thought, she felt heat suffuse her cheeks and quickly turned her attention back to the calico. She wondered if he could bathe with his clothes on. It would save her the trouble of washing them. "Uh, no, you're not too late."

"Hey, Mr. Rhodes!"

She turned to see Micah's little legs churning as he raced across the general store. He slammed into a display of hoes at the end of the aisle and sent them—and himself—crashing to the floor.

Abbie rushed to his side and knelt beside him. He

glanced around as though he couldn't figure out how he'd ended up where he was. "Micah, you've got to watch where you're going," she chastised gently.

"I think he was," Grayson said quietly as he crouched beside Micah.

Abbie jerked her head around. "What?"

She watched the Englishman scrutinizing her son as though searching for an elusive shadow.

"Micah, watch your mother," he ordered. He peered at her. "And you watch him."

Micah sat completely still, his eyes on her. Out of the corner of her eye, she saw Grayson flick his fingers near Micah's left cheek. She flinched, but Micah didn't move. Grayson shifted his gaze to her. "I don't think he can see."

Horror mingled with grief swept through her. "You mean he's blind? He can't be blind."

"Not completely," he said in a calm voice. "But I've noticed him running around and the only time he stumbles into something is when it comes at him from the left side."

Placing her hands on Micah's shoulders, Abbie leaned close to her son, studying his perfect violet eyes. "Micah, can you not see properly?"

"How would he know?" Grayson asked. "If his vision has always been less than it should be, he would never realize what he was missing."

Apprehension and guilt gnawed at Abbie. How could she not know that her son could not see? She shook her head. "He's just clumsy. All five-year-olds have two left feet. He's always rushing to get places, and he's not looking—"

Grayson curved his hand over her shoulder, surprising her with the strength she felt within his grasp.

"Is there a physician in this town?"

She nodded mutely. What sort of mother wouldn't notice that her child couldn't see?

Abbie remembered when Johnny was three, he'd gotten the croup. She'd been terrified as the coughing fits had caused his little body to spasm and his fever had raged. She had fought to get broth down him, bathed his burning body, held him, rocked him, and sang him sweet lullabies—alone, late into the night, through the first light of dawn—until his fever broke and he smiled at her.

John's responsibility rested in getting food on the table and tending the fields. Her responsibilities included every aspect of caring for the children, even when the task meant holding death at bay. Alone. Always alone.

So she wasn't quite sure what to make of Grayson Rhodes as he stood beside her, questioning the doctor's examination, assuring Micah that he'd done nothing wrong, and frequently whispering to her, "Not to worry. It's going to be all right."

Micah looked so small sitting in a chair while the doctor wiggled fingers in front of his face. Abbie took a step forward, and Grayson shadowed her movement. "He's all right, isn't he?" she asked anxiously.

"Of course he's all right," Dr. Hickerson said. His graying hair had a tendency to stick up like the petals on a dandelion and looked like a strong gust of wind might send it flying away. "Although I think Mr. Rhodes might be right. I don't think Micah is seeing the world as clearly as he should."

His knees creaked as he stood. He walked to a cabinet, opened a drawer, and began rummaging through the contents. "I don't have much of a selection," he said. He lifted a pair of spectacles, held them up, and peered through the lenses. "But I think these might work."

He turned, the furrow between his brow lessening as his gaze fell on Abbie. She'd always thought he had comforting brown eyes.

"Don't look so worried, Abbie," he said with a smile. "This isn't the croup."

"But Micah needed me—"

"What he *needs* is spectacles," Dr. Hickerson said as he crouched in front of Micah. "Now then, son, let's see how these work."

He set the spectacles on Micah's nose and curled the metal behind his ears. The lenses made his eyes look larger than they were. Abbie's heart tightened and she pressed a fist against her mouth when Micah's eyes widened further with wonder.

"Everything ain't furry," he announced.

She watched the Englishman kneel before her son, angling his head one way and then the other.

"I say, they make you look rather distinguished."

Micah wrinkled his nose and the spectacles rose slightly. "What's that mean?"

"Handsome."

Micah beamed, and Abbie wondered how the man always knew exactly what her child needed to hear.

*   *   *

Her youngest son had needed spectacles. All this time she'd simply thought he was awkward.

Night was closing in and she wondered if his world had been as dark before this afternoon. She heard him scramble to his knees in the back of the wagon and saw his tiny hand touch Grayson's shoulder.

"Lookit!" he said, pointing his finger toward the black heavens.

A warm smile spread across Grayson's face. "The stars. I suppose before tonight they were little more than a hazy blur." Micah nodded and settled back down in the wagon between Johnny and Lydia. Grayson shifted his gaze from the stars to Abbie. "Stop looking as though you're being stretched out on a rack in the dungeon."

"What kind of mother doesn't notice that her child can't see?"

He wrapped his hand around her clenched fist. The warmth and comfort of his touch sent shock rippling through her. In all her years of marriage, John had never held her hand. It was only Grayson's thumb stroking her knuckles, soothing her, that kept her from jerking free of his hold.

"Abbie, it was natural for you to assume he was a bit clumsy and would outgrow it. Any mother would have done the same."

"You didn't," she snapped.

A corner of his mouth curled up. "Ah, but I'm not a mother, am I?"

She didn't want him teasing her, didn't want to see the warmth and understanding in his eyes.

He shifted on the bench. "Abbie, from the moment he was born, you have been in his company. From the moment he was born, he has seen the world as a bit hazy. How could either of you recognize that what you were seeing was not as it should have been?"

Tears burned her eyes. "But you did."

His thumb ceased its stroking, and she felt his hand tighten around hers. He released her and turned his attention back to the road.

"When I was a lad, I found a mangy cat at my father's estate in the country. Someone—I suspect the duke's son—had plucked out its left eye. It was a clumsy creature, always running into things. The duke's wife forbade me to bring it into the house after it knocked over one of her precious crystal vases. So I made a home for it in the stables."

She remembered that he'd told her that first night that he had often slept in the stables. "And you slept with it there."

He nodded. "Whenever I could. As unflattering as it is, watching Micah simply reminded me of the cat."

"Did you have to leave the cat there when you came here?"

"No, he died some years back."

His voice was flat, and yet it contained underlying currents of pain.

"How did he die?"

He shook his head and glanced at her. She saw the sorrow reflected in his gaze. "You don't want to know."

But she did. Suddenly she wanted to know this

man, to understand what had shaped him into the kind of man who would notice more about her children than she did, who would give them more attention than their own father ever had. "Tell me."

In the moonlight, she saw his jaw clench and his gaze harden. "The duke's son was intrigued with the practice of drawing and quartering. He needed a victim." He leaned toward her slightly. "If you don't know what drawing and quartering is—I'm not going to enlighten you."

Dear God, but she did know. She felt her stomach lurch and pressed a hand to her mouth, swallowing the bile that had risen in her throat. "Your brother sounds horrid."

"He is not my brother. Being born under my unfortunate circumstance, I was not considered a relation—simply a reminder of the duke's folly."

"But you lived with them."

"Yes, my father was adamant about that. Since he was a man of power, wealth, and influence, his generous treatment of me was tolerated."

"And this cruel son will inherit."

He gave her a mocking smile. "Everything."

Shuddering, she shook her head vigorously. "That makes no sense to me. To give everything to someone simply because of his birth."

"Yes, I fear the duke's holdings will go to ruin once his son inherits."

His son. Abbie realized that although he referred to the duke as his father, he did not truly consider himself the man's son. He was the man's bastard— a horrible label to inflict upon a child. How would it feel to grow up always balancing on the fringes of acceptance and love?

"I can't believe the English hand everything over to someone just because of his birth. I think it's stupid," she said, feeling an irrational anger at the circumstances that had brought this man to Texas.

"I find it difficult to fathom myself. Take Kit for example. His brother emerged from the womb two minutes ahead of him so Christopher will inherit. Knowing Kit, he was probably first in line but stepped aside to let his brother pass."

"Is *his* brother horrid?"

He smiled warmly. "No, but neither is he wise. Unknown to the Earl of Ravenleigh, Kit was forever advising his brother on the best manner in which to handle his affairs. Kit is as levelheaded as they come and his brother's thoughts are constantly scattered upon the wind. Kit is a tad worried now that he's not there to watch over him."

"Surely he didn't have to come—"

"You have to understand the world in which we were brought up. We are governed by obligation. When our fathers told us that they had made arrangements for us to come here, we came because it was expected that we would bow to their wishes."

"You're better off here," she said indignantly.

His smile grew, his eyes warmed until Abbie almost felt them as a caress.

"Yes," he said quietly. "I am beginning to believe that we are."

5

"Gray! Gray! You gotta get up. Hurry!"

Groggily Grayson awoke from a deep sleep, vaguely aware of the jerking on his shoulder and the frantic voice. He squinted against the yellow glow of the lantern until Johnny's worried gaze came into focus. He bolted upright. "What is it, lad? What's wrong?"

"We gotta go fishin'."

Grayson's heart slowed to a normal pace as he glanced toward the opening in the loft where stars sparkled against the blackened sky. "Good God, boy, it's the middle of the night."

"No, it ain't. It's four in the morning."

He cringed at Johnny's enthusiasm. "I thought today was supposed to be a day of rest."

Smiling brightly, the boy bobbed his head like an apple in a bucket of water. "It is. That's why we can go fishin'. Ma's gonna milk the cow for me."

Grayson buried his face in his hands and sighed

81

heavily. "No respectable fish would be awake at this hour."

The lad's laughter echoed across the loft. "Come on. You're burning daylight."

Grayson lifted his head. It looked to him as though daylight had already burned to a cinder. Johnny hurried to the ladder and scrambled over the edge, calling, "Come on!"

With a groan, Grayson reached for his boots. Whatever had he been thinking when he agreed to go fishing?

Without bothering to straighten his clothes, he climbed out of the loft and stumbled from the barn. The only advantage to getting up at this ungodly hour was that it afforded him the opportunity to see Abbie a little sooner in the day.

Smiling warmly as he approached, she extended a cup. "Thought you might need a little something to get the blood moving."

"The blood's moving. It's the rest of me that would rather still be abed."

She laughed softly, and he thought the sound rivaled the beauty of a nightingale's song. He took the cup from her and drank deeply of the black coffee, grimacing as he did so.

"Is it too strong?" she asked.

"Yes, but it seems to have worked."

"Come on, Gray!" Johnny yelled as he bounded out of the house, Micah following closely on his heels.

"Johnny, call him Mr. Rhodes," Abbie admonished.

"I've given the children permission to call me Gray," he said.

"It shows a lack of respect on their part if they use your first name."

"Or a depth of caring, a bond of friendship. Besides, I'm certain some rule exists that says you can only go fishing with someone if you call him by his first name."

Within the pale light of the lantern hanging from the porch, he saw her blush and reveal the tiniest of smiles as she lowered her gaze to the porch. "It's not proper."

"It would please me greatly if you'd call me Gray as well," he said quietly, ignoring her flimsy argument.

Her blush deepened. "I prefer Grayson."

The shaft of pleasure that pierced him took him by surprise. "To whom do you prefer me?"

Horror swept over her face as she backed up a step. "No, I meant I prefer the name Grayson over Gray. I don't prefer you over anyone."

Studying Abbie's flustered state, he was hit with the sudden realization that the woman knew nothing of flirtation. She took everything at face value. It was a wholesome yet disconcerting discovery. She wasn't like the bold women he'd known in England who understood the risks and gambled with wit and flirtation to gain a moment's pleasure. A careless word or gesture could hurt Abbie more readily than a sharpened rapier.

He extended the cup toward her. "I was only teasing, Abbie. I meant no harm."

He was astonished to feel a slight trembling in her fingers as she took the cup from him.

"I never know what to make out of half the things you say."

"I assure you that they're all innocent. When they aren't, you will have no doubts whatsoever." He could almost see the thoughts spinning through her mind as she tried to decipher his words. She truly was a delight and if she didn't have three children hanging onto her skirts, he would have thought she was as innocent as a newborn babe.

"Come on, Gray!" Johnny yelled.

"You'd best go," Abbie suggested.

Unexpectedly, he loathed leaving her. "You're not coming?"

She shook her head. "Lydia and I will join you later."

"I'll look forward to your arrival." He caught a glimpse of the red creeping beneath her collar before he began strolling toward the woods. The odd thing was—he was telling her the truth.

Abbie whipped the needle and thread through the material, effectively closing off the opening through which she had only moments before stuffed goose down and feathers. She tied a knot and bit off the thread. Then she stroked the pallet. It would provide some padding between Grayson's body and the straw. She felt the heat scald her cheeks as she thought of him sleeping where her hand now rested.

She clenched her fists to stop them from trembling. She'd never in her life thought about a man as much as she found herself thinking of Grayson. Her heart had sped up at the sight of him rumpled from sleep this morning, and she had fought an incredible urge to comb his golden hair off his brow.

She had never felt these things around John—had never anticipated greeting the day with the sight of him, had never felt a sorrow when night took him beyond her vision. Her life with John had been practical, routine. She doubted that Grayson Rhodes had ever had a practical thought or a routine day. She squeezed her eyes shut and tried to bring forth an image of John smiling. With a sadness, she realized she'd never seen her husband smile.

"Mama, I think the biscuits are burning," Lydia said.

"Oh!" Abbie cast the pallet aside and bolted out of the rocker. Kneeling before the hearth, she wrapped a towel around the pan and brought the biscuits off the shelf. She tapped the dark brown bread. "I think they're fine."

"Were you sleeping?" Lydia asked, as though the very notion was unbelievable.

"No, I was thinking about your father," she said quietly.

Lydia wrinkled her nose. "I don't remember him much. Was he like Gray?"

"No!" Abbie said much too quickly, with too much force.

Lydia's eyes widened as though surprised by her mother's outburst. Abbie took a deep breath. "Your father . . . your father was a very serious man. Most of the men around here are. The Englishmen have never faced the possibility of starvation or crops not coming in if the weather doesn't cooperate. Life shapes men differently.''

"Do you miss him?" Lydia asked.

Abbie felt her heart tighten. She didn't want to deceive her daughter, and she didn't want her to misinterpret the truth. She set the biscuits aside, stood, and tugged one of Lydia's blonde braids. ''Your father has been gone a long time. I missed his presence at first, but I began to accept his absence as part of my life. It's best not to hanker for what we can't change.''

Lydia nodded with a child's understanding. ''It won't change anything if you miss him. It'll just hurt.''

"That's right. Now we'd best pack up the breakfast before your brothers get hungry and start eating their bait."

"Oh, Ma!" Lydia screeched, sticking out her tongue. "Worms!"

Smiling, Abbie reached for the biscuits, wishing she wasn't anticipating seeing Grayson quite as much as she was.

Abbie's chest tightened, her heart pounded, her palms grew damp, and her step faltered as she neared the area where she knew her boys liked to fish. She wondered briefly if perhaps she were ill. She gripped the handle on the wicker basket more securely and pressed the quilt hanging over her arm against her side. She heard the rushing water of the river and her boys' harsh whispers.

"Remember to be quiet," she said to her daughter trudging along beside her. "We don't want to frighten the fish away."

"If there's any fish to scare. Johnny and Micah make enough noise to keep them away."

Abbie peered through the foliage. She saw her sons sitting at the edge of the bank, their poles dangling over the river. Nearby, Grayson was stretched out on the green clover, his hands folded beneath his head. Her mouth suddenly went dry.

She'd never been completely comfortable around John once she realized what passed between a man and a woman during the darkness of the night. Her reaction to the sight of Grayson was stranger than anything she'd ever experienced around John. It was downright ridiculous. She wasn't married to Grayson—had plans to never again marry. Nothing would ever pass between them during the night.

She stepped into the clearing. Johnny jerked his head around, and she pressed a finger to her lips. He glanced at Grayson, and she saw his shoulders roll forward as he fought back his laughter. She crept toward the Englishman. His eyes were closed, his face relaxed. With his blond curls serving as a halo, he almost reminded her of an angel—a wicked angel who teased with a gleam in his eye and a smile that made her forget her name. She wished he'd stop teasing her—wished he would tease her more. Wished he'd leave—wished he'd stay. Wished he'd say her name—

He opened his eyes and lifted the corners of his mouth. "Abbie."

Her heart pounded. "I thought you were sleeping."

"Not with the boys so near the river."

"They know not to go into the water."

He lifted a brow. "What a boy knows and what a boy does aren't always one and the same."

She suddenly realized that she'd instinctively known he'd keep a careful watch over her sons. "Is that the voice of experience talking?"

"Most definitely."

She glanced at the fishing pole resting on the ground beside him. "You'd have more luck catching fish if you put the hook in the water."

He shook his head. "It seems we are responsible for baiting our own hooks. I had no desire to touch one of those squishy creatures." He sat up and pointed toward her basket. "What have you there?"

"Breakfast."

"Wonderful. I'm starving." He unfolded his body and took the quilt from her. She watched him open it with a snap and settle it into place over the clover—so simple a task, a gesture John had never done for her. He took the basket from her and set it in the center of the quilt. Then he took her hand.

Abbie jerked free, cradling her hand against her chest. "What were you doing?"

He narrowed his eyes. "I was going to assist you in sitting on the quilt. It's my understanding that it's easier for a woman to sit with a man's help."

She glanced over to see Lydia staring at her, her youthful brows drawn together to form a deep crease.

She didn't want her only daughter to grow up harboring her mother's fears.

"It means nothing, Abbie. Only a courtesy. The women I've known appreciated a man's attention."

She wanted to snap that she didn't need a man's attention, didn't want it. Instead she looked at his hand. A week in the fields had shaded it a golden brown. He twisted his hand slightly, presenting his palm as an offering. His gesture hinted at nothing threatening, and yet the action terrified her. She felt like a horse that was being gently tamed to accept the saddle. An image of this man riding her swept through her mind, and the panic increased. She lifted her gaze to his. Something flitted through his eyes— an understanding perhaps.

With a seamless movement, he turned to Lydia and bowed slightly. "Miss Lydia."

Giggling, Lydia covered her mouth with one hand, but her glittering eyes revealed her smile. She slipped her hand into Grayson's and with an elegant dip, eased down to the quilt.

Grayson released her hand and tilted his head slightly. "You are supposed to say, 'Thank you, kind sir.'"

Smiling brightly, Lydia mimicked his words. Abbie wondered if she'd ever warmed to a man's attention like that.

Grayson raised a questioning brow slightly. She fought back her doubts and gave a shaky nod. He smiled warmly and wrapped his fingers around hers. The action could not have been more devastating if he'd wrapped his entire body around hers. She dropped down to the quilt. When she tried to pull her hand away, he tightened his grip. She jerked her head up and glared at him. He seemed to be waiting.

"Mama, you're supposed to thank him," Lydia reminded her.

Abbie forced herself to smile. "Thank you, kind sir."

She had expected him to release her hand. Instead, she was shocked to watch him lean over slightly and brush his lips over her knuckles.

"You are most welcome, gentle lady," he said in a low voice, his warm breath skimming over her skin.

Then, mercifully, he let go of her hand and knelt beside her. "Was that so horrid?"

Ignoring him, she glanced over her shoulder. "Boys, come eat."

The boys scrambled up from the bank. She lifted the lid on the basket and removed a bundle. Her hands were shaking so badly, she was surprised she was able to bring back the edges of the cloth to reveal biscuits slathered with butter and stuffed with crisp bacon. Each of the children grabbed a biscuit. She extended the bundle toward Grayson. "Help yourself."

He took a biscuit, studied it from all angles, and began to eat. Abbie removed a jar from the basket and unwrapped the towel from around it before passing it off to Johnny.

The silence was awkward and suffocating. How could she have felt so comfortable with this man at dawn and so uneasy around him now because of a simple touch? John had only ever touched her within the intimacy of a bed.

"How many fish have you caught?" she asked.

Johnny wiped the back of his hand across his mouth before passing the jar to Micah. "None. Had some nibbles, though."

Micah gulped the milk before passing the jar to Lydia. Reaching across, Abbie wiped the white mustache away from his lip.

"Lookit," he said, baring his bottom teeth. With his tongue, he moved one tooth forward. He looked different, not so much like her little boy with the spectacles sitting on his face. He'd worn them to bed, and she'd had to gently remove them after he fell asleep.

"A loose tooth. You are growing up, aren't you?"

He nodded, beaming.

She took the milk from Lydia. Turning slightly, she offered it to Grayson, his intense gaze causing the breath to back up in her lungs. She wondered what he was thinking, even though she'd never ask. "Would you like some?"

He dusted his hands over his trousers. "Thank you."

He lifted the jar to his mouth, and she watched his throat muscles work as he took a long, slow swallow before handing it back to her. Taking a shaky breath, she set the jar on the quilt.

"What's England like?" Lydia asked.

"Much cooler than Texas," Grayson answered.

"Do you have any brothers or sisters?"

Abbie's heart tightened as she watched Grayson study his biscuit.

"No," he said quietly before popping the last of his breakfast into his mouth.

"You're lucky. I wish I didn't have any brothers."

"You'd feel differently if you had no brothers," he assured her.

She shrugged. "Maybe."

"I brought apples," Abbie told everyone, taking one from the basket and handing it to Grayson.

He scrutinized it as though he'd never seen one. He ran his thumb and forefinger along the length of the stem. "Lydia, would you like to know who you'll marry when you grow up?"

Lydia's eyes widened with wonder. "You can tell?"

He shifted closer to her and gave her the apple. "You twist the stem," he explained, "while I recite the alphabet. When the stem breaks, you'll marry someone whose name begins with the last letter I say."

Abbie sensed Lydia's excitement as her daughter held the apple in one hand and grabbed the stem with her delicate finger and thumb. With her brows furrowed in concentration, she gave the stem a twist.

"A," Grayson announced.

Another twist.

"B."

She twisted, and he called out the letters until the stem broke off at the letter I. Lydia wrinkled her nose. "I? What names begin with I?"

"Lots of names," Grayson assured her.

"Name one," she commanded.

Grayson looked at Abbie. She drew an absolute blank. She rolled her shoulders forward, shaking her head slightly. Grayson turned his attention back to Lydia. "Ichabod."

Johnny guffawed. "Lydia's gonna marry a man named Ichabod!"

"Ain't neither," Lydia said.

Abbie hated to see her daughter's disappointment. Why couldn't he have skipped the awkward letters? Then she brightened. "Irwin!"

Lydia rolled her eyes, and Johnny laughed harder. Grayson smiled at her. "Good try."

She tilted up her nose. "It's better than Ichabod. Why would you saddle my daughter with someone named Ichabod?"

"Ivanhoe, then."

"Ivanhoe?" Lydia repeated.

"Don't you know the story of Ivanhoe?" Grayson asked. "He was one of the bravest knights in all of England."

"What's a knight?" Micah asked in his deep voice.

"A knight was a soldier of sorts and he wore armor to protect himself from the blows of a sword—"

"Is a sword like a saber?" Johnny asked.

"It's similar, but it's bigger and heavier ... and ... don't you children go to school?"

"After the crops are in, I go for a spell. I can write my name," Johnny said with obvious pride.

Grayson supposed in all fairness the children didn't need to know history in order to harvest cotton, but he couldn't imagine living without education. Dear God, but his father had given him far more than he'd realized.

"My pa was a soldier," Johnny suddenly blurted. "He killed a thousand damn Yankees."

"Johnny," Abbie scolded. "Don't swear and don't stretch the truth."

Grayson gave the boy an indulgent smile. "Did he?"

The lad averted his gaze, nodded briskly, and began to pull weeds from the ground. Grayson remembered how much he had admired his father, the tall pedestal upon which he'd placed him—and how much it had hurt when he'd toppled off, and he'd realized that his father was only a man. Johnny need never see his father topple. "Sounds as though your father was a worthy opponent. If he were English, he would no doubt have been knighted."

Johnny jerked his head up. "I reckon so, too." He jumped to his feet and ran toward the stream.

"Can I go, too?" Lydia asked.

With a wave of her hand, Abbie sent the two remaining children to the river, an apple in each hand.

"If you'll watch the children, then I think I'll take a nap," Grayson said. There was something to be said for stretching out on a bed of clover and listening to the babble of the flowing stream. With his hands folded beneath his head, Grayson watched as clouds drifted by, barely visible through the abundant scattering of leaves above. Closing his eyes, he was beginning to have an understanding of why men had fought to claim this land.

Abbie dared a glance at Grayson. Without his intense gaze focused on her, it was much easier to apologize. She considered waiting until he began to snore, but she didn't think an apology counted if the person it was directed to was asleep.

"I'm sorry I jerked away from you . . . at first, when you were trying to be a gentleman," she said, her voice low, not certain she wanted him to hear her apology.

"No harm done."

She tossed out the milk and put the empty jar into the wicker basket before stuffing the remaining biscuits inside. "I . . . I just . . ."

He rolled to his side and lifted up on an elbow. "You don't owe me any explanations, Abbie." He gave her a disarming smile. "I wasn't trying to be a gentleman. I was searching for an excuse to touch you." He reached toward her, and she thought he might touch his finger to her cheek, but he retreated. "You're quite right not to trust me."

"It's not you so much . . . It's . . ." She studied the wrinkles in her apron, thinking how her life seemed as untidy. She smoothed out her apron. "I was sixteen when I married John. I wanted to marry him, to be his wife, to take care of his house . . ." She felt the heat scald her cheeks as she kept her gaze averted. "I didn't know . . . everything a wife does for her husband."

The incredible silence stretched between them, blocking all sounds until she no longer heard the children. Why had she told him that embarrassing truth?

"Did you love him?" he asked quietly.

She wrung her hands in her lap. "He was my husband."

"But you didn't love him."

She felt the tears burn the backs of her eyes. She pressed trembling fingers to her lips and shifted her gaze to him. "I tried . . . but I just couldn't."

His blue eyes darkened with concern. "Did he hurt you?"

She shook her head vigorously. "He was a good man. And wise. He knew when to plant the cotton. You see, you don't plant it at the same time every year. You have to be able to read the weather, and the moon, and the signs of nature. You compare that with the almanac. No one planted a crop until John Westland began to plant his."

"He sounds like a remarkable man."

Turning, she looked at her children. "I should have loved him."

"You respected him, admired him—that's much more than some men get."

She met his gaze. "Is it? It hardly seems enough. I think of him dying with no one loving him—"

"In England, among the nobility, marriages are seldom a love match. My father married a woman because she was his social equal. Her father was a duke. She was a biddable female who understood obligation. I don't think the duke ever visited her bed once she gave him an heir."

Abbie drew her brows together. "Where did he sleep?"

Grayson smiled. "He had his own room. It's quite fashionable for a husband and wife to have separate rooms. Wouldn't you have preferred to have your own room?''

She gnawed on her lip. She had never welcomed the physical joining of her husband's body to hers, but still she had found comfort in his presence through the night. Although she had slept alone for five years now, she still huddled on the edge of the bed, recognizing the portion that her husband's large body had claimed. A thought struck her from out of the blue. ''Did you leave someone behind?''

Grayson sat up. ''I beg your pardon?''

Abbie balled her fist around the hem of her apron. ''Were you betrothed or married . . . or was there someone you cared about that you wanted to come with you?''

His smile turned melancholy. ''No, but that's an interesting way to turn the subject off you.'' He picked up the apple stem that Lydia had dropped on the quilt and popped it into his mouth.

''You don't have to eat that. I brought plenty of apples,'' Abbie said.

He shook his head. ''I only want the stem,'' he mumbled around the object in his mouth.

''Why?''

He pointed to his lips. ''Watch.''

She stared intensely at his mouth, fascinated by the ebb and flow of his lips, lips that looked as soft as his hands had felt less than a week ago. Although he'd sealed his mouth, she could tell that something was going on. His movements caused hollows to form and recede within his cheeks. Then he placed his fingers to his mouth and removed the stem—tied into a knot.

He smiled triumphantly. "Not bad, eh?"

Dumbfounded, she couldn't prevent herself from gawking at his accomplishment.

He leaned toward her, a wicked gleam in his eye. "You should see what else I can do with my tongue."

"What?" she asked.

His smile faltered. "What?"

"What else do you do with your tongue?"

He scrutinized her as though she were the one who had stupidly tossed an apple stem into her mouth. What purpose did tying it into a knot—

"You honestly don't know to what I'm referring, do you?" he asked quietly.

"Should I?"

With a deep sigh, he tossed the knotted apple stem over his shoulder. "No, I suppose not." He looked toward the river. "So what are the plans for the remainder of the day?"

Abbie finished putting everything into the basket, stood, shook out the quilt, and tucked it beneath her arm. "I need to cut that calico I bought yesterday into pieces for Lydia's dress. Henhouse needs to be cleaned, barn needs some repairs—"

Grayson jerked his head around. "I thought today was supposed to be a day of rest."

Abbie wrapped her fingers around the handle of the basket and lifted it. "We're not working in the fields. That's as close to a day of rest as we get."

6

"Did you know that if a snapping turtle bites you, it won't let go until it hears thunder?" Johnny asked.

Trudging toward the house as the early afternoon sun beat down on him, Grayson glanced down at Johnny's serious face. He had eventually succumbed to the boys' pleading and threaded a hook through a wiggling worm. It was either do that or return home where a chicken coop needed to be cleaned.

"Truly?"

"Yep."

As he walked next to Johnny, Micah was jerking his head up and down to emphasize the truth of his brother's words regarding snapping turtles. They had been imparting words of wisdom most of the morning.

"Once a snapping turtle bit Ezra Jones's grandpa right on the finger." Johnny pointed his index finger at Grayson for emphasis. "Weren't a storm cloud in the sky. So he took an axe and chopped off that

99

turtle's head." Johnny's eyes widened. "And he still hung on!"

"Amazing," Grayson conceded.

"Amazing," Micah croaked beside him.

"You know what Ezra Jones's grandpa did?" Johnny asked. He didn't wait for Grayson to answer. "He chopped off his own finger!"

Grayson skewed his face into an appropriately horrified expression even though he suspected Ezra Jones's grandfather had lost his finger through carelessness and not a desire to rid himself of a turtle's head. "I shall take great care to never place my finger near a snapping turtle."

"Next time we go fishin', me and Micah will try to find a snapping turtle so you'll know what one looks like," Johnny offered.

"Perhaps next time, we should try fishing later in the day," Grayson suggested as they reached the edge of the woods. "I'm certain fish are practical creatures that arise at a decent hour."

Johnny's face split into a wide grin. "You don't like gettin' up early, do you?"

"Not particularly."

"What did you do all day before you come here?" he asked.

Ah, God, what had he done? "Well, I might visit with friends or take a ride through a park—"

"What's a park?" Micah croaked.

Grayson spread out his hands. "Within the city, it's a place with trees and flowers, a place where people stroll or ride in a carriage—don't you have parks here?"

Both boys simply stared at him.

"Of course not," he mumbled. "Whatever was I thinking."

"It's a lot different here, ain't it?" Johnny asked.

"Yes, lad, it is."

"Do you like it here?"

The boys' faces held such high expectations that Grayson decided to fudge a little with the truth. "It's an adventure, and I've always liked adventure."

"Me, too!" Johnny exclaimed. "But every time I try to go on an adventure, Ma comes after me and brings me back home."

"You should be grateful that you have a mother who cares enough—"

The scream shattered the peace of the afternoon. In a frenzy, birds flew from the trees. Grayson's heart slammed against his ribs.

"That's Lydia!" Johnny cried.

"Indians!" Micah yelled, his raspy voice giving the word a threatening edge.

Indians! He'd read stories of renegade attacks—

"Bloody damned hell!" The fishing pole slipped from his hand as he tore into a run, heading for the farm. He heard another scream—Lydia again—followed by another frantic cry. Abbie!

Why hadn't Abbie told him about the dangers? Why hadn't she and Lydia stayed with them at the river? He heard the boys' footsteps echoing his.

The house came into view, the curtains billowing through the windows like a woman waving her handkerchief to get a man's attention. The horses were prancing around the corral—but where were the Indians? Where was Abbie?

Another shriek sounded—from near the barn. Grayson grabbed a pitchfork that was leaning against the front wall of the barn and rounded the corner with a heathen yell that would have done his medieval ancestors proud.

And froze, staring at the tableaux in front of him. Abbie was sweeping hogs.

At least that was his initial impression. With a broom, she had been patting the backside of a hog before she stilled and stared at him as though he were a madman.

He felt like a bloody damned fool!

He lowered the pitchfork until the prongs dug into the ground. A mistake. The hog she'd been swatting now had no guidance so it turned abruptly and charged—toward him.

He had seen the hogs in the pen, but outside of their enclosure, they looked enormous; their grunts and squeals sounded frightening. This one was snorting until it sounded like a bloody train barreling down the tracks.

He tossed the pitchfork aside and was on the verge of saving his ass when Abbie cried, "Catch it!"

"With what?" He had no time to think, little time to react. He simply flung himself at the charging beast, wrapping his arms around its thick neck. It squealed loudly, right near his ear, and he was certain he'd lose his hearing on that side. Then the damnable beast reared up as much as its portly body would allow before rolling onto its side, pinning Gray beneath it. The air rushed out of him in a painful whoosh, and he wondered if the duke would feel any remorse when he received word that Grayson had died—squashed by an immense sow.

The duke's heir apparent would no doubt laugh his fool head off.

Then an angel swept down with a vengeance, mud caking her cheeks, strands of hair flying wildly about her face, her chest heaving as she gasped for breath, her violet eyes wide with fury.

"Get off him, you stupid hog!" she yelled, bringing the broom down on the beast's back.

The animal jerked its massive frame, snorted, and rolled to its feet. In an agonizing rush, air filled Grayson's lungs. He watched the hog trot toward the pen, Abbie chasing after it, applying the broom repeatedly to its backside.

Grayson struggled to his feet and staggered to the pen, still fighting for breath, wondering if he'd broken a rib. The hog went into the pen and abruptly did an about-face.

"No, you don't!" Grayson roared as he blocked the animal's path, dropped to his knees, and flung his arms once again around the hog's neck. With a twist, it slid free. Before he could catch his balance, Grayson found himself lying face-down in the mud. He heard the hog snort, followed by the loveliest sound to ever touch his ears.

Abbie's laughter.

He pushed up to his elbows, used his fingers to drag the mud from his eyes, and glanced back. Her shoulders rolling forward, she pressed a fist against her stomach, her smile bright as the laughter trickled out like the clear water of a spring flowing over sparkling rocks.

Dear Lord, he'd never realized before how beautiful Abigail Westland truly was.

"Think it's funny, do you?" he asked.

She bobbed her head in the same manner that Johnny often did. He glanced quickly around the pen. The hog had decided to content itself with its slop. Grayson looked back. Tears were running down Abbie's face, and she dirtied her face further each time she tried to swipe them away.

Without warning, quicker than lightning could flash, he grabbed her hand and tugged her down. She released a startled screech and slid to the ground beside him. With a wide grin, he rolled halfway over her, tucking her body beneath his, his hands curling around her arms. "Think it's funny now?" he asked in a low voice.

He watched the joy in her eyes slowly fade into fear. No, not fear, not something that extreme. Apprehension perhaps, wariness. Her breath came in short, halting bursts. "Please, let me go."

He felt the tremors racing through her body. "Abbie?"

She pounded her fists against his shoulders. "Get off me. Oh, God, please get off me."

He rolled away and watched as she frantically struggled to her feet, slipping in the mud, desperate to escape the pen—to escape him.

"Ma! We got the other hogs!" Johnny cried as he

and Micah guided the three remaining hogs toward the enclosure.

"Good," she said, wrapping her hands around the gate until her knuckles turned white. "Mr. Rhodes, you'd best get out," she said without looking at him, her voice shaking.

The mud cloying at him, he brought himself to his feet and shuffled out of the pen. The boys guided the snorting hogs home. Abbie slammed the gate and set the latch.

"Children, you need to see to cleaning the henhouse," Abbie threw over her shoulder as she strode toward the house.

Grayson heard the children groan before walking off, dragging their feet. He flung the mud from his hands, running the past few moments through his mind. What had happened?

Using the pump out back, Abbie began filling the bucket. She needed a bath—badly. It didn't have to be hot, just wet. She heard the squishy sound of soaked, muddy shoes and pumped harder, faster.

"Abbie?"

She squeezed her eyes shut. "I'm going to take a bath. You need to go to the barn."

"Because I touched you? I won't leave until you tell me why you're upset."

He took a step toward her. Releasing the bucket, she skittered back. It banged against the pump before splashing water over the ground. Her heart was beating like a wild thing, her hands trembling as she stood covered in mud, staring at a man who was also

covered in mud. Her chest felt as though someone
had tied a rope taut around it. "I know what you
need," she ground out. "You're not gonna get it
from me."

He should have looked ridiculous with the mud
streaking his face. Instead he looked incredibly foreboding as he narrowed his eyes. "What do I *need*?"

Her gaze darted to his trousers and back to his
eyes. How innocent they both looked, but she knew
differently. "I know what I felt when you were on
top of me. I know what you want."

Bending, he picked up the bucket and began to
work the pump. "You think I want to ravish you?"
he asked quietly.

She nodded jerkily.

He stilled. "You're right. I can think of nothing
I'd rather do than lay you down on the cool clover,
remove your clothes, and make passionate love to
you. It's what I *want*, Abbie. It's not what I *need*."

"I'm a widow. I know for a man there's no difference between wants and needs. I'm never getting
married again. I'm never going to have a man in my
house, in my bed—"

"Did your husband rape you?"

Abbie staggered back. What in God's name was
she doing discussing this subject with this man? How
could she explain the dread of hearing the bed creak
beneath his weight as he rolled toward her . . . the
humiliation of having her gown lifted, the initial pain.
"No, he never forced me, but—"

"But perhaps he led you to believe you had no
choice when it came to *his needs*. With me, you will

always have a choice. Even if I am unable to control my body's reaction to your nearness, I can control my actions." He dumped the water over his head, washing away some of the mud. Then he gave her a look that she thought might have scalded her had she been standing any closer to him. "Remember that, Abbie. Should anything ever happen between us, it will be because it is what *you want*."

She watched him walk away, the mud that still clung to his clothes making his movements stiff. She thought about yelling after him that women didn't have wants and needs with respect to *that*, but if that were the case, why did she suddenly find herself wondering exactly what it would feel like to lay naked upon clover?

It felt damn good to be clean.

Grayson walked from the back of the house where he'd indulged in a hot bath after helping the children clean the henhouse and the stalls in the barn.

He knew Abbie would call them into the house for dinner soon. The sun was easing over the horizon, but he was too weary to appreciate its beauty, too grateful to know the day of rest would soon be over. He did not consider the English to be a lazy lot, but by God, they did know how to appreciate a day of rest. How in God's name did these Texans continue day after day when nothing awaited them but toil and hard work? Why should a man work his fingers to the bone if he never had a moment to appreciate what he had attained?

Grayson strolled into the barn and watched the

dust motes waltz lazily around him. His body craved a few moments of hiding away and doing absolutely nothing. He climbed the ladder toward the loft. Just a few moments of solitude when his hands weren't in constant movement, his mind reeling with possibilities. The top of the loft came into view and he stilled.

Abbie sat in the loft, framed by the opening, looking for all the world like an ethereal painting. Her feet were tucked beneath her, her hands caressing his book as though it were a lover. His stomach tightened as he was suddenly hit with the ridiculous notion that he wished he were a book. Although he could only see her profile, awe was clearly written within every line and curve of her face.

The ladder creaked as he hoisted himself into the loft. She jerked her head around. The wonder in her eyes very nearly stole every bit of breath from his body. She held her find toward him. "It's a book," she whispered reverently.

"*Ivanhoe*," Grayson said quietly, not wishing to shatter the fragile moment. "It's my favorite."

She trailed her fingers over the leather cover. "I've never seen an honest-to-gosh real book before. Except for the Bible . . . and John's almanac."

Her statement held no great surprise. So many of the things he'd taken for granted in England were sought-after luxuries here. "Would you like me to read it to you?"

He saw desire and doubt swirl within her eyes, and at that moment, he would have given his soul to have the desire directed toward him. "I could read it to you and the children after the evening meal.''

Her eyes brightened. ''Oh, they'd like that.''

It surprised him to discover that he would as well. He'd once spent the evenings drinking, gaming, womanizing, and he could suddenly think of nothing more alluring than sitting before a fire in the evening and reading to Abbie and her children. ''I'll look forward to it.''

With great care, she set the book into the exact spot where he'd left it the night before. Then, reaching out, she touched the newest addition to his home. ''I made you the pallet I promised. Stuffed it with goose feathers. Thought it would be more comfortable than just lying on quilts on the straw.''

''I can't recall ever receiving so fine a gift.''

''It's not a fine gift, but it's practical.''

''I was referring to your smile as you held the book. You don't smile enough, Abbie.''

Her cheeks flamed red. ''I need to get supper going.''

Although he preferred to stay where he was, out of respect for her apprehensions he moved aside so she could scramble past him. She was well out of sight before her head suddenly popped up, her brow furrowed. ''You won't forget to bring the book, will you?''

He smiled warmly. ''I won't forget.''

She disappeared over the edge. He crawled across the loft and glanced out the opening. He couldn't give a name to the stirring in his chest that grew as he watched Abigail Westland—widow, cotton farmer, mother of three—skip to the house with joyful abandon.

He only knew that even in hell, a man could find snatches of heaven.

Grayson had spent his life longing for attention, adoration, the warmth of family. As he sat in a chair before the hearth with an enraptured audience before him, he had never felt more content. The children were stretched out on the floor on their stomachs, their eyes wide, their attention riveted on him.

Abbie had begun the evening sitting in a chair across from him, sewing in hand. It had pleased him greatly when her hands finally stilled as she became absorbed in the story. He wished he'd brought a hundred books.

And he wished he could read through the night, but the day had taken a toll on him and he knew tomorrow would be no easier. He read the final words of the chapter and closed the book.

Johnny scrambled up, his brow deeply furrowed. "You're done?"

"For this evening. It's quite late."

Abbie looked toward the clock on the mantel and her eyes widened. "Oh, my goodness. It's almost ten. I can't believe it." She stood. "Children, say good night to Mr. Rhodes. It's long past time for bed."

The children grumbled, but they dutifully thanked him before shuffling across the room. Lydia went through one door, the boys through another. One door remained closed, and Grayson knew it would be the door into Abbie's bedroom. He had never given much thought to where she slept, but suddenly he had a strong desire to extend this feeling of family . . . to follow her to her room and take her into his arms—

An action to which he knew she would strenuously object.

"Thank you for reading to the children," Abbie said, wringing her hands as though she'd realized the direction his thoughts had traveled.

He stood and set the book on the table. "It was my pleasure. I'll leave the book here."

He wanted to prolong the moment, but knew no good would come of it. He crossed the room, opened the door, and stepped into the night. He heard her quiet footsteps and turned to see her standing within a shaft of pale lamplight, one hand gripping the edge of the door.

"The children will probably dream of merry England tonight," she said hesitantly.

He took a step toward her. "What will you dream of, Abbie?"

"I don't dream. Do you dream of England?" she asked hastily.

"No."

"You don't dream either?" she asked.

"I dream, but the truth of them would probably frighten you."

"You have nightmares? Are they from your childhood?"

"They aren't nightmares, and they are most certainly not the dreams of a child. I rather enjoy them actually."

She shook her head. "You're not making any sense."

"I dream of you," he said quietly. He saw the shock ripple through her eyes and knew he was right to think the admission would unsettle her.

"You shouldn't say that," she scolded.

"But you asked," he pointed out, wishing he had indeed kept his mouth shut. Conversations held with her were as fragile as hand-blown glass, and it took very little to shatter her trust.

She pulled back into the house slightly and the door closed a little. "You can't help it, can you?"

"What?"

"You can't help being a rogue."

"Afraid not. I fight it where you're concerned, but I'm a weak man."

"Not so weak, I think," she said quietly. "And you're kind."

"Dear God, don't tell anyone that. It'll send my reputation to hell."

She bowed her head. "I'm sorry about this afternoon. I think . . . you were only trying to tease me when you pulled me into the mud. I . . . I'm no good at flirting or teasing—"

"For which I'm incredibly grateful one moment and deeply frustrated the next."

She snapped her gaze up to his.

"You're honest and so open," he explained. "I've never known anyone like you. You always have the slightest look of bafflement on your face when I tease you, as though you aren't quite sure how to react.

Rest assured that I am harmless . . . until you give me permission to be otherwise.''

Before she could protest, he leapt off the porch and threw over his shoulder, "Good night, Abbie. Have pleasant dreams.''

7

"**Y**ou want to make sure you cover the roots," a deep voice rumbled over Grayson's shoulder.

Grayson nodded at Abbie's brother. "I appreciate the advice."

He returned to chopping the weeds away from the cotton stalks, but he felt James watching him as though he were an irritating gnat that needed to be squashed. "Am I doing something else wrong?"

"Amy and I . . ."

Grayson straightened, bending backward to work the painful knots out of his lower back. "You and Amy?"

"We've got an extra room at our house. We plan to use it for the baby when we have one, but right now it's empty. Thought you might want to come live with us."

Grayson smiled slightly. "I'm quite content in Abbie's barn. Thank you."

All attempts at good humor fled the man's face. "I don't want to see Abbie hurt."

"I have no intention of hurting her."

James took a step closer, and Grayson had little doubt that before the war had battled the man down to skin and bones he was a formidable size. "I don't know how things are done in England, but we live by different rules here. If you hurt Abbie, I'll kill you."

Grayson arched a brow. "So you're the one who killed her husband?"

Horror sweeping over his face, James jerked his head back as though Grayson had punched him. "No! Yankees killed him."

"Yet you had no objections to her husband hurting her. You just don't want an Englishman to hurt her."

"John never hurt Abbie—"

"Then why is she fearful of a man's touch?"

"She's not—"

"She is," Grayson insisted. "When I did nothing more than offer her my assistance Sunday, she acted as though my hand were a snake." What had transpired at the hog pen was a matter he saw no need to divulge.

He could see James contemplating his answer as he looked toward the house where Abbie and several women were preparing the noon meal. "I don't think John . . . She would have told me . . . John wasn't . . ."

He turned his attention back to Grayson. The concern reflected in his eyes came as a surprise. "You think he hurt her?"

"How could he not? Dear God, man, she was only sixteen when she married him."

"That's not unusual. A lot of women get married young—"

"She wasn't a woman. She was a child."

James dropped his gaze to the ground and mumbled, "Too many mouths to feed."

Grayson leaned forward slightly. "What has that to do with anything?"

With guilt reflected in his eyes, James met Grayson's gaze. "My parents had eleven children. Crops weren't doing well. Pa thought it would be better on the older girls if they took a husband, had someone else to feed and clothe them. Daniel had been courting Elizabeth so that was no problem, but Abbie . . . well, she hadn't caught anyone's eye."

Grayson assumed the community had consisted of fools who wore blinders instead of hats.

James shrugged. "John was a bit of a loner but he was the most prosperous farmer around."

Grayson allowed his gaze to roam to the small clapboard house and back to the fields. This was prosperity? Dear God, and his father had expected him to become a man of means here? "So your father sold her?"

"No. He just gave John permission to ask for Abbie's hand. She was excited about being his wife."

I didn't know everything a wife does for her husband.

"Yes, well, I'm afraid that excitement might have died on her wedding night—along with her innocence."

"I hope you're wrong."

"Perhaps I am. Perhaps her husband didn't hurt

her, but someone did. Of that, I'm sure."

James clenched his jaw and gave a long slow nod. "If you're right, I'll find out who it was and if he's still alive, I'll kill him." He turned, started to walk away, stopped, and glanced over his shoulder. "And if you hurt her, I'll kill you."

Grayson watched him make his way to the end of the furrow. Texas seemed to lack not only civilization but civilized people.

Abbie felt the hand clamp onto her shoulder. With a tiny shriek, she spun around. She pressed her hand above her pounding heart. "Dear Lord, James, you scared me to death."

Her brother narrowed his eyes. "Who did you think I was?"

"I had no idea who you were, but I'm not used to being grabbed." She turned back to the heavy cast-iron caldron and stirred the simmering beans.

"Is the Englishman bothering you?"

She snapped her head around. "Where in the world did that question come from?"

Her brother's gaunt cheeks flamed red. She wondered if John had grown as thin before he was killed.

James ducked his head slightly. "I've seen the way the Englishman watches you."

Abbie's heart fluttered like the wings of a butterfly being spread for the first time. "Exactly how is he looking at me?"

James' face became even redder. "You know, Abbie."

She planted a hand on a hip. "No, James, I don't."

"He looks at you the way a man does when he's . . . thinkin' things he shouldn't.''

Abbie shifted her gaze to the fields. She could see little more than the hat that she knew Grayson was wearing. She tucked a stray strand of hair behind her ear. "I have no interest in him, and he knows it. So he can look all he wants. Nothing will come of it.''

"He says John hurt you."

She snapped her gaze back to her brother. "What?"

"He thinks . . . Why did you jump when I touched you?''

"I told you. You startled me.''

He lifted his hand, and she jerked back slightly. A sadness touched his eyes. "Why didn't you tell me you were unhappy with John?''

"I wasn't unhappy. He was a good man.''

"But was he a good husband?''

"Let the dead rest in peace, James. I have three children that I love." And memories that did no more than haunt her.

Grayson heard the clanging iron that meant Abbie had finished preparing the noon meal. He thought briefly of the tiny brass bell the duke's wife chimed whenever she was ready for a servant to serve another portion of the meal. Here someone only clanged the iron once because more often than not only one dish was served.

Each day, more men worked the fields, the vanquished returning home with little or no fanfare. Some men introduced themselves; others simply took up a hoe and chopped at the ground as though they'd never left. No one spoke of the war that had taken him from family and home.

He strode toward the house, falling into step beside Harry. "When are you going to take a razor to your face?"

Harry rubbed his hand back and forth across the dark bristle coating his chin. "When we've made our fortune."

"I would think a beard would be unbearably hot in this climate."

"It's not that bad, and it offers some protection from the sun." He slanted a glance toward Grayson. "Besides, the time I would spend shaving, I can spend sleeping."

The laughter flowed from Grayson. He and his friends had stayed up until all hours of the night and morning when they were in England. Why did they resent the early hours so much here? "Good God, but we are a lazy lot."

"There has to be an easier way to make a living," Harry admitted.

"Don't you think these people would have taken it up if it existed?" Grayson asked.

"No. I think they're all masochists. I can't understand why—once they got a notion of what they were getting themselves into—they didn't return from whence they came."

"Perhaps this was better than what they had," Grayson pointed out. "Even in England, not everyone lives the life of luxury that we took for granted."

"They bloody well should."

Grayson chuckled. He didn't think Harry was nearly as shallow as he appeared. "Saw you and some gents resting behind the barn earlier."

"We weren't resting. We were doing a bit of wagering."

"Oh?"

Harry grinned. "The lovely Widow Denby shall have a new roof on her barn by Sunday."

"Dear God, Harry, you'd best take care that these people don't learn that you're a master at sleight of hand or they are likely to chop off your fingers." It amazed him to see how many men continued to wear their weapons—guns and knives—as though they expected the enemy to jump from the bushes at any moment.

"Don't worry about me. I have a feeling James would like nothing more than to blind you for the way you look at his sister."

Grayson grabbed his friend's arm and jerked him to a stop. "What's wrong with the way I look at her?"

"Nothing's wrong with it. Just keep in mind that we *will* be leaving." Harry resumed strolling toward the house.

Grayson matched his stride. "This isn't such a bad place—"

"There's no opportunity here, Gray."

"We could make the opportunity—"

"Why go to the trouble of making it when it already exists in abundance elsewhere?"

"It would be no trouble. All this land belongs to Abbie. If she were to marry—"

Harry shook his head. "Watch yourself around the Widow Westland, Gray. She's not really your type."

"Oh? Exactly what do you consider my type?"

"Married."

Grayson stumbled to a stop while Harry continued on. With no conscious thought, he searched for Abbie among the women who had begun to serve the meal to the men. Harry was right. Grayson had always been drawn to married women—they were safer.

Marriage for himself was something he'd never contemplated because he could not content himself with a woman who lacked rank, and he was not suitable marriage material for any woman whom he might have thought worthy of him. His father had always told him that he set his sights too high. Here he was, away from England, away from its social mores, unable to tear his gaze from a woman who could not even read.

He had always enjoyed reading, but not nearly as much as he had the past few nights. Abbie's rapt attention while he read gave him an incredible sense of satisfaction, a measure of joy that he'd never before experienced. He felt as though each word he spoke aloud was a gift to her. His only regret was that the words had come from Sir Walter Scott's heart and not his own.

He ambled to the makeshift planked table. Abbie's gaze met his and she blushed slightly. "Sit down, Mr. Rhodes."

Mr. Rhodes was it? He hated it when she got formal with him—which she did whenever her neighbors were here.

"Abbie, I can see no reason for you to wait on these men as though you are little more than a common serving girl."

The air suddenly filled with a hushed silence and a quivering of expectancy. Abbie's cheeks flamed red, and he regretted any embarrassment he might be causing her, but he was damned tired of watching her work so hard. The only respite she got from labor was when he read to her in the evenings—yet even then she was darning socks or sewing clothes for the children or mending her own clothes.

"The men work hard—"

"And you don't?" He grabbed the caldron of beans from her and nearly fell over with its unexpected weight. He dropped it on the table with a loud bang. He thought he might possibly have heard some wood split. "Sit down, Abbie."

She planted her hands on her hips, a mutinous gleam in her eye. "I don't know how you do it in England, but here we wait on our menfolk."

She wrapped her fingers around the handle of the pot. Grayson laid his hand over hers. She snatched her hand back as though he'd set a burning torch against her wrist. "I don't imagine there is a person here who gets up any earlier than you or works any harder. You're wearing yourself down to skin and bones and I don't like it."

She jerked her chin up and the violet in her eyes deepened. "I don't care what you don't like."

He quirked a brow and a corner of his mouth. "That's too bad, because until you stop waiting on these men, I'm not reading aloud in the evenings."

The sadness that delved into her violet eyes almost brought him to his knees.

"You can't do that," she whispered hoarsely.

"You're right. I can't." He grabbed the pot of beans. "I'll serve the meal. You sit and rest."

He felt a tug on the pot and snapped his head around. Smiling, James took the pot from him. "He's right. No reason we can't serve ourselves." He slapped beans on his plate and passed it to the next man.

Abbie heaved a defeated sigh. "Reckon I'll sit and eat." She took a step toward the table where a few women sat with the children.

"Not there," Grayson said. "Here."

Her eyes widened. "That table is for the men."

"Why?"

She looked as though he'd thrown a bucket of icy water on her. "What do you mean, why?"

"Most of these men have not been home in years. Why would they want to sit at a table with men when they could sit with their families?"

"I like the way you think, Rhodes," James said as he stood. "You can have my seat, Abbie. I'm going to sit with Amy."

More men stood to join their wives until the only men left were those who had no wives. Women who had no husbands suddenly found themselves without a place to sit at the table that had once been for women only. Grayson watched the men at the bachelors' table smile as women shyly sat beside them.

"What have you done?" Abbie asked.

Grayson smiled broadly. "Made the meal more enjoyable. Sit down."

For once, she did as he instructed. Careful not to touch her or give her any reason to jerk away from him, he dropped on the bench seat beside her. She sat ramrod-straight. He stood. "Scoot to the end, Abbie."

She did until there was nothing on one side of her but the warm Texas breeze. Awkwardly, Grayson worked his way between her and the man who had been on her other side. She relaxed only a little, but it was enough to give him hope.

"You told James something you had no business telling him," she whispered, her gaze riveted to the beans on her plate.

"My apologies, but I was attempting to deflect the accusations he was throwing my way," he said in a low voice.

She twisted her head around, her brow furrowed, her gaze scrutinizing.

"He thinks I mean to harm you," Grayson explained.

She nodded. "I told him that wasn't the case."

He was completely unprepared for the joy that shot through him, like a star bursting from the sky. In spite of her wariness, she trusted him—believed in him when no other woman ever had.

He started to speak and realized something had lodged in his throat. A lump of emotion the likes of which he'd never felt before. He swallowed hard, and gave her a slow, lazy smile. "I appreciate that."

The pot of beans finally made its way back to

Grayson. He slapped the beans on his plate. If his stomach wasn't on the verge of growling like a maddened dog, he'd do without. He longed for something—anything—that had a thick, creamy sauce poured over it.

"I would have been here sooner had I known the segregation of males and females had come to an end," Kit said as he dropped down beside Harry. He smiled at Abbie's sister as he reached for the beans. "A lady's company always makes the meal so much more enjoyable."

Elizabeth snorted and rolled her eyes. "You're wasting your flirting on me, Christian Montgomery."

He placed his hand over his heart. "I am deeply wounded that you would consider my sincere sentiment to be no more than flirtation."

She dropped her elbow on the table and rested her chin in her palm, meeting his gaze. "Are you telling me that you weren't flirting?"

"Of course he was flirting," Harry said. "That's all he ever does."

"Stay out of this, Bainbridge," Kit warned.

"You gents got fifteen minutes before you need to get back to the fields. You'd best stop your bickering and get to eating," Elizabeth reminded them.

"You are a hard taskmaster, Mrs. Fairfield," Kit said.

She gave a brusque nod. "Don't you forget it."

Grayson slanted a gaze at Abbie, who was watching her sister as though she didn't quite know her. He wondered if she'd ever seen couples flirt, ever witnessed the easy camaraderie that could exist between a man and a woman.

He leaned forward slightly. "Tell me about the cattle."

Abbie snapped her gaze to his. "What cattle?"

"When the boys and I were on our way back from our fishing excursion, I saw some cattle. Rust-colored. Enormous horns. Why weren't they in an enclosure, fenced in?"

Abbie shrugged. "I don't know much about the cattle."

Grayson glanced down the table. "Does anyone?"

Andy Turner nodded. The wiry man still wore his Confederate uniform, as if he'd returned home with nothing else. Grayson didn't think the man was any older than twenty-five.

"What do you know?" Grayson asked.

"Well . . . afore the war, a lot of ranchers were herding them cattle north, but they just set a lot of 'em free when they went off to war."

"So they don't belong to anyone?" Harry asked, and Grayson could tell by the way Harry sat a little straighter that he had an interest in the conversation.

"Depends," Andy said.

"On what?" Harry asked.

"On whether or not it has a brand on it. If'n it does, it belongs to the man that owns the brand."

"And if it doesn't, it's free for the taking?"

"Yep."

"So why aren't we gathering up the cattle?" Harry asked.

" 'Cuz they're about as valuable as Confederate

money," a man at the far end of the table said. Grayson thought the slump-shouldered man's name was Sam.

"Why?" Grayson asked.

"Takes months to herd 'em to market. Ain't worth the trouble. Cotton's better."

"If there were ranchers before the war, they must have felt differently," Kit suggested.

Sam, Andy, and every other farmer at the table simply lifted a shoulder and returned to eating.

Grayson, Harry, and Kit exchanged glances.

"Might be an avenue of income worth pursuing," Kit suggested quietly.

"Not until the cotton is picked," Abbie said adamantly.

Grayson looked at her, surprised by the fierceness of her gaze.

"Not until the cotton is picked," he assured her.

Grayson stood, his arm raised, hand braced against the inside wall of the barn, his gaze focused on the pale halo of light spilling into the night from the back of the house. For over two weeks, he'd kept vigil here, wondering if Abbie were bathing in the moonlight, thinking of the warm water caressing her flesh.

The woman was driving him to distraction. He wanted to see laughter reflected in her eyes instead of weariness. He wanted to purchase her the finest gowns, made with the softest material.

He'd never known anyone like her, never known someone who thought of her own needs last—if she thought of them at all.

Grayson enjoyed reading to the family in the evenings, watching the way Abbie's gaze would drift over her children. In the beginning, he'd wanted her attention to remain on him but as the evenings came one after another, he began to realize that when her attention wandered away from him, he lost nothing for he still had her presence.

Dear God, but he had emerged from selfish surroundings. He had come here wondering how he might best benefit. In less than a fortnight, he had seen what hard labor truly was. He wanted to ease the burden Abbie carried, not only the burden of caring for a family and maintaining a farm but he also wanted to ease the burden of her heart.

He had only once heard her laughter; he seldom saw her smile. She hadn't any idea how to enjoy life.

A corner of his mouth quirked up. Well, perhaps she had a small inkling of an idea—after all, she took her baths surrounded by moonlight.

Except for tonight. The faint glow coming from behind the house puzzled him. He was certain she'd taken baths other nights because she smelled like a freshly plucked rose each morning. He was fairly certain she took her baths outside. At least his imagination had her taking baths outside.

But never before had there been a light—not even the first night when he'd unwittingly discovered her indulgence.

Shoving his hands into his trouser pockets, he turned and walked toward the ladder that led to the loft, to his humble abode.

Bloody hell. He spun around and stalked from the

barn. He'd honored his word for two damnable weeks which was longer than any respectable rogue should honor anything. As he neared the house, he lightened his step. The last thing he wanted to do was alarm her. He just wanted to ensure that all was well.

And if he happened to catch a glimpse of her in the lamplight . . . so be it.

Holding his breath, he peered around the corner. Abbie's back was to him. She was nestled deep within the tub, her head back against its edge. A lantern on a crate near the tub illuminated the book she held within her hands, high above the water.

His book!

He rounded the corner and snatched the book from her grasp. She released a tiny screech and the water splashed over the sides as she sank further within its depths.

"You're going to get the book wet and ruin it," he scolded as he scrutinized it, grateful to see no water stains.

"I was careful," she said, her voice breathless.

He shifted his gaze from the book to her—and wished to God that he hadn't. She had piled her hair on top of her head. Flaxen strands framed her face and trailed along the slender length of her neck. The light from the lantern shimmered over the dewy drops of water that covered her face, her throat, her bare shoulders . . . the swells of her breasts that only became visible when the water ebbed and flowed. She was an illiterate farm girl and he'd never wanted anyone more. His fingers tightened on the book. Not illiterate.

"I thought you couldn't read."

Her brows came together into a deep furrow. "Why would you think that?"

"When I found you with the book, you were simply holding it."

"It wasn't mine. I didn't know if you'd want me to read it."

"If you can read, then why did you look devastated when I threatened to stop reading to you?"

"I love your voice," she confessed softly, and he would have sworn that even within the shadows, he saw her blush. Then her words hit him with the impact of a sledgehammer. She loved his voice. Never, in his whole life, had he had the word love directed toward any aspect of his person.

"Is it . . ." He cleared his throat, trying to sound normal when he had a lump the size of an apple lodged in his throat. "Is it the timbre of my voice that appeals to you or the way I pronounce the words?"

"Both. You sound so . . . so—"

"English?"

He saw the barest of smiles touch her lips. "Yes."

"Then my voice will be at your disposal whenever you wish it."

Her smile grew slightly. "There you go, making me feel like buttermilk again."

Against his better judgment, he smiled mischievously and leaned toward her. "Have I ever mentioned that I simply adore the taste of buttermilk? I have been known to lick the glass clean."

Her eyes widened and before she could react further, he asked, "Have you been reading the book every night?"

"Only the passages you already read to us. I like looking at the words, reading them. But tonight I . . ." She lowered her gaze.

"You what?"

She lifted her gaze, guilt readily apparent. "I read past where you read. I wanted to know if Ivanhoe was going to save Rebecca."

He smiled slightly. "Did he?"

"I don't know. You took the book away!"

Taking a step forward, he grabbed the lantern and walked to the porch.

"What are you doing?" she asked.

"I'm going to read to you."

"I'm bathing."

"Yes, I know."

"You said you'd leave me in peace when I bathed."

"What could be more peaceful than sinking back in the tub and listening to me read? After all, I know you love the sound of my voice."

"Not when I'm bathing."

"Then don't bathe. Simply listen."

Abbie glared at the man for all of a single heartbeat before allowing herself to relax within the steaming water. She did so love his voice, the gentle lilt that made the words sound poetic, much softer than her own voice did.

She found it strange that once she accepted he was going to stay, her body began to feel like the melting wax beneath a lighted candle. She was certain he wouldn't harm her. He would have done so long ago if that were his intent. Despite what he'd told her about his past, he was a gentleman.

Against her better judgment, she liked having him around. She liked to see him first thing in the morning, all rumpled and cross-looking as though he wanted to beat the sun back beyond the horizon. She enjoyed the easy laughter he showered on the children, the way he listened to them, and talked with them as though he valued their opinions. His patience seemed unlimited.

His hair had grown in the time that he'd been here so now it curled over the collar of his shirt and swirled around his ears. The color reminded her of corn silk, and she wondered briefly if it felt as soft.

A part of her felt guilty because she found most of her thoughts of late revolving around Grayson. She had thought of John as well when he was alive, but the images were different. With John, she had wondered when he would be in from the fields, what he wanted to eat for supper, if he would nudge up her nightgown . . .

Slamming her eyes closed, she clenched her fists beneath the water and bowed her head, her breath coming in tiny gasps. Concentrate on the story, she told herself, on Ivanhoe and Rebecca . . . and Grayson's voice bringing the story to life as she never could—

"Abbie?"

Her eyes flew open. He was studying her, the closed book clasped in his hands.

"Are you all right?"

She nodded her head quickly. "I was just listening."

"The water must be cold by now."

"Not very," she lied, wondering when it *had* grown cold. How long had she listened to him, how long had her thoughts wandered?

He lowered the flame in the lantern until it sputtered and died.

"What are you doing?" she asked, hating the edge of panic in her voice.

"I want to enjoy the stars for a moment. They look no different in England. You know, sometimes when I wake up in the middle of the night and look at the stars, I forget that I'm not in England."

Her heart ached at the longing reflected in his voice. She had never strayed far from Fortune. "Do you miss England?"

She could only see his silhouette, his head tilted back as he looked at the heavens.

"Oddly enough, I do, though only God knows why. I was miserable there."

"And here?"

She felt more than saw him shift his gaze to her.

"I can see the potential for happiness here."

He stood and her heart pounded so hard that she was surprised it didn't create waves within the water.

"I'm not going to touch you, Abbie, but I want you to tell me when your heart slows."

"What makes you think it's beating fast?"

"You start breathing in audible, tiny gasps."

She took a deep breath, trying to calm herself. It was disconcerting to know he could easily tell when she became nervous. "You can leave now," she told him, pleased with the even tone of her voice.

"Good," he said briskly before he walked to the bathtub and came to an abrupt halt.

Her heart bounced against her ribs, and the short little pants echoed loudly through the night.

"Have I ever hurt you?" he asked.

"No," she answered on a short gasp.

"Then why are you afraid now?"

"You *could* hurt me."

"But I won't. I give you my word, as a gentleman, that my hands will not touch you."

He planted his hands on either side of the tub and leaned over slightly. The water splashed over the sides as Abbie jerked back, realizing too late that she could not escape without shoving him aside. Why had she let her defenses down? Why had she indulged in a bath when she knew he was nearby?

He moved no nearer. His voice, when he spoke, was low. "Tell me when your heart stops pounding."

"It won't stop pounding until you move away."

"Then we're at an impasse because I won't move away until your heart stops pounding."

"Why are you doing this?"

"Because . . ." He leaned closer. She pressed her head against the back of the tub. "I am a man with absolutely no willpower."

He touched his lips to hers. So incredibly soft. And warm. Gently, his mouth moved against hers, easing and increasing the pressure, reminding her of water lazily lapping against the banks of the river. Then with a surety, he slid his tongue into her mouth. She would have jerked back if she hadn't already almost embedded her skull into the tub. The unexpected pressure of his tongue, the full taste of him, surprised her. If he felt her alarm, he paid it no heed. He simply enticed her with a slow waltz, deepening the kiss. When his tongue retreated, hers followed and drew his back. She heard the rumbling groan deep within his chest. His breathing became as loud and as quickened as hers. She would have thought they'd been running instead of doing nothing but moving their tongues, their mouths.

He withdrew slightly. Abbie followed the direction of his gaze. His clenched fist was close enough to her cheek that he would only have to unfurl his fingers to touch her.

He shifted his gaze to her, and she watched his throat work as he swallowed.

"Hell of a time for me to decide to become reputable," he rasped roughly.

Slowly, stiffly, he straightened. "Good night, Abbie."

Jerking her head around, she watched him disappear into the darkness. She sank her quivering body into the cool water until it lapped at her chin. She pressed her trembling fingers to her swollen lips while scalding tears stung her eyes.

For one devastating moment, she wished he hadn't been noble.

8

*Kissing Abbie had been a mistake. Indulgences al-*ways came at a heavy cost. Last night's price had been to go the remainder of the night without sleep.

The heat had intensified, and his body had ached with desires left unfulfilled. The woman was not an innocent virgin. She was a widow with three children. She had been without a husband in her bed for at least four years. Common sense dictated that he should offer, and she would readily agree, to a mutually gratifying romp in the hay as it were.

God knew his own carnal needs had always taken precedence over honor. Why did he suddenly feel that possessing her body would leave him empty? Why an irrational need to possess what he could never hold—her heart?

Leaning against the side of the barn, he watched Abbie stroll through the fields in the predawn light. He didn't think Ivanhoe's Rowena could have looked more lovely. She had gathered her blonde hair into one long braid that dipped into the small curve of her back.

She wore a simple dress that he knew she had mended and patched. He thought of the allowance his father had generously bestowed upon him all the years he'd been in England, the money he had spent upon nothing that would last more than a heartbeat. He would give anything to have a portion of it back, to have enough to purchase Abbie one gown of the finest cloth. Her feet stirred up the dirt, creating a billowing cloud around her bare ankles. He thought of all the shoes he'd thrown away because of a single scratch.

He bowed his head, wondering how he had become such a shallow man who valued nothing beyond a moment's pleasure.

He lifted his gaze and slowly ambled toward the field, toward a woman he feared may have never known a moment's pleasure. Or perhaps she knew more than he did. He thought of the lovely smiles that graced her face when her fingers touched her children's hair or the rapture in her eyes when he read to her. What in God's name would he see in her eyes if he made love to her?

As he neared, she bent over, her fingers cradling a delicate blossom the color of cream. Similar blossoms were abundantly scattered over the fields.

"Where did the flowers come from?" he asked.

"They unfolded during the night." She looked at it in wonder as though she'd never seen one when he knew she had probably seen thousands. "It's so delicate," she said softly. "Tomorrow, they'll turn a deep red like the blood that coats your hands when you're picking. By tomorrow evening, the petals will die and fall away, leaving behind a boll." With a sigh, she straightened. "Reckon it's laid-by time."

"What does that mean?" he asked.

Avoiding his gaze, she said, "We stay out of the fields until the cotton bolls burst open and invite us back in."

"Dare I hope that during this time, we simply sit in the shade?"

He felt an unfamiliar tightening in his chest when a corner of her mouth curled upward.

"We'll slaughter hogs, preserve vegetables, pickle—"

"Look at me, Abbie."

Ever so slowly, she turned her face toward him. The faintest hint of a blush adorned her cheeks, and the slight curve of her smile disappeared. He suddenly felt like a bully instead of a man accustomed to charming women into his bed. When he teased, she felt threatened. What meant nothing to him meant everything to her. As much as he loathed leaving her, some minute aspect of being a gentleman embedded in his character insisted that he no longer stay. "Abbie, about last night—"

"He never kissed me," she blurted out.

Grayson felt as though someone had just delivered a stunning blow to his midsection. "What?"

She shook her head slightly as tears welled within her eyes, creating violet pools of anguish. She pressed one trembling hand to her lips and wrapped an arm around her stomach. She looked toward the fields, and he watched helplessly as a solitary tear slid along her cheek.

"He gave me three children," she rasped, "but he never gave me a kiss."

"I know it's rude to speak unkindly of the dead, but your husband was a bloody fool."

"He didn't love me. I was a possession, like the land. Something to be looked upon with pride, something to yield a harvest, but he gave more to his land than he ever gave to me. If the land had needed a kiss . . . he would have dropped to his knees and pressed his mouth . . ."

Slowly, carefully, he drew her into his embrace. He felt the tremors traveling through her, heard the wretched sob that broke free, felt her body stiffen as she fought to stifle another one. Dear Lord, but she felt wonderful within his arms, tiny, but sturdy from years of battling the land. What sort of man was he to be grateful for anything that made her drop her reserve and brought her this close to him?

A far better man than her husband. He could not help but wonder with bitterness what else the man might not have given the woman within the circle of his arms. He pressed his cheek against the top of her head. "Abbie," he cooed in a low voice. "Abbie, it's all right."

She shook her head without moving away from him. "I wasn't glad when he died. I wasn't."

"Of course you weren't glad—"

"But I was . . ." He felt a spasm rock her body. "Relieved."

The word was spoken agonizingly low, as though she'd forced it past the burden of guilt. He brought his arms more tightly around her. "There's no sin in that, Abbie."

He felt the slightest yielding of her body against his, as though his simple statement had lifted a heavy weight from her heart.

"It was wrong of me to marry him—"

He cradled her face between hands that had become coarse over the weeks and tilted her head until he could gaze into her eyes. So slowly, his thumbs gathered the tears that adorned her cheeks. "You were sixteen, Abbie. What did you know of marriage or love?"

He refrained from telling her that the fault rested with her husband. He had spoken ill of the dead once, and he had little doubt he would do so again, but not where she could hear.

The doubts plaguing her tore at him as nothing had in his entire life: not the cruel taunts that he'd received as a child or the snubs he'd received as an adult, not the absence of love or the shattered dreams.

"There are a thousand marriages which contain not the tiniest seed from which love can grow. You must have cared for him some or it would not haunt you now that you think you did not."

"But it wasn't enough."

"Why?"

Her gaze flitted to his mouth, her blush deepening before she again met his gaze. Something deep within him burst forth as he'd heard others describe the ripening of cotton—like a tiny explosion that resulted in a glorious unfolding. Guilt gnawed at her this morning because last night it hadn't. Her tongue darted out to lick lips that he longed to taste again.

Having no desire to abrade her soft skin, he

touched his knuckles to her cheek, knowing a moment's regret that his palms were no longer smooth and unmarred. She neither flinched nor moved, but simply watched him as he had once seen a cornered fox await the arrival of the bloodthirsty hounds.

He felt completely inadequate to the task of giving to her what he feared she may have never experienced, never known—and he'd never wanted anything more in his life than he wanted to share with her all his worldly knowledge.

He moved his thumbs to the corners of her mouth, felt her stiffen, and knew if he moved too fast, he'd lose the tentative trust he'd gained.

"Let's play today," he said, and saw the trust retreat like the sun before a storm. "You, me, and the children," he hastily added.

Confusion swam within her eyes. "You do know how to play, don't you?" he asked.

Her chin came up. "Of course I do, but we have chores—"

"That will keep until tomorrow." Reaching down, he took her hands and brought them to his lips, placing a kiss on fingers that were as rough as leather. "What's the point in working so hard if you never enjoy the fruits of your labors?"

He heard the rumble of a wagon, and she pulled away from him, wiping her hands over her skirt as though to remove the evidence of his touch. There was a time when he would have taken her actions personally—but no longer. He didn't think it was his touch she wanted to erase, but that of her husband.

She waved and he saw a forced smile spread across her face. "James! It's laid-by time."

Her brother brought the wagon to a halt and leapt down before helping Amy. He walked toward the fields, his gaze flickering between Grayson and Abbie. "Rhodes," he acknowledged curtly.

"Mr. Rhodes was saying that maybe we've worked hard enough to spend the day playing," Abbie said.

James gave him a suspicious glance. "Well, I don't suppose it would hurt to relax a little today."

It didn't take Grayson long to realize that "relaxing a little" meant not relaxing at all. Every neighbor who arrived greeted the idea of not chopping in the fields with unbridled enthusiasm—and then set about working elsewhere. The men argued about when the first boll of cotton would erupt, then set off to slaughter a hog. Children scrambled through the household garden, gathering tomatoes and onions and assorted other vegetables. Men dug a pit and built a fire within it. The unfortunate swine was spitted and draped over the low-burning fire to roast.

Grayson stood beneath a tree, feeling like an intruder. Everyone seemed to know their place, seemed to know what needed to be done without a single order being issued, while he and his friends seemed to be the only ones relaxing.

Harry stood beside him, his arms crossed over his chest. "I thought I heard someone say we were going to play today."

Grayson nodded. "I think all this activity is their idea of playing. I'm beginning to wish I hadn't suggested it. Abbie is working harder today than she usually does.''

''She seems to be enjoying it,'' Kit observed.

''That's not the point,'' Grayson said. ''I wanted her to spend the day doing absolutely nothing.''

''What you want and what she wants may not be the same thing,'' Kit said.

''We want the same thing—she just doesn't know it yet,'' Grayson said.

Kit raised a brow. ''Oh?''

''Don't go getting sweet on her, Gray,'' Harry ordered. ''As soon as the cotton is plucked, we are on our way to Galveston.''

''I'm not sweet on her, but I've been a long time without a woman—''

''And might as well go with one who knows the ropes,'' Kit said. ''A woman with three children certainly shouldn't be offended by a brief affair.''

Grayson shoved his hands into his trouser pockets and rocked back on his heels. ''Have either of you ever made love to a woman and *not* kissed her?''

''Careful, Gray,'' Kit warned. ''You're beginning to sound completely unlike yourself.''

He wondered what his friends would think to learn that he wasn't exactly *acting* like himself either. For the life of him, he couldn't figure out why he hadn't touched Abbie's cheek last night—or better yet, dove into the bath with her.

''I'll be back shortly,'' he mumbled before shoving away from the tree and heading to the house.

He stood within the doorway watching Abbie flutter around the kitchen like a schoolgirl who had been given a holiday. She softly hummed a tune with which he was unfamiliar, but he could well envision a mother cradling a babe within her arms and rocking the child to sleep.

An assortment of pies adorned the table, the aroma of apples and cinnamon wafting through the room. She turned a tin pan upside down, placed it on a plate, and tapped gently. When she lifted the pan, a dark chocolate cake remained on the plate. Then she went about whipping up some icing within a bowl, her humming growing louder as her hand quickly circled the bowl with her movements.

"When I suggested that you play today, I was thinking more along the lines of you not working at all," Grayson said.

She snapped her head around, the humming continuing until she spoke. "I haven't baked any pies or cakes in a good while."

"But it's work, Abbie."

She smiled softly. "I enjoy it." She began to slather a thick chocolate concoction over the cake. He watched her quick efficient movements. She placed the cake so near the edge of the table that he was surprised it didn't topple off. He reached out to shove it back. She grabbed his hand, her warm fingers wrapping tightly around his. Her cheeks pinkened as she gave her head a quick shake. Humming loudly, she walked to the hearth. He followed. "Abbie—"

She quickly placed a finger to her lips. Over her shoulder, she pointed to the table with her other hand. Grayson shifted his gaze, noticing for the first time the little urchin crouched beneath the table. Micah scooted forward, came out from beneath the table like a turtle from its shell, swiped a finger across the cake, and ducked back beneath the table, the icing tucked into his mouth before he'd fully disappeared.

"He thinks I don't notice him sneaking in," she whispered low, a conspiratorial smile gracing her features.

Humming again, she strolled back to the table. She stomped her foot. "I thought I'd already put icing on this cake."

Grayson heard Micah release a throaty chortle and saw him wrap his arms around his drawn-up knees as though he could make himself smaller and increase the effectiveness of his hiding place. But as soon as Abbie walked back to the hearth, Micah uncoiled his body and headed for another taste of the forbidden. Grayson found himself wondering what forbidden pleasures Abbie might be willing to sample.

The game went on for several minutes before Micah's laughter grew too loud to ignore. Abbie looked beneath the table. Had Grayson pulled Micah's prank within the duke's kitchen, he would have had his ears boxed. After his discovery beneath the table, Micah received a sound tickling and the bowl of remaining icing.

As Micah loped out of the house with his reward, Grayson thought Abbie had never looked happier. He imagined the glow he would see upon her face if she really knew how to relax and play. He was determined to find a way to bring that radiance forth.

*   *   *

Floating on her back, the waters of the river lapping around her, Abbie studied the billowing clouds in the blue sky. Grayson had seemed incredibly pleased when someone had suggested everyone go for a swim.

The afternoon sun warmed her as she remembered the disbelief that had washed over his face when he'd discovered that the men were to take a different path to another swimming hole. Surely he didn't expect the men and women to swim together. A smile touched her lips. Yes, she imagined he did, rogue that he claimed to be.

But how many rogues would have willingly taken on the responsibility of watching over two active boys? She had planned to keep Micah with her because his swimming skills were limited to splashing, kicking, and screaming. But Grayson had interceded on her son's behalf, and smiling brightly, Micah had tromped off alongside the men and older boys.

Joy had shot through her at the sight of her son's happiness—along with a measure of hurt. She didn't resent that he wanted to be with the men, but it was hard knowing that her baby was growing up.

She sighed deeply, closed her eyes, and thought of Grayson's kiss. She wondered how many women he had enticed into his bed with little more than the persuasion of his lips.

Not that she was tempted to illicitly clamber into the loft one night. But she did find herself wondering what he looked like, farther down the river, with drops of water rolling over his bare body. She imagined he was a powerful swimmer, cutting a path through the river toward her—

She halted her errant thoughts, swam to the bank, and trudged up to the shore. Snatching her towel from a low-hanging tree branch, she briskly dried herself. She was surprised Grayson had stayed at the farm as long as he had.

But picking time would be the real test. Regretfully, she didn't think he'd last more than a day.

Lying on his stomach in the loft, Grayson concentrated on the sound of the milk hitting the galvanized pail—anything to take his mind off the excruciating blaze of fire dancing over his back. He had felt the pricks of pain yesterday evening after they'd returned from the river. He had not realized the agony that would follow.

The Texas sun was unmerciful and it had wreaked its wrath with a vengeance. He heard the creak and moan of someone climbing the ladder. A halo of light crept over the edge of the loft.

"Gray, you comin' down to breakfast?" Johnny asked.

"No, lad. I'm hoping Fate will be kind and I shall die before the meal is served."

From the corner of his eye, he saw the light increase and felt the slight trembling as Johnny scrambled into the loft.

"Gawd Almighty!" Johnny cried.

"That bad, eh?"

"I'll get Ma."

He closed his eyes. He could think of nothing

sweeter than holding a woman's hand as he died. Especially if that hand belonged to Abbie. She had actually been smiling broadly when they'd all met up after their swim in the river. He decided he could take credit for that smile. Even though the day had not been spent doing nothing, she had looked relaxed and much younger as evening drew near. He had nearly given in to the temptation to draw her into his embrace and kiss her soundly.

He felt the slight vibration as someone climbed the ladder, and then he smelled the sweet fragrance of roses.

"Oh my Lord," Abbie whispered, the anguish in her voice easing the pain throbbing through his shoulders. In all his life, he couldn't recall anyone caring that he might be experiencing some discomfort. When he was ten, he'd broken his arm and received a tongue-lashing for inconveniencing everyone.

He forced his eyes open. Kneeling beside him, she furrowed her brow so deeply that he could have planted seeds within the folds. She combed her fingers through his hair, lifting it away from his face with a gentleness he'd never known.

"Your back is burned and your shoulders are blistering. What were you thinking yesterday?"

"Obviously, I wasn't." She began to gnaw on her bottom lip. "Don't fret so, Abbie. I'm certain it looks worse than it is."

He watched as she reached into her pocket and brought forth something green. "What's that?"

She leaned forward slightly, rolling one across her palm. "It's a stem from a plant."

He thought the thick object looked more like a branch. She squeezed it and a small bit of juice eased onto her finger. She shoved it toward his face.

"I don't know what it is, but my ma taught me to use it on burns. It'll ease the hurt." Her gaze shifted to his back. "But I don't know if I've got near enough."

He considered telling her not to bother, but he could only think of one way for her to apply whatever the hell it was to his back and shoulders. He wasn't certain he could endure the pain that her touching him might cause, but neither did he want her *not* touching him. He closed his eyes. "Just do the best you can."

Abbie stared at his back. He'd spread out his arms, bent his elbows, and tucked his hands beneath his cheek so his back was fanned out, revealing its breadth. He seemed completely comfortable with his partial nudity. No doubt countless women had rubbed their hands over his back. She had just never expected that she might be one of them.

Swallowing hard, she wiped the sweat from her palms using her apron. Then she took one of the stems she'd torn from the plant and squeezed out the juice, drawing a small squiggly line across his back. A back much broader than she'd realized. She wondered if working in the fields had added bulk to his frame. Lightly, she touched her fingers to nature's balm, gently spreading the salve over his back, feeling the heat radiating from his skin. She was surprised he didn't cry out from the agony she knew he had to be experiencing. She had burned her hands too many times while cooking not to know how painful a blister could be.

"How does that feel?" she asked.

"Heavenly," he murmured.

She squeezed the juice from another stem and continued the procedure. "Did you sleep at all last night?"

"No."

"Why didn't you come and get me?"

"I didn't imagine there was anything you could have done for me. Tell me about this laid-by time. Will your neighbors come over again today?"

"No. They won't come back until I send word the cotton is ready to be picked. They'll all be getting ready for the winter."

"What is winter like here?"

She squeezed out more balm. "Cold some days. Warm mostly."

"Snow?"

"Not usually, although I've seen it a time or two. But it doesn't stay long."

"I know you were born in Texas. Were . . . you born here?"

His voice sounded sleepy, causing her to smile. "Nearby. James lives in the house where we were all born."

"He said there were eleven of you—where are they all now?"

"Dead. Diphtheria came through here the year after I married John. Took them all. Reckon it would have taken me, too, if I hadn't been with John."

"So something good came from your marriage."

"That and my three young 'uns. I don't want you thinking badly of John. He wasn't a bad husband."

He opened his eyes, piercing her with his gaze. "But neither was he a good one."

"He had his moments."

"Tell me one, just one."

She angled her chin defiantly. "When Johnny was born, he brought me a whole passel of wildflowers."

Groaning, Grayson struggled to sit up. He cradled her cheek. "If you were mine, I'd bring you a bouquet of flowers every day."

Jerking back, she snorted. "That's easy enough to say—probably easy enough to do—when you don't have to worry about putting food on a table or clothes on a body's back. You're just here playing at being reputable. Working the fields is a game to you and your friends, but to us it's life. You don't work the fields, your crops don't come in, and you go hungry. You ever been hungry, Mr. Rhodes?"

"No." He had the grace to look slightly embarrassed which should have lessened her anger, but only served to increase it.

"Well, I have. I've been so hungry that my stomach was gnawing at my backbone. Until I married John, I had one dress and it changed when Elizabeth outgrew the one she was wearing and handed it down to me." She shoved the remaining stems into his hands. "So don't go plying me with your fancy words and your quick promises. You're not here for the long haul, Mr. Rhodes, so don't pretend you are."

She scrambled across the loft and clambered down the ladder before he saw the tears welling within her eyes—before he realized that a part of her wished he might stay forever.

9

*G*rayson found Abbie in the family garden, jerking carrots from the ground and hurling them into a nearby wicker basket. He rather imagined she would have preferred that the carrots were his head.

How strange that she had grown up with affection and lacked food while he had a constantly full stomach, but lacked affection. He would have traded places with her in a heartbeat . . . and she would probably have traded with him. The grass was always greener until one had lain upon it.

"Abbie?"

She jerked around. Dirt streaked her face where she'd attempted to wipe away tears. His stomach knotted; he knew he was the cause of the tears. Her gaze darted to the scraggly bouquet of wildflowers he halfheartedly extended toward her.

"Why are you doing this?" she asked softly.

"When I was a lad, I thought the duke's heir was the most fortunate child I'd ever known, not because he would inherit the duke's estate and title and all the respect that came with it—but because one day, I saw the duke's wife embrace him. I thought it would be the most wonderful thing in the world to be loved so much.

"I have known married women who did not love their husbands. They invited me into their beds, caring not one whit whether their husbands discovered their duplicity. I happily accepted what they offered, knowing full well that the invitation was not for *the long haul*. These women lived lives of wealth and privilege, but not one of them gave her husband half the devotion in life that you give yours in death. I made the mistake of confusing you with them. For that, I humbly apologize."

She shook her head. "There you go, making me feel like buttermilk—"

"You are the cream, Abbie. Never think that you're not."

She blushed. "If I am, I'm sitting in a cracked pitcher."

He glanced around, his gaze touching on the three children who stood nearby watching, eyes wide and round. "No, sweetheart, you're sitting in the finest china." He extended the bouquet toward her. "You are correct. I will not be here for the long haul, but while I am here, I would cherish your friendship."

He noticed the slightest hesitation before she reached for the flowers, their fingers touching briefly before he relinquished his gift into her keeping. She blushed profusely, averting her gaze, and he feared he might have inadvertently given her his heart as well.

* * *

"What in God's name are we looking for?" Kit asked.

"I'm not sure," Grayson said as he guided the horse through the woods. "But I'll know when I see it."

"I thought we were going into town, to the saloon," Harry said.

"We will," Grayson assured him, "as soon as I find what I'm looking for."

"Can you give us a hint?" Kit asked. "It might hasten our finding it."

Grayson rubbed his shoulders with a vengeance. The skin was peeling off in clumps and it itched like bloody hell. "I want a place where we can hold a tournament."

"A tournament?" Kit asked. "What in the bloody hell are you talking about?"

Grayson drew his horse to a halt and turned to face his friends. "I read *Ivanhoe* to the children. Certain things simply cry out to be seen."

"Where do you think you're going to find knights?" Kit asked.

"For the most part, I expect the older lads would take on those roles, although they will need examples by which to learn."

Kit narrowed his eyes. "Is there a reason you're looking at me when you say that?"

Grayson smiled. "I thought the three of us might each have a team."

"The sun not only baked your shoulders, it cooked your brain," Harry said.

"The real reason," Kit said.

Grayson slammed his eyes closed. It infuriated him that Kit never took anything at face value. He opened his eyes and glared at his friend. "A few days ago when I suggested we have a day to play, Abbie worked as hard as she does any other day. I want to give her a day where she has nothing to do. I want it away from the house so she won't be tempted to work. I want . . . I just want to give her something that no one else has."

"You're planning on staying." Kit's voice contained no censure, no question.

Grayson averted his gaze. How could he possibly be falling in love with a woman he had not yet bedded? "I don't know." He looked back at Kit. "I just know that I want them to remember we were here. I want us to leave our mark."

"You don't think leaving our sweat and blood in the fields is mark enough?" Harry asked.

Grayson shook his head. "Not for me."

Kit nodded. "I know a place."

"Why didn't you say so earlier?" Harry demanded.

"Because Gray didn't tell us what we were looking for." Kit turned his horse. "Come on. Follow me."

Grayson urged his horse forward. He knew Harry would grumble, Kit would roll his eyes, but in the end, they would humor him.

Abbie enjoyed laid-by time most of all. Although she knew that the cotton crops brought in the money, she liked knowing that the other things she did touched her children in tangible ways. She prepared the foods that would last them through winter and into the spring. She had a little more time to sew and moments when she could simply watch her children.

She knew Grayson had not understood how much she had enjoyed the day when they'd all played. Relaxing to him was doing nothing—to her, it was doing something she enjoyed.

Their recent days had settled into a routine. In the early morning, they walked through the fields in quiet camaraderie, inspecting the crops. He was fascinated with the bolls. She could barely wait for that first morning when one popped open, and she could share the moment with him. Sometimes their hands would accidentally brush, and he would look at her as though he wished it were more.

He no longer voiced the comments that had once made her uncomfortable, and Lord help her, she missed the teasing, missed the way his eyes would sparkle just before he said something wicked—like licking buttermilk.

He did whatever chores she assigned him without complaint, and in the late afternoon, he always went riding with his friends. He had begun taking her sons with him. She was torn between being grateful that they had a man to influence them and wishing they'd never let go of her apron hem. Especially Micah. But the violet eyes that the spectacles enlarged had never shined more brightly.

A part of her feared the grief her children would

experience when Grayson moved on, but grief was part of life—as was saying good-bye.

If only she'd had a chance to say good-bye to John—perhaps then she might look toward the horizon more freely.

Standing on the front porch, she saw the silhouettes of Grayson and her sons as they rode in from the west. Unlike some communities, theirs had an abundance of fine horses. Their men had decided that they could best serve the Cause as an infantry unit, and they had not taken the horses with them when they had marched off to war. Abbie had heard of another community whose men had taken the horses with them, only to have them returned within a month. She would have thought having horses would have aided their journey. She knew so little about war—or men.

Each day, Grayson looked less like the stiff-collared Englishman who'd stepped foot on her land weeks ago, but he would never look like a man shaped by the land—for the genteel refinement had a way of shining through.

He and the boys drew their horses to a halt. He dismounted and extended a bouquet of wildflowers toward her. "My lady."

She felt the heat creep into her face as she took the flowers. Although he did it every day, she seemed unable to become accustomed to the idea. "I reckon it's a good thing you'll be gone before the flowers are."

"What's good about it?" he asked quietly.

"I've come to expect the flowers and if you were

here and they weren't . . . I'd be disappointed that you couldn't bring me flowers.'' She stared at the delicate petals, hoping her reasoning didn't sound as stupid to him as it did to her.

He tucked his finger beneath her chin and lifted her gaze to his. His eyes grew warm and she thought she would think of him whenever she looked at the blue sky of dawn.

"If there were no flowers, I would find something of equal worth to bring you.'' He dipped his head and brushed his lips over hers, so briefly, so softly, that she wasn't even certain she could call it a kiss. But her heart was pounding so hard that she didn't think it could have been anything else. He stepped back as though he, too, were trying to determine what he'd just done.

"I need to put these in water,'' Abbie said, wondering where her breath had run off to. She scurried into the house, wishing she had a crystal vase instead of a chipped Mason jar in which to place them. She removed the wilting plants that he had brought her yesterday and slipped their replacements into the jar. She broke off the dried blossoms as she crossed the room to the desk where John had determined the planting of the crops. She removed the family Bible, opened it, and slipped the blossoms between the pages before closing the heavy book.

Keeping them was a silly thing, but when he left, whenever she read the Bible, she'd be reminded of him.

As though she'd need reminders.

*　　*　　*

"Ma, watch!" Johnny cried. "I'm gonna be a knight!"

Abbie strolled to the edge of the porch and wrapped her fingers around the pillar. Micah and Lydia dropped onto the steps beside her. Johnny sat on a brown gelding, his face serious.

Her gaze strayed from her son to the man sitting astride a bay stallion. The battered hat sat at a jaunty angle on his head as he talked with her son. He pointed toward the three poles that he'd embedded earlier in the ground along the road that led away from the farm. The poles were set an equal distance from each other, a metal ring dangling from each pole.

She wrapped her arms around the pillar, the way she had never wrapped them around a man, the way she often found herself of late thinking of wrapping them around Grayson. He possessed a sturdiness that she hadn't noticed when she first met him. He always grumbled at the ungodly hour they awoke—yet he walked the fields with her in the predawn. She anticipated those quiet moments, enjoyed his presence. She couldn't give a reason behind her feelings—they simply existed. Feelings she'd never experienced, frightening her as much as they excited her, causing a dull ache whenever she thought of Grayson leaving.

And leave he would. She knew that. For there was nothing here to entice a man such as he was to stay.

She watched as Grayson lifted his makeshift lance. Johnny bobbed his head as he listened intently. Grayson sidled his horse away from Johnny's, leaned over the horse's neck, and with one hand on the reins, the other on the lance, he urged his horse into a gallop.

Abbie's breath backed up within her lungs. She didn't know a man in Fortune who couldn't ride like the wind, but Lord, they weren't nearly as graceful as he was. He slipped the lance through a ring, snatching it from the pole. Excitement rippled through her, and even when the lance only bounced off the second ring, it did nothing to diminish the thrill of watching Grayson gallop down the road. He snagged the third ring and turned his horse, galloping back toward the house.

Smiling broadly, he drew his horse to a halt. "What do you think?"

"I didn't expect you to ride so well," she admitted, returning his smile.

He laughed. "Dear God, Abbie. Sometimes I get the impression that you think I did little more in England than lounge in bed and drink wine all day."

"Where did you learn to ride?"

"Hunting foxes can get rather vigorous. One must learn to move with the horse." He slid the two rings off the lance. "Micah, do you want to help me put these back into place so Johnny can have a go?"

Micah hopped up from the porch. Grayson handed the lance off to Johnny before lifting Micah onto the horse. Then he urged his horse back toward the poles.

"I sure do like him, Ma," Johnny said.

"He won't be staying," she told him, reminding herself as well.

"He might if you asked."

"Women don't ask men to stay."

"How come?"

"It's just not done." She watched Micah reach up and hang a ring. She heard his deep throaty laughter and wondered what Grayson had told him.

"We sure laugh a lot more," Johnny said.

Abbie nodded, deciding she'd find a way to keep the laughter even if she couldn't keep the man. Grayson brought Micah back to the porch and lowered him to the ground before turning his attention to Johnny.

"Ready, lad?"

Johnny nodded so hard that Abbie was surprised his head didn't go flying off. She couldn't remember a time when her children had been so eager to do anything.

"You want to keep the lance tucked in close to your body," Grayson said. "Keep your gaze focused on the rings."

"Can we add more rings?" Johnny asked.

"Let's master these first, and then we'll see about adding rings for the tournament."

Abbie furrowed her brow. "What tournament?"

Grayson cleared his throat. "I thought that perhaps before we begin picking the cotton, we might have a day of celebration. A picnic. Some games. A tournament. I found a pretty piece of land that would serve us well."

"Just us?"

"That's what I was thinking."

"Don't you think it would be more fun if we invited the whole community?"

"Not if the men and women split up halfway through the afternoon."

Abbie laughed. "You're still upset about the afternoon we went swimming."

"I'm not upset. I simply prefer not to miss any moments when you might actually be enjoying yourself. Your eyes too seldom carry a sparkle, and I can't hoard the memories if I'm condemned to spend the afternoon in the company of men."

Happiness was fleeting. She knew it, and yet she couldn't for the life of her remember any time when she'd felt such joy. "I think it would be more fun if everyone were invited."

She thought she saw disappointment touch his eyes before he nodded brusquely. "Very well. Invite the whole bloody state, but I don't want you working to feed the lot of them."

"I promise I'll only work to feed you and the children." Her words didn't seem to appease him, so she added, "If we invited everyone, we could have music."

His eyes brightened. "Music? Where in God's name would you get an orchestra?"

"Some of the men play fiddles, harmonicas—"

"Fiddles and harmonicas. I suppose beggars don't have the luxury of choosing."

"We make do with what we have. Nothing is gained by wishing for what can never be."

"I disagree, Abbie. I think wishing is responsible for some of the greatest accomplishments of the world. Long ago, men walked to the edge of the land and stared at the ocean. What if no one had ever wished to cross it?"

"Wishing breeds discontent."

"Is that why you don't dream, Abbie?" he asked quietly.

She felt her children's gazes on her and wondered how this conversation had ever managed to travel the road that it did. "I dream," she insisted.

"What do you dream?"

"That my children will never go hungry."

"And what do you dream for yourself?"

She searched her mind for a reply, wanting desperately to find something. But all she found was empty desires.

He leaned low, and she met his gaze. "Not to worry, sweetheart. I'll teach you how to dream for yourself. Being the selfish man that I am, I'm an expert."

She felt her breath hitch. She didn't know which melted her heart more—when he called her Abbie or when he called her sweetheart. Turning his horse away, he urged it toward Johnny. He gave her son further instructions, and she wondered why he considered himself selfish. He gave far more to her and the children than he ever seemed to take.

She saw Johnny give a curt nod before urging his horse into a gallop. Lydia jumped to her feet. "Ride, Johnny!"

Her heart clenched when the lance fell short of snatching the first ring. She grimaced when the lance missed the second ring and knocked the third to the ground. Johnny dismounted, picked up the fallen ring, mounted, and slipped it back into place before loping back toward them. "I'm going to try again," he said.

It took him three tries to get a ring on his lance. He returned with his face beaming, and Abbie felt her heart swell.

"Well done, lad," Grayson said. "A little more practice and you'll be getting them all."

"Don't you think I should have armor for the tournament?" Johnny asked.

"It'd be too cumbersome," Grayson said. "Perhaps your mother could sew you a surcoat."

Johnny wrinkled his brow. "What's a surcoat?"

"It's clothing that's open on the sides and slips over your head. You'll have to design a coat of arms."

"We can do that tonight after supper." Johnny snapped his head around. "Can you make me one, Ma?"

"I'll make one for everyone." She looked at Micah. He sat on the porch steps, his elbows on his knees, his chin in his palms, looking like a dog someone had just kicked. "Would you like to have a surcoat, Micah?"

He pushed out his lower lip and shook his head.

"Are you ready to take a run at the rings?" Grayson asked.

Micah jerked back his head. "I ain't big enough."

"You're big enough to help me." He reached toward Micah. "Come on, lad."

Micah jumped up and grabbed Grayson's hand. Grayson hoisted him onto the saddle. He took the lance from Johnny and handed him the ring. "Put this back."

While Johnny did as instructed, Grayson spoke

quietly to Micah. She watched her son's eyes widen
and sparkle like a new star in the sky. His tiny fingers
closed around the lance that Grayson securely held.

"Ready! Go!" Micah yelled, and he and Grayson
loped along the road.

Abbie urged them on when they snagged the first
ring. Clapped when they snagged the second. Jumped
up and down with delight when they snagged the
third. She didn't imagine any knight could have
looked more victorious than Micah did at that moment as Grayson brought the horse to a halt near the
porch and lowered Micah to the ground.

"I gotta kiss the queen of the tournament!" Micah
cried as he threw his arms around Abbie's legs. She
lifted him up and he planted a wet, sloppy kiss on
her cheek.

Abbie looked past Micah to Grayson. The warmth
in his gaze was as powerful as a touch, as devastating
as a kiss.

Abbie knelt at the edge of the field and gently cradled the open pod in her hand. She could see a scattering of white laced through the fields. She heard
the soft footfalls, and from the corner of her eye, she
saw Grayson crouch beside her.

"So that's cotton," he said quietly.

She nodded. "When the boll bursts open, it reveals
five locks of cotton." She curled her free hand and
touched each finger to a lock.

"Uncanny."

"Nature's perfection makes it possible to slip your
fingers between the cotton and the tines and pluck

out the cotton in one sweep.'' She demonstrated, taking pride in the swiftness of the motion and the fact that she came away unscathed. She twisted slightly and offered the cotton to Grayson, only to discover he wasn't looking at the cotton at all, but was watching her with an intensity that set her heart to pounding.

''We'll start picking soon, working from can-see to can't.''

''Then we should probably have our picnic in the next day or so,'' he said.

''I reckon day after tomorrow would be best. That'll give me time to make us a proper picnic.''

A corner of his mouth quirked up. ''And what, pray tell, is a proper picnic?''

''I've got a surprise or two planned. Reckon you'll just have to wait and see.''

''Reckon I will at that.''

She released a small giggle and slapped a hand over her mouth.

''What's the matter, ma'am?''

She dropped her hand and jerked up her chin. ''You're making fun of the way we talk.''

His smile withered. ''No, Abbie. Only wishing I wasn't quite so foreign to you.'' He cradled her cheek and slowly leaned toward her.

Her heart pounded so hard that she was certain he could feel it vibrating through her flesh, traveling to the tips of her fingers. The blue of his eyes darkened, reminding her of a sky before a thunderstorm. His lips touched hers, and she thought of the time she'd seen lightning strike the ground.

His free arm wound around her waist and drew her hard against him, so that they were kneeling in the dark soil, the good earth. He drew away and rubbed his thumb over her swollen lips, still throbbing from the persuasiveness of his kiss.

It seemed the most appropriate place in the world for love to take root.

Abbie stood at the side of the house, peering around the corner, watching Grayson shave. His burned shoulders had healed, leaving a few scattered freckles in their wake. He seemed a little broader, his muscles more toned—from working the fields and chopping wood for her, she supposed.

He angled his chin up and scraped the blade along his throat, the scraping sound echoing in the silence.

"You can come out of hiding, Abbie," he said, not removing his gaze from the small mirror.

Feeling like a child caught snitching a cookie from the jar, she jumped, clutching her offering more closely against her breast. "I didn't want to startle you and cause you to cut yourself."

Grinning, he swiveled his head slightly. "And here I thought perhaps you just enjoyed the view."

She felt the heat scald her face. "Your thoughts are terribly wicked."

His grin grew. "Terribly."

She angled her head slightly, studying him. "Your back seems darker than I remember. Have you been going without a shirt?"

"A few minutes each day. I have no desire to let the sun catch me unawares again."

But he had certainly caught her unawares. She found the bronzed tone of his skin incredibly . . . attractive, which was the last thing she wanted him to realize.

"The children are so excited about the picnic."

His smile warmed. "I'm glad."

"I finished their surcoats last night."

"Wonderful. Now they can pretend they are real knights."

"Did you pretend you were a knight when you were a boy?"

"I pretended—but not that I was a knight."

"What was it that you wanted to be?"

"Loved."

Her heart felt as though someone had just clamped a hand around it. He turned back to the mirror and began scraping away the remainder of his whiskers.

"Forget I said that," he said quietly, his gaze latched on his reflection.

But how could she not remember when his eyes had told her the answer long before he spoke the word. "I'm sure your father loves you."

His hand stilled, the razor resting just beneath his chin. "Yes, I suppose he does. In his way. He gave me a generous allowance, an exceptional education—" He slid his gaze toward her. "And a journey into hell."

"The hottest fires forge the strongest metals."

He raised a brow. "Is that so?"

She thought it was, but wasn't completely certain so she simply angled her chin defiantly. "Whenever a blacksmith needs to reshape iron, he thrusts it into the hottest fires.''

''My father is not a blacksmith.''

''But you needed reshaping.''

The laughter rumbled from deep within him, and Abbie wanted to sing out.

''Yes, I suppose I did need a bit of reshaping.''

''And you'll have some reminders of England today.''

With a towel, he wiped the remaining lather from his face. ''That's true.''

She took a step closer. ''I . . . I made this for you.''

He turned his head slightly and looked at her as though she'd spoken in Spanish. He set the towel aside. His footsteps echoed across the porch nearly as loudly as her heart. He took her gift and shook it out, twisting it, turning it, studying it from all angles.

The early morning sunlight seemed to emphasize every flawed and faulty stitch. ''It's a shirt,'' she said, wishing now that she hadn't sewn it. Compared with the linen shirt he'd been wearing the day he'd arrived, it looked as though it were better suited to holding potatoes. ''Something to wear in the fields—''

His gaze shifted and captured hers. ''I wouldn't dream of wearing it in the fields.'' He leaned toward her, and she would have sworn he was going to kiss her, but instead, he simply touched a finger to her cheek. ''No one has ever made a gift for me before. I shall take great pleasure in wearing this today. Thank you.''

Backing up a step, she wiped her sweating palms

on her apron. "I'd best put the finishing touches on the food."

"I'll get the wagon."

She watched him watching her, and suddenly couldn't remember what it was she was supposed to do. He stepped off the porch, and she wondered if she'd ever noticed how long his legs were. He needed only two strides to reach her, only one movement to cradle her cheek, and one swoop to press his lips to hers. She leaned into him as though she were a willow bending with the wind. His lips trailed along her cheek and came to rest beside her ear. "Make no mistake, Abbie. Today you are my lady."

She drew away, heat flaming her face. "I don't know how to play the flirtatious games—"

"No games. Just try to enjoy my company today as much as I enjoy yours."

She nodded and scurried away with the shameful thought that she was the mother of three and had never given her heart away—but at least now she knew why. It hurt to do so.

10

Grayson drew the lumbering wagon to a halt. He would have gladly sold his soul for a carriage—and a decent road—that he might have used to escort Abbie to the day's festivities in a manner she deserved instead of the manner to which she was accustomed.

Wearing the shirt she'd sewn for him, he wished he had something of equal value that he could have bestowed upon her. She wore the bonnet that normally graced her head as she worked the fields—not a plume, a colored ribbon, or a bow to be seen except for the one tucked beneath her chin to keep the plain thing in place. Abbie's dress had faded to leave nothing but a shadowy reminder of the colors it might have once possessed. Yet he thought she had never looked more beautiful.

Lydia proudly wore a new dress. Following alongside the wagon, Johnny sat astride the horse he would ride in the tournament. Micah was perched behind his brother, his arms wrapped tightly around

Johnny's waist. The boys wore shirts that resembled Grayson's.

Grayson climbed from the wagon and reached for Abbie. She blushed becomingly before placing her hands on his shoulders. His hands spanned her waist, his thumbs touching, and he wondered how the mother of three could be so tiny. His gaze delving into the violet of her eyes, he slowly brought her to the ground. Christ, but he wanted to kiss her.

"I dislike that bonnet."

Her hand flew to the brim that reminded him of a duck's beak. "It keeps the sun from turning my face into leather."

He narrowed his eyes. "How much harm could one day without it cause?" Without waiting for her answer, he grabbed the end of the faded ribbon and tugged the bow loose of its moorings. Her blush deepened but she did nothing to stop him. He slipped a finger between the ribbon and her throat and felt the rapid beat of her pulse. He was tempted to press his lips against her fluttering flesh. He loosened the ribbon and tugged the bonnet from her head.

She quickly pressed a hand to her head, touching different areas of her upswept hair as though to make sure everything was in place. A touch of vanity, perhaps, and it pleased him beyond measure.

"What are we gonna do first?" Johnny asked.

"Stake a claim to some shade beneath a tree," Abbie said as she walked to the back of the wagon and fetched a quilt. "Come on. Everyone needs to help."

They tended the horses, then Grayson and Johnny each carried a large basket to the shade of a towering tree that Abbie had called "perfect." Grayson heard the babbling of a nearby brook, but he had no desire to swim. He wanted nothing more than to spend the day in Abbie's company.

She spread the quilt beneath the tree—a lone star quilt, she called it—and he wondered how many of the diamond-shaped scraps of cloth had once been a portion of her clothes.

By the time they'd finished setting up, several families had arrived.

"Ma, can me and the boys go play?" Lydia asked.

"Yes, but stay together and within sight."

Holding hands, the children scampered away.

More people began to arrive, and Grayson reluctantly admitted that Abbie had been right—the atmosphere was more jovial with friends in attendance. He had not realized how much a part of the community he had become.

Before Texas, even with Kit and Harry as friends, he had hovered on the fringes of acceptance. He had always wondered at first if Kit and Harry had accepted him into their circle simply because having him as a friend was so incredibly scandalous.

He remembered the first time Kit had taken him to Ravenleigh. The earl had looked as though something sour were sitting on his stomach when Kit had introduced Grayson to him.

"Now, whose son are you?" he'd asked.

"He's no one's son, Father," Kit had piped up. "He's a bastard."

Grayson had prayed fervently that the stone floor of the manor would crack open and he'd disappear. Instead the carriage door had been flung open, and he'd found himself back in the carriage, traveling to Eton.

He had been staring out the window when Kit had quietly said, "I hurt your feelings—"

"You knew he wouldn't let me stay."

"Yes, and I knew he'd send me packing right along with you. I apologize for using you, but I had no wish to spend the holiday at Ravenleigh."

Grayson had slid his gaze to Kit. "Why?"

"Because there I am nothing. My father never sees me unless I'm into mischief and causing trouble." He shrugged. "So I decided to cause trouble from the beginning and be done with it."

Grayson had realized then that not only bastards belonged to no one.

"Rhodes!" someone called, and Grayson turned to see Andy Turner walking toward him. He was dark-haired, dark-eyed, and tanned. Like many others, he'd returned from the war quietly. He and Grayson had worked in the fields together, occasionally lamenting the heat. "Interested in some horseshoes?"

"I don't think so." Grayson cast a look Abbie's way. "Your horses don't need shoeing, do they?"

She smiled brightly, her eyes crinkling at the corners. "Horseshoes. It's a game."

"Ah. Do you think I can beat Andy here?"

"Probably." Her eyes gleamed with a challenge. "But I don't think you can beat me."

He held his arm out to her. "We shall see, my lady."

She slipped her hand around his arm, and he tucked it in close to his body. He could almost imagine that they were strolling through a park. The green leaves were breathtaking as they lay against the azure sky. The constant breeze ruffled the loose-fitting shirt she had sewn him, cooling him as much as it was able. They neared a spot where several men stood about, and a steady clanging like a blacksmith's hammer could be heard.

Grayson watched a man swing his arm like a pendulum as he gripped a horseshoe. Bending slightly, he tossed it. The inside curve of the shoe hit a metal stake in the ground a few feet away, ringing loudly before thudding to the ground.

With a nod of understanding, he said, "Seems easy enough. I accept your challenge, Andy." He leaned toward Abbie. "After which, I shall challenge you."

To his regret, she released her hold on him and stepped aside. Realistically, he knew he could not play with her hanging onto him—but still, he would have been willing to give it a go.

Several stakes had been set up. He and Andy moved to a pair that was unoccupied. Andy handed him a horseshoe. Grayson tested the weight. It was evenly distributed. It seemed too fine a piece of workmanship to be tossed around.

"You go first," Andy said.

Grayson peered at Abbie. She held up her hands, fingers crossed—for good luck, he supposed. Not that he would need it.

He brought his arm back, then forward, and released his hold on the horseshoe. It sailed through the air, past the stake, and landed with a thud some feet away.

Straightening, he cleared his throat. "The weight carried it a bit farther than I anticipated."

With a broad grin, Andy picked up a shoe, squinted one eye, and tossed it. One end clanged against the stake. Andy spewed forth a stream of tobacco. Grayson had noted that many of the men harbored that vile habit.

"Care to make a bet on the next set?" Andy asked.

"What sort of bet?"

Andy looked at Abbie. "You paying on the number of sacks picked?"

She nodded. "That's the way John did it. I reckon I'd do it the same."

Andy looked pleased as he slanted his gaze back to Grayson. "I'll bet you a full sack of picked cotton that I can get my horseshoe closer than you can."

"You're on."

Abbie grabbed Grayson's arm. "No, don't do this. You don't know how much work is involved in filling a sack of cotton."

"She's right, Andy. It wouldn't be fair to you to have to sacrifice your hard labors to me."

Andy threw his head back and laughed. "She ain't worried about my hard work, she's worried about yours. Come on, Abbie. If'n he wins, he'll get my sack."

It stung Grayson's pride to see the look Abbie bestowed upon Andy—she didn't think Grayson had a chance in hell of winning. Grayson strode to the far stake and picked up both horseshoes. "Come on, then, lad, you can have the first go."

With a confidence to his step, Andy sauntered to the line.

"Andy Turner, you're taking advantage—"

"Aw, Abbie, it's just a little wager."

She crossed her arms beneath her breasts, throwing the gentle swells into delightful relief.

Andy tossed his shoe. It hit the stake dead center and did a half-turn before dropping to the ground. Andy folded his arms across his chest, smiled broadly, and rocked back on his heels. Grayson contemplated his strategy for a full minute before throwing his horseshoe. It fell short of the mark.

Andy released what Grayson thought was termed a rebel yell. Abbie looked as though the defeat were hers instead of Grayson's. Grayson extended his hand. "Good job, Andy."

Andy rubbed the side of his nose. "Hell, with Abbie lookin' at me like that, I feel like I took advantage of you."

"Nonsense," Grayson assured him.

"Andy, you aren't really gonna make him hand over a sack of cotton—"

Grayson gave her a glare that stopped her words cold. "A gentleman always pays his debts."

Andy pumped his hand. "Well, hell, then, you want to play again?"

Grayson smiled. "No, the next game is Abbie's." He strolled to the stake, picking up his shoe along the way before retrieving the one Andy had thrown.

"What shall we wager?" he asked.

"Nothing. The fun is simply in winning," she said.

"But a wager adds to the excitement. If I win, you will allow me to unpin your hair, and you shall wear it loose for the remainder of the day."

She thrust out a hip and planted her hand on it. "I've seen you play. You're not going to win."

He contemplated her stance, wondering what he could offer her that would ensure her desire to wager. "If I lose . . . I shall give *Ivanhoe* to you."

"The book?"

"The book."

"For keeps?" she asked breathlessly.

"For keeps."

She snatched a horseshoe from his grasp. "You made a mistake wagering something that I covet."

He smiled lazily. "I shall be the judge of that mistake. But since what I am wagering means so much to both of us, I hate the thought of losing it on a single toss. Would you be willing to go best two out of three?"

"That seems fair."

He angled his head. "You may go first."

He stood to the side and a little behind her. She furrowed her brow and pressed her lips into a straight line, concentrating on the stake at the far end. She swung her arm back and forth, back and forth. She bent over slightly, giving him a lovely view of her backside. She released her hold and the horseshoe glided through the air, hit the stake, and bounced back marginally, close enough that the open end framed the stake. Smiling broadly, she turned to him.

"Well done," he said, hating the thought of seeing that smile disappear, but his strategy would no doubt demand it.

He stepped to the line, balancing the horseshoe between both hands, before bringing his arm back and tossing the shoe with a fluid movement. The curve caught the stake, clanged, and slid to the ground.

He turned, swallowing back the laughter at the incredulous expression on Abbie's face. "Well, it seems I might have mastered the technique."

Her narrowed gaze darted between the stake, him, the stake, and finally him, suspicion lurking in her eyes. "The best two out of three, right?"

"Absolutely."

With her arms swinging as though she were warming up for the toss, she marched to the other end of their field. Grayson caught the gazes of a few people watching them. She snatched up both horseshoes and handed one over to him.

"You can go first this time," she said.

"No, ladies first." He leaned toward her. "The gentleman in me insists."

"I've got a feeling it's not the gentleman I'm playing, but the rogue."

He placed a hand over his heart. "You wound me. Perhaps the last toss was simply fortune smiling upon me."

She pivoted and faced the far marker. Closing her eyes, she inhaled deeply and released a slow, quiet breath. Then she opened her eyes and tossed the horseshoe. It slammed against the stake and fell to the ground. Grayson moved into position, sighted the target, and threw the shoe. It hit the stake, circling it as it made its way to the ground, landing on top of Abbie's shoe. She charged over, Grayson in her wake.

His shoe had hers beat by a thumbnail. She snapped her fiery gaze up to his. "You won."

"It appears so." He reached for a pin and she jerked back, pressing her hand to her head.

"What do you think you're doing?"

"Receiving my prize."

"You sure got good awfully fast."

"Remarkable, wasn't it? You shouldn't have wagered something that I coveted. Now you must pay up."

He slid a pin from her hair, then another, and another until her hair tumbled down her back and curled over her hips. In his wildest dreams, he had not imagined it so thick, so glossy as to truly look as though it had been woven from moonbeams.

"Beautiful," he whispered reverently.

He saw the doubts flit across her face. She touched her slender fingers to the flowing strands.

"If I leave it loose, it'll be tangled by nightfall."

"I'll brush out the tangles for you."

"Gray!"

He jerked around at the sound of Harry's voice. He watched Kit and Harry stride toward him, each wearing the clothes of a gentleman: trousers, starched white shirt, and a jacket. He would have thought the two of them believed they were back in England.

Bending over, Harry picked up a horseshoe.

''Horseshoes?'' He turned to Abbie. ''Have you seen Gray toss one of these? He's quite good—''

''Harry!'' Gray interjected, but knew he'd cut off his friend too late.

Abbie angled her head, a speculative gleam in her eye. ''Is he good?''

''He has an excellent aim,'' Harry confided.

''Harry,'' Gray warned.

''If you are so talented, why didn't you beat Andy?'' Abbie said.

''Would you have wagered against me if I had?''

She studied him a moment before shaking her head. ''You think you're so clever. You'll regret both wagers once you discover how much work goes into filling a sack with cotton.''

He watched her walk away, her hair cascading around her, and knew he would have willingly traded ten sacks of cotton for no more than a glimpse of her hair unfettered.

Abbie stayed angry for all of two minutes. Then she felt a thrill of pleasure such as she'd never known ripple through her as she remembered the adoration in Grayson's eyes as he'd reverently removed the pins from her hair. She'd barely been able to breathe. He looked as though he might devour her on the spot.

She should have been frightened. Instead, she wondered if he truly would brush her hair come nightfall.

When he joined her and the children for lunch, she knew he felt no remorse for his earlier duplicity. It was the rogue within him, the rogue that constantly warred with the gentleman. She feared she might be falling in love with both.

When he finished eating and stretched out beside her, she couldn't stop herself from wishing he'd laid his head in her lap, as James had with Amy.

Grayson released a sigh of deep male contentment. "Now, this is how a holiday is supposed to be spent—doing absolutely nothing."

"Aren't you bored?"

He opened one eye. "Relax, Abbie. Watch the clouds roll by or listen to the leaves rustle."

She heard thundering feet. Johnny and Micah tore toward the tree and dropped to their haunches beside Grayson. "When are we gonna have the tournament?" Johnny asked.

"Later, lad."

"When?"

Grayson closed his eyes. "When I'm rested."

"When will that be?" Micah asked.

"In a bit."

Her sons exchanged anxious glances. She had found it difficult to get them to sleep last night. They had talked constantly of the joust, asking her over and over about their surcoats until she'd finally relented and allowed them to sleep in the costumes.

"Why don't you boys take a little nap as well?" Abbie suggested. "You didn't get much sleep last night."

Johnny scrunched up his face with distaste, but Micah bent his small body over and laid his head on Grayson's stomach. Grayson's eyes flew open, and he tucked in his chin as he stared at Micah, on whose face was an innocent smile.

Gently Grayson unwound Micah's spectacles from around his ears. "Let's remove these for the time being, shall we?" He folded them and placed them on his chest.

"How long we gonna sleep?" Micah asked in his gravelly voice.

"Until we're rested."

Johnny jumped to his feet. "I'm gonna go play with Ezra."

She watched her older son run off before turning her attention back to the man and boy who had stayed behind. Their eyes were closed and Grayson's large hand had come to rest against the back of her younger son's head as though to support and protect him.

A rogue indeed.

She leaned against the tree, thinking she'd never been happier.

The tournament was scheduled to begin in the late afternoon, but the third time that Micah asked of Grayson, "Are we rested yet?" he got the answer he wanted.

"Yes, lad, as rested as we'll ever be."

Six poles were set at equal distances apart along a path cut by wagon wheels over the years. Johnny sat astride the bay horse he'd ridden to the picnic earlier. On a makeshift stage, with pennants ruffling in the slight breeze, three judges sat. Abbie stood along the sidelines with the other spectators, her heart leaping with excitement and worry.

She didn't want Johnny to be disappointed. He'd only ever practiced snatching three rings. She feared his arm would be too tired by the time he reached the sixth ring.

With pride, she studied the intensity on her son's face as he bent over slightly to receive final instructions from Grayson. Her heart tightened at the sight of their heads almost touching—dark brown against pale blond. Soil against wheat.

With a final nod, Johnny beamed and straightened. Grayson patted his knee before stepping back and lifting Micah onto his shoulders. Even though Micah would not participate in the tournament, he proudly wore a surcoat bearing the simple coat of arms they'd wanted: a red cross.

Abbie took Lydia's hand and squeezed lightly as Grayson strode toward her.

"Don't look so worried, Abbie," Grayson scolded.

"I'm not worried."

"The lad will do fine."

Johnny did more than fine. On his first pass he caught three of the six rings, on his second pass he slipped four onto his lance, and the third pass found him carrying five rings to the judges. None of the other boys matched his efforts. Amid cheers and clapping, he was announced the winner.

"Hey, English," Andy called out, grinning, "think you could take on a Texan born and bred?"

"Without a doubt," Grayson replied, lifting Micah off his shoulders.

James stepped out from the crowd. "Andy, if you're gonna challenge one, you gotta challenge them all."

"What will you wager?" Harry asked as he came forward.

"Ain't winning enough?" James asked.

"No," Harry answered. "In England, if a knight was challenged and he lost, he had to forfeit his armor and his horse to the victor. We'll settle for your horses."

James rocked back on his heels. "What do we get since you don't have any horses?"

"Credit for all the cotton we pick the first day," Grayson said.

Abbie grabbed his arm. "Grayson—"

He slanted his gaze toward her. "Have you no faith?"

"You don't know how hard it is to pick cotton—" The look in his eyes stopped her. "You don't know how well they ride."

He merely lifted a brow.

"Men are so stubborn," she muttered as she reached into her pocket, withdrew a lace handkerchief, and held it toward him.

"What's this?" he asked, taking it from her.

"Isn't a lady supposed to give her knight a token of her affection?"

The molten heat of his gaze almost turned her knees into jam.

"Am I your knight?" he asked quietly.

She backed up a step. "You're going to work too hard for that cotton. Don't let them win it."

"My lady, I wouldn't dream of it."

He walked away with a careless stride, and she wondered how he could appear so relaxed. Johnny gladly handed over the horse he'd used, along with his lance. A lump rose in her throat as she watched Grayson tie her handkerchief around the end of the lance, a flag in the breeze.

Johnny rushed up to her. "They're gonna do it like a team—just one pass each—but everything will add up. Gray's gonna go last. He'll make 'em win."

She didn't think anything except all of them pulling together would make them win. The Englishmen didn't have any trouble deciding who would ride because there were only seven of them, but her brother and his friends were having a difficult time trying to decide who would have the honor of accepting the challenge. For a moment, the men reminded her of the way they'd been before the war: eager to prove themselves, excited, laughing, anticipating the opportunity to win. She hoped her sons would never have to answer the call to arms.

They had no trumpets so someone blasted a sound from a harmonica. The Texans removed their shirts and hats. The Englishmen quickly followed suit. Tanned skin against golden. Not at all what she'd expected. The English looked less like nobility every day.

But then they lined up their horses, shifted in their saddles, and hundreds of years of ancestry were reflected in their proud and magnificient posture.

Her brother went first, releasing a rebel yell, snagging four of the rings. After that, she paid no attention to the riders, but kept her gaze focused on Grayson as he apparently discussed strategy with his two friends. She wondered if she should have warned her brother that these Englishmen tended to be much better than they let on.

Then it was Grayson's turn and she could hardly think at all.

"No one's gotten all six yet," Johnny announced, jumping up and down as though he were as young as Micah.

Abbie lifted Micah onto her hip. His face was incredibly serious.

Grayson's horse snorted and pawed at the ground. Someone must have said something to him, offered advice maybe, because he gave a quick nod of his head.

"What's the tally?" Abbie asked.

"He'll have to get all six for the English to win," Elizabeth said beside her. "Wonder what they'll do if they tie."

"Probably have a sword fight," Abbie mumbled.

Johnny jerked his head around. "You think so? Gray would win. I just know it!"

Her son's adoration for the man was touching and worrisome. How would he feel when Grayson left?

The harmonica sounded and Grayson kicked his horse into a gallop. She thought he looked magnificent, leaning low over his horse's back, holding the reins with one hand, the lance tucked under his other arm.

She didn't realize until he'd slipped the sixth and final ring onto the lance that she'd been holding her breath. The air filled with groans and moans as well as jubilant cheers. He was supposed to take the rings and present them to the judges.

Instead he guided his horse through the crowd and brought it to a halt before Abbie. A fine sheen of sweat covered his face and chest. She could hardly take her eyes off him. His gaze held hers as he slowly tipped the lance.

She thrust her hands out in time to catch the rings as they slid from the lance. When she lifted her gaze back to his, she read within his eyes a devastating truth.

He knew . . . he *knew* that he had not only captured the rings . . . but he had captured her heart as well.

They began playing the music at twilight, peaceful melodies that had not sounded since the war. Abbie had always listened to the gentle strains with longing because John had claimed to have two left feet—and they had never danced.

Out of loyalty to him, she had politely refused the few offers that came her way.

Tonight her only loyalties were to herself, and it somehow seemed appropriate—right—that when Grayson looked at her, a question in his eyes, she stepped into his embrace with her answer.

She had known, even though she had never before danced, that within his arms the movements would come to her, like the cotton growing from the earth with nothing but the sun, soil, and rain for guidance.

"Your brother has a fine horse," he said quietly.

"He *did* have a fine horse. Now it belongs to you."

He gave her a smile lacking in shame. "They issued the challenge. What could we do but accept?"

"You could have missed the last ring so it would have ended in a tie. Then no one would have lost."

"I considered it, but with you watching I knew I had to give it my best."

"So it's *my* fault my brother lost his horse?"

"No, it's only your fault that I wanted to show off."

She allowed his words to wash over like the first gentle rain of spring.

"I was wrong about you Texans," he said quietly as his steps followed the strains of the fiddles.

"In what way?"

"I thought you knew nothing about playing."

She smiled. "We work hard. We play hard."

"But you work more than you play."

"We don't have a choice if we want to provide for our families. I guess when you finish picking the cotton you'll return to your life of leisure."

"Not quite, although there must be an easier way to make a go of it here."

She shrugged. "Cotton is all I know."

"Did you enjoy today?" he asked quietly.

She nodded. "Very much. But it'll be a long while before we have another day to play."

"Then we should make the most of what's left of today."

She hadn't paid attention to where he was guiding her, and she only now realized they were at the edge of the circle of dancers. Without a word, he stopped dancing, took her hand in his, and led her into the copse of trees.

She followed in silence, not knowing where the journey would end, but knowing with a certainty how it would end.

It ended in a clearing, where wildflowers carpeted the earth, and the sunset swept across the sky.

Releasing her hand, he turned to face her. Softly, he touched his fingertips to her hair. "Thank you for being such a good sport about the wager and keeping your hair down."

"Thank you for giving my children as much attention as you did."

"I would give more attention to you if I didn't think it would cause you to retreat."

She licked her lips, her heart hammering. "I wouldn't mind a little more attention."

His blue eyes darkened as he lifted his hands and cupped her face. "I'll try to keep my distance," he rasped as he lowered his mouth to hers.

Warmth. Wetness. Tenderness. Respect. They all flowed from his lips to hers. Even with her eyes closed, she felt the brilliance of the sunset, flowing through her as he deepened the kiss, his tongue sweeping inside her mouth. She felt his fingers clench, then relax as though he'd meant to pull her to him . . . and remembered the fears she harbored, the doubts that plagued her.

But the heat of his kiss sent the fears into oblivion, the doubts circling on the wind. With one hesitant, awkward step, she wound her arms around his neck and pressed her body against his. Against her breasts, she felt the deep rumble within his chest as his fingers clamped her head and angled her mouth so he could delve more deeply into the kiss.

She'd never felt the flickering heat of desire, had never known what it was to want . . . to want . . . dear Lord, what was it that she wanted? She wanted to cry out from frustration, from ignorance, from this need that she didn't understand. And she knew this man could provide the answer to the question burning deeply within her.

Breathing heavily, he tore his mouth from hers and trailed his lips along the column of her throat. "Damn the rogue in me," he ground out as he pulled back and turned away from her.

Devastation swamped her. She wanted him back, wanted his arms around her, his mouth on hers. "Grayson?"

He held up a hand. "Give me a moment, sweetheart."

She heard him release a slow harsh breath before he slowly turned and walked behind her. He wrapped his arms beneath her breasts and brought her flush against his body, laying his chin on top of her head. "The sun will be gone shortly, and we'll need to leave," he said quietly.

She nodded and placed her hands over his. "I'll remember this day until I die," she said softly.

"And I shall remember you."

11

Abbie lay in bed, listening to the night, listening to her heart. She had bathed outside, hoping that Grayson might make an appearance. But he hadn't.

She had slipped on her nightgown with thoughts of his hands skimming over her body filling her mind. The night was warm, but it was the fire burning inside her that was unbearable, that kept her from sleeping.

She had never before felt this . . . this urge to have a man's body cover hers.

And she knew beyond a doubt that Grayson had a man's needs. She had felt those needs pressing against her as he'd kissed her. She understood a man's needs because John had explained them to her—the way a man's body ached when he needed a woman and there was no woman about.

"I need you tonight, Abigail," he'd say as he lifted the hem of her nightgown.

Her heart pounded with the memories, with the humiliation—

She squeezed her eyes shut and a solitary tear trailed along her cheek. She had never fought her husband, had willingly endured the mortification because he provided for her. Now she provided for herself. She didn't need a man.

But perhaps, she thought, a man needed her. She would endure anything because she loved him.

She slipped from beneath the sheet. Quietly, she tiptoed from the room and looked in on Lydia. The bed creaked as her daughter rolled to her side. Abbie glided away and peered into the boys' room—her knights. What a day Grayson had given them . . . and her. She'd never felt as cherished.

Closing the front door behind her, she stepped onto the porch. She saw the silhouette of a man standing in the doorway of the barn. Even from the distance, she felt his gaze latched onto her. Her stomach knotted, and she swallowed hard with the knowledge that he, too, was unable to sleep.

Wearing only her nightgown, she stepped off the porch into the pale moonlight, knowing that she was sealing her fate. He would expect exactly what she was willing to give. She could only hope that he would never realize what it was costing her.

She strolled across the expanse separating them, surprised by the peace that settled over her as she grew nearer. He stepped out of the shadows, his un-buttoned shirt waving in the slight breeze like a flag of truce.

As she approached, he reached out, took her hand, and drew her against him. She pressed one hand against his bare chest while the other arm wound around his neck. His mouth swooped down to capture hers and she was lost.

Lost to the sensations swirling around her: hot mouth and warm flesh. She heard a throaty groan rumble deep within Grayson's chest, felt the vibration beneath her fingers. He tore his mouth from hers.

"God, I want you, Abbie." He blazed a trail of kisses along the column of her throat as she arched her head back.

Want. Not need. Had she ever been truly wanted? She didn't know. She only knew that she had never felt as precious as she felt at this moment. His journey along her throat came to an end, and he straightened, capturing her gaze.

The desire burning within the depths of his eyes made her breath hitch. "If I could, I would lay you down upon silk, but all I have to offer you is straw. I will certainly understand if you decide against following me into the shadows of the barn."

"I'm here, aren't I?"

The warm smile he bestowed upon her set her heart to racing. He touched a finger to the top button of her nightgown. "Yes, but I somehow sense that you are wearing armor."

She felt the heat scald her face. "I'm not any good at this."

A wealth of tenderness reshaped his features as he brought her hand to his lips and pressed a kiss to the tips of her fingers. "I am."

She slammed her eyes closed. "Grayson, I'm no good at the games. I can't be like the other women you've known—"

"I don't want you to be," he said, skimming a finger along her cheek.

She opened her eyes.

"I want you to be only who you are—what you are. But I want you to understand that if you come with me, we'll do a lot more than kiss."

She nodded, wondering why it seemed that he was trying to talk her out of this. "I thought you were disreputable."

"I am, but where you are concerned, I prefer not to feel guilty." He intertwined his fingers through hers. "If you change your mind, simply release my hand, and I'll continue walking without looking back."

But she knew that if she released his hand, she would forever look back. Would forever wonder. He stepped into the shadows. Her hand tightened around his, but she knew no hesitation. He had given her the choice—follow or leave.

She found the knowledge liberating because in her marriage, she had known no choice. She did not consider her relations with John to have been forced. They simply were what was expected.

Moments with Grayson were filled with the unexpected.

He came to a stop beside the ladder that led into the loft. His lips found hers as unerringly as the summer rain found the parched earth. When he drew away, he guided her onto the first rung of the ladder. She gathered the hem of her gown into her fist and clambered up into the loft, his hand resting easily against the small of her back, balancing her.

The fragrance of flowers wafted around her as she scrambled over the ledge. She stopped, sat in the straw, and stared at the blossoms strewn over the hay, captured by the moonlight. Grayson knelt beside her.

"How did you know I'd come tonight?" she asked quietly.

"I didn't."

She turned her head slightly. He cradled her cheek within his palm. "But I hoped. I've hoped every night since the first time I kissed you."

Tears stung the backs of her eyes. "You brought flowers up here every night?"

"You deserve so much more, and I have nothing else to give you." He led her to the feather pallet she'd sewn for him. Moonlight glided through the opening in the loft and created a halo that would circle them in its pale glow.

Her heart leapt into her throat. She had expected a darkened corner. She turned to suggest that they move to the far end of the loft. He took her in his arms, lowered his mouth to hers, and all thoughts save one flew from her mind: she loved the way he kissed her. Slowly, leisurely, as though time held no meaning, as though there were no crops to harvest, tools to mend, seasons for which to plan.

She twined her arms around his neck like a vine searching for a place to take root. With a throaty groan, he deepened the kiss and flattened her body against his. She felt the beat of his heart thundering against his chest, her breast, and hers answered in kind. All her doubts melted away. He wanted her, and if she were honest with herself, in spite of all she'd have to endure . . . she wanted him.

Desire was a stranger to her, but as it knocked with intensity, she warily opened the door and invited in the unknown.

Warmth spiraled through her, warmth that had nothing to do with the late August night. A thousand sensations sparked to life, flared, and slowly died.

Grayson's kiss lost its patience, became demanding, his tongue sweeping through her mouth the way the first storms of autumn swept across the fields, clearing away the harvest that had come before. Surprising herself, she returned his kiss with equal fervor, hoping his mouth would never leave hers.

But it did. Hot and moist, it blazed a trail along the column of her throat, his tongue tracing what she was certain was a heart-shaped path in the hollow at the base of her throat, before his mouth continued its sojourn. She had been unaware of Grayson loosening the buttons of her gown, but the material parted and he continued his journey along the inside swell of her breast. His warm breath fanned her flesh—so deliciously wicked.

His tongue circled her nipple and she dug her fingers into his shoulders. His mouth and all the heat it carried covered the hardened tip. Her breath came in small panting gasps. When he gently suckled, she dropped her head back and her legs gave way beneath her. "Oh, Lord."

He wrapped an arm around her, supporting her, laying her on the pallet. With a speed that belied his earlier lovemaking, he whisked her nightgown off her body. When she started to curl on her side, his hands spanned her hips, holding her in place.

"Don't turn away," he rasped.

Within the moonlight spilling through the opening in the loft, she saw the intensity of his gaze as it roamed over her exposed body. "We're supposed to do this in the dark."

He snapped his gaze up to hers. "Why?"

Silence reigned for the span of a heartbeat before he said quietly, "Do you have any idea how beautiful you are, Abbie?"

She felt the heat warm her cheeks. Beautiful was not a word anyone had ever associated with her.

Stretching out beside her, he took the braid draped over her shoulder and began to unravel the strands. "No, I can see that you don't know." He combed his fingers through her hair, smoothing it over one side of her body as though it were a blanket. "I intend to make you feel beautiful."

His mouth met hers with an urgency that sent waves of heat coursing through her. She tightly squeezed her eyes shut, concentrating on his kiss, blocking out the feel of the movements that she knew meant he was removing his clothes.

Where was the blessed darkness? Why hadn't she insisted that they move to the shadows?

She felt the heat of his body pressing against her side, burrowing against her thigh. He took her hand. "Touch me, Abbie."

Her eyes flew open. Curiosity warred with fear. He wanted things of her that John had never asked—and oddly, she found herself wanting to give more to him than she'd ever given. Her fingers momentarily tightened around his before they unfurled and reached down to touch him as he'd asked. Closing his eyes, he released a long slow moan.

"See how beautiful you are, Abbie?"

She furrowed her brow, her hand closing around him. "This isn't me."

A corner of his mouth quirked up as he opened his eyes. "No, sweetheart, it's not. But your beauty certainly makes it stand at attention."

She released her hold as he rolled between her thighs. She stiffened, bracing herself for the discomfort that always came at the beginning. He pressed a kiss to the pulse beating at her throat. Then he moved her hair aside and nibbled on her ear. She wrapped her arms around him, grateful for the distraction, wishing she could be as relaxed and comfortable with her body as he was with his.

He nipped at her shoulder, his tongue swirling over her collarbone. He moved lower and she thought of his comment that he'd been known to lick up all the buttermilk. His roughened palm cupped her breast and she felt his callused thumb skim over her nipple, drawing it up, causing it to strain for another touch, a touch that was answered with his mouth closing and suckling. Pleasure speared her. If his body wasn't pressing down on hers, she would have curled into a ball that had nothing to do with embarrassment. He gave the same tender ministrations to her other breast before moving lower. He dipped his tongue into her navel, then pressed a kiss to hollow of each hip.

He moved lower and kissed her intimately. She

drew her knees up, pressing her thighs against his shoulders. He slipped his hands beneath her hips and lifted her slightly. His tongue darted and swirled.

If he heard her startled cry, he ignored her. If he spoke, she did not hear the words as sensations rocketed through her. She braced her hands on either side of his face, needing to touch him as she'd never needed anyone. Her body curled, coiled, tightened. Her shoulders came off the pallet as the pleasures increased. And then she felt as though everything within her exploded as her back arched and she cried out.

Gasping for breath, she stared at his blond curls wrapped around her fingers. Slowly, he lifted his head. And she wished she had died. "I'm sorry," she whispered.

He furrowed his brow. "Sorry?"

She nodded jerkily. "I don't know why I did that ... I ... I ... Oh, God." Tears welled in her eyes as the embarrassment slammed into her. She squeezed her eyes shut and felt the tears roll along her temple. How could she ever again meet his blue gaze? "I'm so sorry."

Grayson moved up and cradled Abbie within his arms, drawing her against his bare chest, feeling the warm tears trailing along his skin. He was not a man prone to violence, but right this moment he had never known an anger so intense. Abbie had three children and although he knew her husband had never kissed her, he had hoped beyond reason that the man had not withheld the pleasure from her as well.

He felt the shudders wracking her body and

wanted every movement to be the result of pleasure, not embarrassment or shame. He cupped her cheek and lifted her face away from his chest. Her eyes were squeezed closed so tightly that he feared she might never open them. "Abbie, look at me."

She shook her head slightly. So he spoke the words that he knew would make her look at him. "I love you."

Her eyes flew open, and he saw the doubts swirling within the violet depths. Regretting his roguish ways as never before, he combed the stray strands of hair behind her ear. "Know that I have never spoken those words to another." He released a derisive chuckle. "Have never even considered speaking them before I met you. I've never known anyone like you. You give everything to others and never ask anything for yourself. I fear you came to me this evening expecting to receive nothing in return. That you would willingly give so much to me humbles me." With his thumb, he captured a solitary tear that trailed from the corner of her eye. "It was my intent to gift you with pleasure . . . not embarrassment."

He saw her lower lip tremble. "I . . . I never . . ."

"I know that now, sweetheart."

"Elizabeth told me once that it was different when you loved the man. I didn't come here tonight as a sacrifice. I came here because I love you."

Nothing in Grayson's life had prepared him for the impact of those three little words slamming into him. Not all the years he'd longed for someone to say them to him, not all the nights when he'd wished to hear them directed his way. Cradling her face, he

pressed her against his chest, hoping that the pounding of his heart wouldn't bruise her delicate skin.
"No one ever has."

"I don't believe that. There's too much about you
to love. Just because they didn't say the words
doesn't mean they didn't feel the love."

Perhaps he did possess his father's love, but he
knew beyond a doubt that she was the first woman
to ever love him. Christ, but it was a joyful burden
to bear. "Tell me again."

"I love you."

He felt as though someone had just delivered a
well-aimed punch to his midsection. "Even if I'm
disreputable?"

"I don't think you're disreputable at all." Drawing
away from his chest, she gave him a shy smile. "But
your mouth and tongue are terribly wicked."

He grinned. "The rest of me can be terribly wicked
as well."

Raising her hand, she threaded her fingers through
his hair. "I don't doubt it." He watched as her teeth
tugged on her lower lip, something he'd seen her do
often. Only now did he realize it was a sign that she
was nervous. "Show me," she whispered.

"With pleasure, sweetheart," he said as he rolled
her back onto the pallet and kissed her as tenderly as
he knew how. Like her, all the women in his life had
been married. Unlike her, they'd all been experienced. The romps had been designed to bring the
greatest amount of pleasure in the least amount of
time—before their husbands came home.

He wanted with Abbie nothing that he had ever

shared with any other woman. He felt the need to protect her innocence, the desire to maintain her simplicity. Her faint scent of roses followed him as he nestled himself between her thighs. His hands outlined her curves. His mouth taunted the swells, the peaks, and the valleys. He rejoiced when he heard her breath catch, smiled inwardly when her low moan accompanied the slight roll of her body against his.

When she welcomed his body into hers, he'd never felt more complete. It took every ounce of willpower he possessed not to explode at that very moment. But he'd be damned before he gave to her less than she deserved.

"Open your eyes, sweetheart."

She did as he bade. "No shadows tonight, Abbie."

She nodded, and even with the ashen light, he thought he saw the love reflected in her eyes. He rocked against her and watched as her eyes widened with wonder. Her fingers dug into his shoulders, her body straining to meet his. Rising above her, he quickened his thrusts. She writhed beneath him. When she cried out his name, her body arching against his, he felt the wave of pleasure ripple through her, close around him, and he barely had time to withdraw before his body responded. He buried his face between her breasts, spilling his seed into his hand.

Breathing heavily, his muscles quivering, he thought the culmination of fulfillment had never felt so empty. He felt her comb her fingers through his hair.

"Why did you leave me?" she asked quietly.

"Because I won't leave my bastard growing inside you."

Her fingers stilled. "I would love your child."

"That would not change the fact that he is a bastard." He lifted his head and met her gaze. "You told me that you have no desire to marry." He grazed his fingers along her temple. "I promised you that with me, you would always have a choice. Besides, you don't need another child hanging onto your apron strings."

"You don't know what I need, Grayson Rhodes."

He quirked a brow. "Don't I? Watch your tone, sweetheart, or I'll give you a good sound licking."

"You mean a spanking?" she asked indignantly.

"No." He smiled warmly and ran his tongue along the underside of her breast.

He heard her sharp intake of breath. "We can't do this again."

"I can't for a while, but you certainly can." And he proceeded to teach her of things she'd never dared dream.

Abbie stared at the white tufts dotting the fields. Lord, but she did not want to pick cotton today. She thought she might never want to pick cotton again.

She had lain through the night with a man who wasn't her husband. She should feel shame. Instead, she found herself wondering how sinful it would be if Grayson slipped through the window into her room at night. She couldn't imagine anything finer than waking up in his arms in the morning.

She thought she might simply curl up and die when

he moved on, and he certainly seemed to have it in his head to do so. But living through a war had taught her one thing: you never knew what tomorrow would bring.

Maybe he wasn't the marrying kind, but her heart didn't care. She did think he loved her, and she knew she loved him. For now, it was enough.

She saw a movement out of the corner of her eye. Turning slightly, she watched as Grayson strolled across the field. Her mouth went as dry as the cotton. She folded her arms beneath her breasts. "Morning."

He smiled warmly. "Good morning."

"We'll start picking the cotton today. I imagine people will start arriving soon—"

"Then I'd best not delay."

Before she knew what he was about, he'd taken her in his arms and lowered his mouth to hers. Standing on the tips of her toes, she wrapped her arms around his neck. She reveled in his throaty growl and tightened her hold, wondering how she'd keep her mind on picking cotton when all she wanted was to think about him.

He drew back, his gaze holding hers. "I didn't sleep a wink after I walked you home last night."

It was almost dawn before she'd returned to the house. He'd walked her to the front door and gave her a kiss that almost had her going back to the barn with him. She felt the heat fan her cheeks as she ducked her head and lifted a shoulder. "You're not going to tell anyone, are you? I don't want anyone knowing that we sinned—"

She felt him stiffen before he drew his arms from

around her. "Believe me, sweetheart, no one will have a clue, but think on this. You made love to a husband you didn't love. You made love in a hayloft to a bastard you claimed to love. Which is the greater sin?"

He spun on his heel and began walking toward the barn. She dashed after him, caught up to him, and grabbed his arm. He came to an abrupt halt.

"Do you think your father sinned with your mother?" she asked.

"Until last night I did. But if he loved her half as much as I love you, then I think the greater sin lies in the fact that he married a woman he didn't love simply to gain a legitimate heir."

"You think I sinned with John?"

He released a great gust of air. "No. I don't think you could sin if the devil sat on your shoulder and whispered the instructions in your ear on how to do it." He cradled her cheek. "I think I'm simply too sensitive about my lack of my parentage—"

"But you had parents, and it doesn't matter to me that they weren't married—"

"But it matters to me."

12

*G*rayson shifted the heavy sack off his shoulder as Abbie took his hand and began to wrap thin strips of linen around his fingers. He thought it was uncanny the way the cotton formed five little pads—five pads for five fingers—and those with experience were whipping those little balls off the plants. It was the little tines that had protected the cotton while it grew that he hated. The damn things were constantly pricking him.

"You want to be more careful," Abbie said as she tied off the linen. "Blood on the cotton lessens its value."

"Well then, we certainly don't want to get my blood on the damned cotton."

She snapped her head up. "How's your back?"

"It hurts worse than my hands."

"Don't bend over to pick the low-growing cotton. Drop to your knees—"

"If I drop to my knees, I'll never get back up to my feet."

The smile she gave him made him want to take her in his arms.

"I wish I could tell you that it'll get better—"

"But it's only going to get worse," he finished for her.

She nodded.

"How long will we be picking?" he asked.

"If the weather holds, a month."

"If the weather holds?"

"Sometimes a storm comes up from the coast. The cotton becomes worthless if it gets hit with a heavy rain. That's why we pick as fast and long as we can."

"There has to be an easier way to provide for your children."

She gave him a sympathetic smile. "When you figure it out, you let me know. Meanwhile, watermelon is waiting for you at the end of the row. When you get there, just break it open and eat the heart."

He didn't know what watermelon was, but he'd seen men stacking the large green balls at the end of the rows. "Sounds positively barbaric."

"You won't think so when you get to the end of the row."

He watched her stroll away, her hips swaying provocatively. Yesterday his body would have reacted at the sight; today nothing. Good God, he hoped all this hard work wasn't going to turn him into a eunuch.

"Wool," Kit mumbled.

Grayson turned. Kit approached each boll of cotton as though he thought it might bite him. Wise man. "What did you say?"

Kit glanced over his shoulder. "From now on, I wear only wool. Let the sheep do all the work."

"I've worked with sheep," Harry said, plucking the cotton with an efficiency that had Grayson envying his friend. Little wonder he could whisk a card from the center of the deck. "I've seen that shearing the buggers is damn hard work."

"Silk then," Kit said. "I can't imagine that working with worms can be that much of a chore."

"Do you know which end of the worm the silk comes out of?" Harry asked.

Kit placed his hands against the small of his back and bent backward. "No."

"Neither do I, but either way I find it rather disgusting."

"You need to stop your gabbing and get to work. You're burning daylight," a smoky, indignant voice commanded.

Grayson turned to see a young woman with fiery red hair glaring at Harry. He had never seen her before, but then a lot of people who had not worked the fields before today had come to help with the harvest. "I don't believe we've met."

She narrowed her gaze, and he suddenly felt like a slug inching over the ground. "If you're a friend of his, then I consider myself blessed not to know you."

She spun around and tromped through the fields. It was embarrassing to note that despite her small size, her sack was almost full.

"Who was that?" Grayson asked.

"Jessye," Harry said, humor laced through his

voice. "Her father owns the saloon and on occasion, she serves the drinks."

"Harry thought she served more than drinks," Kit said with a chuckle.

Harry straightened into an indignant stance that usually meant he found no humor in a situation. "In my own defense, you must admit that it is not uncommon in England for a serving wench to offer her services—"

"Yes, but when she tosses the ale in your face, it means no."

"It was whiskey, not ale, and I thought she was playing hard to get."

Kit grinned and gave his head a jerk in Harry's direction. "That's why he grew the beard."

Grayson stared at his friend. "He told me it was to protect his face from the sun."

"No, he was attempting to cover the bruise she gave him when she said no the second time."

"She hardly seemed your type," Grayson commented.

"I'm desperate. There are no houses of ill repute in this whole area. That's the business we need to go into—a bloody brothel."

Grayson began plucking the cotton from the vines. "It's hardly a reputable undertaking."

"When have we ever worried about our reputations?" Harry asked.

"Perhaps it's time we did."

"Why?"

Kit studied him. "Has your interest in Abbie grown?"

Grayson looked down the row. He saw Abbie

kneeling in the dirt, Micah beside her, as they snatched the cotton and stuffed it into their sack. Grayson had never before considered that laws should exist to prevent children from working in the fields— or the factories at home. But if it was work or go hungry, he supposed there was little choice. And here, all the children worked. Even if that work often entailed nothing more than carting water to the workers.

Abbie had no concerns about his bastardy, and he wanted none of his actions to bring her shame. He remembered a time when he would have bragged to Harry and Kit about his conquests. But Abbie was not a conquest. He couldn't explain his relationship with her to himself, much less to his friends.

"Grayson only has affections for married women," Harry said.

"A widow is not that far from being married," Kit pointed out.

"But she is not safe; she could easily decide that she wants marriage," Harry replied.

"She's watching," Kit said.

Gray jerked his head around to find Abbie's gaze fastened on him. He gave her a brief nod before returning to his task. "I imagine she's wondering why we aren't working, since our efforts will determine how well her children eat this winter."

"And while her children are eating, we'll be in Galveston," Kit said.

Grayson's fingers faltered and he stabbed his finger with the sharp tine that cradled the cotton. With a harsh curse, he stuck his finger into his mouth, biting down on the wound to staunch the flow of blood.

Galveston's appeal dwindled with each passing day.

"Dear God, I want desperately to make love to you," Grayson said. "But I'm too damned tired."

Closing her eyes, Abbie leaned her back against his chest, nestled her head within the crook of his shoulder, and enjoyed the warmth of the water lapping around them. The bath had always been her private sanctuary, a place in which she could escape the demands of being a mother and a wife. How strange that the sanctuary seemed as private when shared with a lover. "Tomorrow will be worse," she whispered.

"I don't see how it can possibly be worse."

"You will."

He groaned and she felt the rumble of his chest against her back. She swallowed her laughter.

"You're laughing."

She shook her head. "I'm trying not to."

He pressed a kiss to the curve of her shoulder. "I don't know how you've managed all these years, Abbie."

He slipped his hands beneath the water as though to hold her, moaned low, and placed his hands back on the edge of the tub. She wrapped her hands around one of his and brought it to her lips, placing a kiss on his swollen fingers. "You got cut up bad today. We need to be sure we put some iodine on the scratches so you don't get an infection."

"Wonderful. I suppose an infection out here could be ghastly."

"A few years back a man got gangrene. He wouldn't let the doctor cut off his hands and he died."

"Lovely. That's just what I want to hear."

She turned slightly, pressing her hand just above his pounding heart. "I'll watch your hands closely. I won't let that happen to you."

Leaning forward, he kissed her tenderly. "You know, it's fortunate for you that I don't pick cotton with my tongue."

Her eyes widened as a realization suddenly hit her. "The apple!"

"What?"

"That day you tied the knot in the apple stem—" The laughter bubbled out of her. "—I didn't understand why you thought it was such an accomplishment."

"The ability to do so gives me a very nimble tongue. You, sweetheart, benefit from that exercise."

"You are so terribly wicked!"

The moonlight reflected off his smile. "Terribly."

Snuggling against him, she felt his body's reaction to her nearness. "I thought you were too tired."

"If we go slow and lazily, I should be able to manage."

The water splashed around them as he stood and climbed out of the tub. She watched the play of moonlight over his body as he rubbed a towel over his arms and legs, completely at ease with his nudity. She had only ever caught a glimpse of John's chest, never his entire body. She had never gazed upon him with appreciation as she did with Grayson now.

Grayson's hands stilled. "See something you like?"

She lifted her gaze to his. "Everything."

He tossed his towel aside and reached for the one that was still folded on the porch railing. As he approached, she rose from the water, surprised by her boldness, her lack of self-consciousness in his presence. She could not recall ever looking at her naked body in a mirror. Yet here she stood with the water rolling over her flesh, her nipples puckering as the night air whispered across them, with no desire whatsoever to shield herself from his gaze, a gaze that warmed her like the sun. He draped the towel around her shoulders, placed one arm around her back, the other beneath her knees, then lifted her and cradled her against his chest.

As he strode away from the house, toward the barn, with her nestled within his arms, she had never felt more treasured.

The days melted one into another, and the nights passed by much too quickly. Abbie often joined Grayson in the loft, but usually he did little more than wrap his arms around her and drift off to sleep.

When he awoke, she was gone.

He had never known such bone-deep weariness or such exaltation as his hands grew more accustomed to the chore and his deftness increased. The first day that he picked over a hundred pounds of cotton, he was tempted to write his father, and if his fingers hadn't ached so badly, he would have.

But he had no idea how he could explain to a man

born into wealth the riches that were earned by a man's own sweat and blood. Here he was not judged by his lack of parentage or his background. The nods of acceptance he received from the other men came about because of his accomplishments, because of his labors, his increasing skills.

There were times when he actually felt that he stood above the highest man of rank in all of England, and when he thought his labors in the field could earn him the right to stand at Abbie's side.

Every moment of every day, in spite of the weariness and the pain, she filled his mind, made all that he endured worth every second of discomfort. When she glanced at him and smiled, his joy was unfettered and he worked even harder to please her, to give her another reason to smile.

But at night when he awoke alone in the loft, surrounded by nothing but the stench of farm animals, he knew an emptiness that stretched toward eternity, and he wondered how he would survive when the last of the cotton was picked and his services were no longer needed. And he knew that time was at hand for the white fluffs were disappearing like a wave retreating from the shore.

Hefting the bulging sack onto his back, he strode to the barn and hoisted the bag onto a fourth wagon. Three wagons were already filled to capacity, sheltered within the barn. He'd never seen anyone worry about rain as much as Abbie did. He saw her at the far end of the barn, standing near the first wagon, her arms folded beneath her breasts.

Even though he knew she'd scold him for wasting

a moment of picking time, he sauntered toward her, intent on stealing a kiss.

"Abbie, you can't," a deep voice rumbled and he recognized her brother's voice. Grayson slowed his step as she thrust up her chin.

"I most certainly can."

He heard James snort. "It's not a woman's place."

"And who do you think did it last year? A woman. And the year before that—"

"Because you had no choice. Well, now the men are back—"

"It's my land. My cotton. I'm driving it to O'Malley's gin."

"Abbie, it's simply not done."

"Before the war, it wasn't done. But it's done now, James."

Grayson leaned a shoulder against the side of the wagon. Where anger brought out the ugliness in most women, it simply enhanced Abbie's features. Her indignation arose because of a need to hold onto a place in the world that she had earned through toil and labor.

Grayson peered around the corner of stacked sacks. James was glaring at Abbie as though he thought that action would turn the stalemate. "She's quite right, you know," Grayson said.

James snapped his gaze to Grayson. "Stay out of this, Rhodes. It doesn't concern you."

Grayson studied his scratched and bleeding hands before meeting James' gaze. "Funny, I thought it did."

"Not when I overheard your friends say that you

would be leaving as soon as the cotton is picked. Well, the fields are almost stripped clean. You can take your leave at any time.''

Abbie jerked her head around, her gaze searching his. ''You're leaving?''

''Not until we've taken the cotton to wherever it is you want it to go.''

''Like hell,'' James roared. ''Based upon what Winslow told me before he left, I wouldn't trust you with Confederate money, much less the cash we'll get for these crops.''

Abbie spared her brother not a glance. ''I trust you. Will you travel in the first wagon with me?''

''It will be my pleasure.''

''Be a good boy and do everything Aunt Elizabeth tells you.''

Leaning against the front porch railing, Grayson watched Abbie kneel before Micah and draw him into her arms, tears shimmering at the corners of her eyes as though she were sending him off to war instead of to his aunt's for a few days.

Micah nodded before Abbie moved on to perform the same ritual with her other two children. She had explained that they would be leaving well before the sun came up in order to get the cotton to one of the gins that rested along the Brazos River. The heavy wagons would make the journey slow and cumbersome so she'd decided to let the children go home with her sister.

The children scrambled into Elizabeth's wagon and waved their arms frantically. Abbie backed away, her hand imitating theirs with less enthusiasm.

"They'll be fine, Abbie," Grayson said quietly.

"I know, but this is the part of cotton farming that I hate. Being without them for a few days."

"We could take them with us if you like."

She glanced over her shoulder, the gratitude in her eyes almost bringing him to his knees.

"They'd be miserable."

He held his tongue, not commenting that being miserable seemed to be a common state around here.

" 'Bye, Gray!" Johnny shouted.

"Take care, lads," Grayson called out as the wagon began to roll away from the house. "You, too, Lydia."

She beamed as though he'd given her a bouquet of flowers.

"We'll see you in a couple of days!" Abbie cried.

Elizabeth waved while the young man on the wagon beside her guided the horses. Grayson didn't think all the men who had come over with him were as discontented as he and his friends. Some had plans to stay. Hell, he thought one or two might have plans to marry.

Abbie stared after the retreating wagon until it was no longer visible and the wispy clouds of dust had settled. With her arms firmly folded beneath her breasts, she spun around, her cheeks carrying the hue of the sunset. "I'll see to getting supper on the table for you."

She scurried into the house, leaving Grayson to wonder what had just transpired.

*　　*　　*

Abbie sat at the table, the steak she'd eaten lying like a ton of rocks on her stomach. She hadn't been this nervous, this excited since her wedding day.

They were alone. She and Grayson were well and truly alone.

She visited him almost every night in the barn. She had no reason to feel jittery.

They hadn't spoken a single word since he'd walked into the house, but Lord, she'd felt his gaze on her throughout the meal. She wondered what he was thinking. If it had crossed his mind that he had no reason to sleep in the barn tonight. This house had plenty of beds . . . They'd all be empty save one.

Her mouth went dry. A ridiculous thing for it to do—but the thought of actually inviting him into *her* bed, into the bed she'd shared with John—

"Abbie?"

She jumped, knocking her hand against her glass of water, catching it before it tumbled over completely and caused a mess. She glanced at the man sitting across from her. "What?"

He'd placed his elbows on the table, intertwined his fingers—all except his index fingers. They were pressed against his pursed lips.

His hands reminded her of a game she'd played with the children: *Here is the church, here is the steeple* . . .

Did they play that game in England? Maybe she should share it with Grayson.

"Why are you nervous?" he asked, his voice low, steady.

How could he be so calm?

"I'm not." She lowered her gaze to her plate. "I am."

"Why?"

She lifted her eyes to his. "Because we're alone. It reminds me . . . of being married."

"And that was awful, was it?"

"Not awful. I just never seemed to be able to relax. I wanted to please John so badly, to be a good wife. And I couldn't."

"I'm not him."

"I know. I know I'm being silly—"

He shoved his chair back, and her body jerked. He held out his hand. "Take a walk with me."

"Outside?"

He smiled warmly. "Outside."

She rose from her chair, walked stiffly toward him, and slipped her hand into his. When his fingers closed securely around hers, she felt the haunting doubts of her past fade away. She followed him onto the porch. He dropped to the top step and guided her to the step below, bringing her within the circle of his thighs. She leaned back, nestling her head against his shoulder.

The retreating sun was skimming its final rays across the tops of the dark green cotton stalks. The fields were not stripped as clean as John would have wanted them, but she didn't think what remained was worth the effort.

Varying shades of pink, lavender, and orange unfurled across the sky, enticing the blue to give way to the night.

"How can you be so wise?" she asked quietly.

He chuckled low. "Whenever the duke's wife or his son would enter the manor, my heart would pound like a soldier beating the drum to announce the start of battle. Later I went off to school, but when I returned for a holiday, even though they weren't in attendance yet, my heart knew no different. Besides, you looked as though you were eating the last meal you'd ever have before I led you to the chopping block."

"You seem to know me much better than I know you."

He skimmed his knuckles along the sensitive flesh below her ear, along her throat, sending delightful shivers down to her toes.

"Because you built no fortification around your heart, and so you have nothing behind which to hide."

She angled her head until she could meet his gaze. "And you do hide."

"As much as I am able."

"Why, when you know I love you?"

She had told him several times that she loved him since that first night in the barn. He had never repeated his sentiments. He would say that he loved her hair, her smile, her touch. But he had never again said that he loved *her*.

He cradled her cheek, tipping her head back slightly. She saw his nostrils flare in the twilight shadows, then his mouth swooped down to cover hers. She wondered if he found love as disconcerting as she found marriage. She placed her hand on his chest, and felt the thundering beat of his heart.

His lips left hers, trailing deliciously across her cheek, until he was able to nibble on her ear. "Come to the barn with me," he rasped.

"No."

He drew back slightly, capturing and holding her gaze. Swallowing her uncertainty, she said quietly, "Come to my bed."

His eyes darkened to the blue of a Texas sky at dawn, while the day is still only a promise. He tucked stray strands of hair behind her ears. "Are you sure?"

She smiled mischievously. "What sort of rogue are you to always give me the opportunity to back away?"

"One who fears you care for me far more than you should."

She pressed her face against his neck, placing her head in the nook of his shoulder. "I want to put the ghosts to rest."

His arms came around her, helping her to stand as he came to his feet. "Let's bathe first," he suggested.

She merely nodded as he took her hand.

Grayson stood within the shadows, listening to the night.

Their bath had ended as it often did: with them making love. Although he normally carried her to the barn, this evening desperation had hung around Abbie as she'd clung to him and they had made love outside, tangled in the towels and their clothes.

She had seemed relieved afterward as though her obligations for the night had been fulfilled, and he was left to wonder if that was all marriages of convenience entailed: obligations.

Did his father ever look on his marriage with regret? Did he often think of the young actress who had captured his heart?

Grayson's nightly routine included checking on the animals, making certain all was secure, and he had gone about his chores without conscious thought while Abbie cleaned the kitchen. Dear Lord, it was almost as though they were married.

He thought about what it would be like to have nights like this one for the remainder of his life—to know Abbie was inside waiting and would be there when he walked through the door.

He heard the clanging of pots and pans cease, and an unexpected hush fell over the house. The lights spilling from the windows dimmed as though she had lowered the flames in the lamps. He considered strolling to the barn, climbing the ladder to the loft, and lying on his pallet in the straw.

But he feared she would not seek him out. A rusty rapier through the heart would not hurt more.

Bloody hell, he not only wanted her, he needed her. He needed those three little words that she whispered during the height of lovemaking, those words he could not repeat. He had spoken them once—and he had meant them. He did love her. But the intensity of those feelings had deepened to such a magnitude as to be frightening. Dear God, if she ever stopped saying those words, he thought he might well and truly die.

With one hand shoved into his trousers pocket, he

stepped onto the porch and quietly opened the door. She had lowered the flame in the lamp. The doors to two bedrooms stood ajar, and he wondered if she'd looked into the rooms, missing her absent children.

The third door had a barely discernable opening through which lamplight spilled into the larger room. Her bedroom. The room she had shared with another. The gentleman within him loathed the fact that she seemed to have few fond memories of her husband. The rogue rejoiced.

Closing the door, he strode across the room. Very carefully, very quietly, he nudged the door open. Abbie sat in a straight-backed chair in front of a mirrored vanity, brushing her hair, her gaze focused on something beyond the mirror, something far away, a remembrance perhaps . . .

The room surprised him. Other than her person, it seemed to include nothing that was notably her. The oak posts of the bed contained no delicate carvings. The chest was as sturdy and plain as the bureau. Even her vanity did not bespeak the delicateness of a woman.

The room reflected a man's tastes, completely and absolutely.

Against his will, his gaze drifted to the bed. The bed where she now slept alone, where once she had not. His stomach clenched and it occurred to him that perhaps it would be best if he left, if he returned to the barn, returned to Galveston, returned to England.

But then his gaze scanned the room and came to rest on Abbie's reflection, watching him, waiting. He could see the rapid rise and fall of her chest. He crossed the room in slow strides that belied his own beating heart.

"Grays—"

He touched the tips of his fingers to her lips. "Don't say anything, Abbie. Not until you've grown accustomed to me being in this room." He took the brush from her hand and glided it through her silken strands, holding her gaze in the mirror.

"You're trembling. It can't be the cold, since this state apparently doesn't have any."

"It's cold in the winter."

"You're trembling," he repeated. "Why?"

Shaking her head, she lowered her eyes to her lap. "I just feel cheap."

He set the brush aside, knelt beside her, took her quaking hands in his, and pressed her fingers to his lips. "I won't stay if you don't want me to."

She lifted her gaze to his. "That's why I feel cheap. Because I want you to."

She shifted her attention to the bed, and he saw the red creep up past the collar of her nightgown to settle in her cheeks. She released a self-conscious laugh and nestled her forehead against his shoulder. "I'm being silly, I know. I've thought of this a hundred times, inviting you to my bed . . . and I thought you wouldn't come . . . after . . . earlier."

"You hoped I wouldn't come."

With a deep sigh, she lifted her head away from his shoulder. "I don't know why this is so hard."

He did. He could feel her dead husband's presence as though he were sitting in the corner looking on. "What if I just held you?"

She blinked as though he'd just snatched the moon from the sky and handed it to her. "Just held me?"

"I've thought of doing that a hundred times, lying in a bed with you and simply holding you through the night."

"I'd like that."

He stood as she rose to her feet. He watched her walk to the bed and fold back the quilt. They wouldn't need it tonight. He snuffed out the flame in the lamp, leaving only moonbeams to guide his steps across the room. Within the shadows, he saw her hands moving over her nightgown. He stilled, relishing the sight of her gown sliding along the length of her body. With practiced ease, he stripped off his own clothes and left them in a heap at his feet.

He heard the bed moan as she clambered into it and scooted over, giving him room to join her. He groaned as he lay down and the mattress cradled him like a newborn babe. "Ah, I've missed the comfort of a bed." He turned his head until he could see Abbie. "Come here, sweetheart."

She rolled toward him and he drew her within the circle of his arms.

Abbie wanted to tell him that she'd never done this before, lain naked against a man in her own bed, but she thought he probably knew. It seemed everything they did was a first for her. Nothing was a first for him. Well, nothing except maybe having someone love him.

She loved the feel of her body partially covering his. The warmth of the night should have made it unbearable, but the breeze whispered through the open window across their bodies.

"What are you going to do in Galveston?" she finally dared to ask.

She felt him stiffen beneath her before taking a deep breath and forcing his body to relax.

"Find some sort of business venture."

"Like what?"

"Haven't a clue. Cattle perhaps. Whatever it is, it will be high risk, high gain. That's the way Harry likes to play and it's his money that will be funding us."

"Do you think you'll ever return to England?"

"Someday. When I am my father's equal."

She heard the determination in his voice, and had no doubt he would find a way to succeed. His hand began a slow lazy caress of her arm, increasing the intimacy of the moment. "Do you . . . do you think you'll ever return here?"

He shifted his body until they were both lying on their sides. He cupped her face, his thumb stroking her cheek. "Do you want me to?"

She nodded, then realized that he probably couldn't see her movements in the shadows. "Yes." She pressed her face against his chest. "I wish you wouldn't leave at all."

He stilled his thumb. "I can't spend my life living in a barn, Abbie."

Of course he couldn't. She nodded, knowing he could feel her movements even if he couldn't see them.

"You told me that you never wanted to get married again," he reminded her.

She nodded again, stupidly, not sure what she wanted or what she needed. He skimmed his fingers along the length of her spine, down, up, down. Then he flipped her onto her back and nestled himself between her thighs. Bracing his hands on either side of her face, he threaded his fingers through her hair and lowered his mouth to hers. The tenderness of his kiss brought tears to her eyes.

This was how it should be, a coming together of hearts and souls before there was a coming together of bodies. She knew that now, understood the simplicity of love. It couldn't be forced. It couldn't be goaded. It grew out of caring, trust, and respect. Like seeds thrown into fertile soil that could take root and bloom.

Before the war, the seeds had been blown onto a desert with little to nurture the blossoms. She didn't want to lose what she had just gained. She tightened her arms around his shoulders, their breadth always surprising her. He felt much sturdier than he looked; he was a formidable man. It was his mannerisms that set him apart from the rugged men she'd known.

He drew away from the kiss. She felt the intensity of his gaze even though she couldn't see the blueness of his eyes. She heard his ragged breathing, felt the rise and fall of his chest against her breasts.

"Marry me, Abbie."

Her heart slammed against her ribs. Her mouth went as dry as cotton. She nodded her head vigorously.

"I have to hear the word, sweetheart, or I'll never believe it."

"Yes," she rasped. "Oh, yes, but what about Galveston?"

"I never cared much for the salt air."

"What about your friends?"

"Are you trying to talk me out of this?"

"No, but I want you to be sure."

"I *am* sure. I love you more with each breath I take, each beat of my heart, each smile that you bestow upon me." Grayson was astounded to realize that he meant the words. His heart thudded against his ribs and he felt certain that she could feel it.

He dipped his head, kissing her deeply, almost desperately. Never had he expected to find a woman willing to marry him. Never had he thought to find a woman who would love him.

They would live here—in this house. They would sleep in this room.

He wanted to chase the ghosts from every corner, every nook and cranny—not only within this room, but within her heart.

He trailed his mouth along the sleek column of her throat, listening to her throaty purr—a contented cat lapping at the cream. He wanted her as he'd never wanted anything.

She writhed beneath him as he used his mouth and hands, alternately rough and gentle, to carry her to the edge of fulfillment. With one sure stroke, he thrust himself into her welcoming warmth. He stilled, fighting back his own release that was perilously close to betraying him.

She pressed her hands to his shoulders. "Don't leave me," she whispered. "There's no need if we're to be married."

Raised above her, he felt his arms tremble. He lowered himself to her, pressing his cheek against hers. "Promise me that you *will* marry me."

"I promise . . . with all my heart."

He began to move against her, marveling at how well their bodies rocked against each other. He listened to her cries, her sighs. He held nothing back, had no need to keep tight rein on his own pleasure.

When she cried out and arched against him, he followed the way she had come, her body wrapped so tightly around him that it was impossible to think of them as separate.

He pressed his lips against the hollow at her throat, absorbing the impact of what he'd done, the splendor of it. Of feeling as though he belonged. He wanted to tell her, to share with her the exaltation that he felt, but to do so, he would have to speak of other women—something that was completely inappropriate under the circumstances.

So he simply repeated what he had said to no other. "I love you."

When her arms tightened around him, he had never known such completeness, had never felt so wholly at home.

13

Guiding the rumbling wagon over the rough road, Grayson listened as it creaked beneath the weight of the heavy sacks of cotton. The intoxicating sound of money. Soon it would change from a creak into a jingle. He cast a longing glance at the woman sitting beside him, the woman who would be his wife. His only regret was that he could offer her little more than what she already had.

Behind him, Kit, Harry, and James guided their wagons along the winding, torturous route. Abbie had explained that the trail carved by wagons since Stephen F. Austin's colony had first begun planting cotton was designed to circle the hills, to avoid the steep slopes and muddy areas, and to cross creeks where the water was lowest.

Little wonder that late afternoon arrived before Grayson drew the wagon to a halt a short distance away from the designated cotton gin near the Brazos river—O'Malley's gin. At least a dozen wagons waited ahead of theirs. Men milled about beneath the shade of the trees, some talking, some sleeping, some spitting tobacco.

"This doesn't look good," Grayson said.

Abbie heaved a sigh. "No, but I expected it." Her cheeks flamed red. "This is the reason James didn't want me to come. We usually have to stay the night, and he doesn't think it's appropriate for a woman to sleep in the company of men."

"A little fact you neglected to mention."

She shrugged. "It's not like I'm innocent."

He cradled her cheek. "You were before I came into your life."

She turned her face against his palm. "No, you returned some of the innocence to me."

"What the devil is all this?"

Grayson jerked his hand away from Abbie's face and glared at Harry who was staring at the wagons in front of them. "What the bloody hell does it look like?"

Harry snapped his head around. "If I knew I wouldn't be asking, now would I?"

Grayson clambered down from the wagon before helping Abbie to the ground. Kit and James strolled over, their gazes fastened on the gin.

"Based on what I saw coming home, I wasn't expecting to see such an abundance of cotton," James said.

"Why aren't any of the wagons moving?" Harry asked. "Why is everyone just standing around?"

"It takes a while to weigh and process the cotton," Abbie said.

A bell sounded.

"What does that mean?" Kit asked.

"They're closing down for the night," James explained.

"So we just leave the wagons?" Harry asked.

James sighed. "No, we'll sleep on the bales."

There was something to be said for lying on a bale of cotton atop the wagon and watching the sunset, a woman's fingers threaded through his. Grayson had never known contentment this deep, this absolute.

In a way, it was completely overwhelming and frightening, and he feared he might be unable to hold onto it.

"What are you thinking?" Abbie asked quietly.

"That I've never known such peace."

She sighed dreamily. "My favorite time is after the cotton picking is done. All the hard work is behind us for a while and I have such a sense of accomplishment." She turned her head slightly and smiled. "You did a good job picking the cotton. You surprised me. I never expected you to stay."

Rolling to his side, he lifted his hand to touch her face but before he could, she wrapped her hands around his and brought it to her lips. "Your poor hands. You can always tell a picker by the scars."

"Then they match yours."

"They were so soft, so smooth the first time I held them."

"Why did you pick mine to hold?"

In the fading light, he saw her blush and watched as she pressed her lips together. "Because you were so damned arrogant."

"Arrogant? I was hot, tired, and dirty—"

"You leapt out of the wagon and looked down your nose at me—"

"Because you're short. If I'd looked up, I wouldn't have seen you."

"You thought you were better than us—"

"You thought I thought I was better than you. Believe me, Abbie, the one thing I have never thought in my life is that I was better than anyone."

She came up on her elbow and rolled over onto her stomach. "But you do give the impression you think that way. Maybe it's the way you stand or hold your head . . . Maybe you do it without thinking so no one will see that you think you aren't better."

He turned his gaze toward the stars and the moon that had slowly risen to fill the black void. "Perhaps."

"You aren't better than anyone, Grayson. But you are at least an equal."

"Only in your eyes."

"They're the only ones that matter."

Chuckling, he rolled toward her and laid his callused hand against her cheek. "They are that, sweetheart. What do you think the children will say when we tell them the news?"

"They'll be happy."

"Do you want to continue to live at the farm?" he asked.

She nodded. "It's all I know. I can't imagine living anywhere else."

"I've asked Abbie to marry me."

Grayson would have laughed at the comical expressions that crossed his friends' faces—if he weren't reeling from the reality of what he'd just announced and all it entailed. They were words he'd never thought to speak.

"By God, surely you're joking," Harry said.

"I'm deadly serious. Marriage is a fine institution."

"Indeed it is, but who wants to live his life in an institution?"

Grayson's lips twitched at Harry's old adage. Women seldom saw the humor in it. He shrugged. "I've decided it might not be the horrid picture we've painted."

"When will she give you her answer?" Kit asked.

Grayson cleared his throat. "She already did."

Kit raised a brow. "And?"

Grayson supposed he shouldn't be surprised that his friend doubted a woman's desire to accept his offer of marriage. In England, proposing marriage had never been a topic of discussion or hinted at—for any of them.

He drew his shoulders back, trying—probably unsuccessfully—not to look offended by Kit's lack of faith. "She accepted."

"So you're going to haul her and the children to Galveston—" Harry began.

"We have no need to go to Galveston. Abbie has the farm—"

"So through marriage, you'll acquire the land you've always coveted," Kit said quietly, speculatively.

Grayson knew he should explain that it was Abbie

he wanted, not the land, but it was much easier not to bare his heart to these two. They knew the worst about him and accepted him. What difference did it make if they thought he was marrying Abbie for all the wrong reasons? With an air of indifference, he rocked back on his heels. "I've always fancied myself a landowner."

"Well then, I suppose congratulations are in order," Kit said.

"Not too loudly. Abbie wants the children to know first. I told you because it changes my plans for Galveston and might affect yours. I trust you to keep this announcement between us until Abbie has talked with the children."

"Does she expect the children to object?" Kit asked.

"No, but it might be a bit of a surprise to them."

Harry shook his head. "So you'll not only be a husband, but a father. Good God, Gray, who would have thought?"

"Certainly not I," Grayson admitted.

"Are you going to write your father?" Kit asked.

"I haven't decided."

"When do you think you'll actually put on the shackles of marriage?" Harry inquired.

"Abbie would like to be married by the end of the month—before we need to begin preparing the fields for next season."

"I suppose Harry and I could get rooms at the saloon until then. This is one moment I shan't want to miss."

"I'm glad. You were the first person to ever befriend me. It would mean—'' He cleared his throat, the words lodged just above his heart. He couldn't force himself to say how very much it would mean to him to have Kit at his side. ''Would you stand as my best man?''

But he knew from the emotions that flitted across Kit's pale blue eyes that his friend understood all that was not spoken. He should have known. Kit had always been uncanny in that regard—in his ability to comprehend what was not voiced.

''I shall be well and truly honored.''

With a brusque nod, Grayson looked toward O'Malley's gin mill. He heard the thunderous roar of the working mill echoing through the air. He saw the farmers waiting their turn. Abbie was talking with James. He wondered if she'd told him. Once or twice, James cast a glance Grayson's way before turning his attention back to Abbie.

Abbie walked toward Grayson, a bright smile on her face. ''We're next.''

He helped her climb aboard the wagon. He took his place beside her and gave the reins a gentle slap to get the horses moving.

He was hit with the sudden realization that this would be his life for the remainder of his days.

With her promise to marry Grayson echoing through her heart, Abbie reached over and squeezed his hand as he guided the wagon toward home. Dusk was settling in, and it somehow seemed appropriate that they would tell the children of their impending marriage shortly after they gathered around Grayson to hear him read.

When they had arrived at Elizabeth's, she had been overjoyed to see the children greet Grayson with as much enthusiasm as they'd bestowed upon her. She could not imagine that there was anything more difficult than raising another man's children, but she thought Grayson was up to the task. Indeed, the children knew more of him than they knew of their own father.

She heard the children moving about in the back of the wagon. She would have admonished them if Grayson hadn't chosen that moment to thread his fingers through hers, bring her hand to his lips, and press a kiss against her knuckles. His eyes darkened as her fingers tightened on his.

"By the end of the month, Abbie?" he asked, his voice a low caress.

Her heart leapt with unbridled joy. She knew he was referring to their marriage. By the end of the month, he would no longer sleep in the barn. He would sleep in her bed every night, and she'd awaken in his arms every morning. "Shhh. You'll spoil the surprise."

"What surprise, Mama?" Lydia asked as she rose to her knees in the back of the wagon.

Abbie shot Grayson a warning glare. The rogue had the audacity to drop his head back and laugh. How she loved his laughter.

"We'll tell you after supper," Abbie promised, not certain she could wait that long to impart the news. She wanted to shout it to the world. Not telling Elizabeth had been one of the hardest things she'd ever done, but she wanted the children to know first.

Lydia brought herself to her feet. "Who's that, Mama?"

Following Lydia's pointing finger, Abbie turned her attention toward the fields. A man stood between the rows of stripped cotton, the plants hiding much of him, his hat shadowing his face as he looked down. She had seen him before, working the fields . . .

He removed his hat, revealing hair the same shade as Johnny's. Gladness swept through her. She'd never thought to see him again.

He bent down, disappearing within the crops. Abbie's heart slammed against her ribs as stark reality crushed the joy, and she squeezed her eyes closed. It couldn't be . . . He couldn't be . . . Her breath came in short little gasps. Her imagination was running rampant, seeing someone who no longer existed. He was just a soldier on his way home, stopping a moment in her fields—

"Abbie?"

Despite the blood pounding between her ears, she heard Grayson's voice, tranquil and soothing. He always remained serene, calming her in the process. How she needed him.

She opened her eyes, bestowing upon him a quivering smile. Impatiently, Lydia nudged her shoulder. "Who is it, Mama?"

Abbie looked back toward the fields. The man was visible again, strolling between the rows as though he owned the very land upon which he walked.

Which he did.

"It's impossible," she whispered hoarsely.

"Who is it, Abbie?" Grayson asked.

The words clogged her throat, threatening to suffocate her.

Grayson drew the horses to a halt. "If you don't know the fellow, then I'll advise him to leave."

"No." Shaking her head, she released his hand and pressed her fingers against her lips. Stinging tears welled in her eyes. With a slight limp, the man walked beyond the fields and toward the wagon, his hands balled into fists.

"Then you do know him?" Grayson asked.

A warm tear slid along her cheek. "He's my husband."

Grayson felt as though someone had just slammed a hammer into his chest. His throat tightened and a knot rose up to nearly choke him. "I thought he was dead."

Woodenly, she nodded. "So did I." She glanced over her shoulder. "Children, stay in the wagon."

She stood, the first indication Grayson had that she intended to get out of the wagon. He pushed her back down. "Let me help you."

He leapt to the ground and hurried around to help her clamber down. With his hands on her waist, he felt the small tremors rippling through her. "What are you going to say?"

She shook her head, her voice a raspy whisper. "I don't know. I'm having a hard time believing this."

He followed her, his hand on the small of her back as she walked jerkily toward the man who'd come to a stop at the edge of the fields. The man's brown gaze darted to the fields as though he were contemplating returning to them.

Abbie stumbled to a stop. "J-John?"

Grayson saw her fingers tremble as she reached out and touched the man's gaunt cheek. The man studied her as though he'd never seen her before. Grayson found himself filled with an irrational hope that perhaps Abbie was wrong. Perhaps this man was not who she thought he was.

"John? It's me . . . Abbie," she said softly, as though she spoke to a child.

The man clenched his jaw and nodded. Grayson wondered if perhaps he'd lost his ability to speak. He knew the harshness of war had a tendency to age a man, but even with the effects of battle taken into consideration, Westland was much older than Grayson had ever imagined him. A scraggly beard, streaked with white, covered his face. His gray uniform—one Abbie had no doubt sewn for him years before—hung loosely from stooped shoulders so he more closely resembled a scarecrow than a man.

Westland extended his large scarred hands and unfurled thick fingers to reveal several tufts of cotton nestled within his palms. "You left too much cotton."

Stunned, Grayson could do no more than stare at the man. He'd been to war, thought dead, hadn't seen his wife in years and his first words of greeting revolved around the damn cotton? Abbie looked at his hands as though she couldn't remember what cotton was.

"We filled four wagons," Abbie said quietly, almost apologetically, as though all their efforts amounted to nothing.

"Should have been five. Maybe more." John Westland jerked his head toward Grayson. "Who is this?"

Abbie turned to Grayson, and he saw that the tears were gone—along with the joy. Her eyes reflected acceptance. "This is Grayson Rhodes. He's been helping with the fields."

"Not doing a good job of it from what I can see. We'll start picking at first light." He turned his back on them.

Incensed at the man's treatment of Abbie, Grayson took a step forward. "We heard you were dead."

Westland turned, narrowing his eyes. "Well, I ain't. Where you been staying?"

"In the barn," Abbie said hastily. "Seven of the families boarded a worker."

"He can stay." He gave his head a quick jerk toward the wagon. "Are those the children?"

"Yes."

Abbie looked incredibly lost and confused. Grayson fought the urge to take her in his arms and comfort her. After all, she was little more than his betrothed while she was Westland's wife. What in God's name had possessed her to marry this man who had not even asked how she was?

"Johnny, bring your brother and sister here," Abbie called.

Grayson looked toward the wagon. The children were standing, eyes wide. The children—children he had begun to think of as his. He watched them scramble out of the wagon and hesitantly approach the stranger—their father. Grayson clearly recognized the man's features in the eldest boy. He prayed to God that he never saw his mannerisms.

Abbie skirted quickly behind the children, placing her arms around the three of them, drawing them near the way a hen protected her young. "Children, this is your father."

Feeling like an intruder but unable to force his feet to move from the spot, Grayson watched as Westland swallowed.

"You've grown, Johnny," Westland said, his voice thick with emotion, but his expression revealing nothing of what he might be thinking.

Knowing what it was to be overlooked, Grayson interjected, "I imagine they've all grown since you've been away."

Westland nodded, and Grayson saw his throat working as though this moment was not as easy for him as he wanted it to appear. He wished he could be glad that the man had risen from the dead, but the truth of the matter was that the man's presence was a damn inconvenience.

"How come you ain't dead?" Johnny asked. "Ma said you was dead."

"Your name was on one of the lists we received," Abbie said, her voice laced with an agonizing apology.

"Things were confused for a while," Westland murmured. "See about getting supper on the table, woman.'' With a slight limp, he walked toward the house.

Grayson watched him disappear within the waning twilight and wondered if perhaps he were in the midst of a nightmare. He turned to Abbie. ''Woman? He hasn't seen you in four, five years—''

She shook her head vigorously and crouched in front of her children.

''I don't like him,'' Micah announced in his deep, throaty voice.

Smart lad. Grayson didn't much like Westland either.

Abbie brushed the dark locks of hair off Micah's furrowed brow. ''You don't really know him. He's a stranger. You were just a baby when he left, but he's your father and we should be . . . grateful that he's home and that he wasn't killed.''

''Why did they say he was dead if he wasn't?'' Johnny asked.

A good question, lad. I'm wondering the same thing myself. But Grayson held his silence for he could not imagine this moment was easy on Abbie. Her hands had yet to stop trembling. He resented like the devil that her husband had left her to handle the children alone, as though they were not his concern, his responsibility. Westland had held the damn cotton in his hands, but not his wife or his children.

Abbie licked her thumb and rubbed a spot of dirt off Johnny's face. ''I don't know. I don't imagine war is very orderly, and someone made a mistake is all.''

Is all? Someone's mistake was on the verge of

bringing untold grief to those Grayson cared about. He watched Abbie force a smile that came nowhere close to touching her eyes.

"Go be with your father while Mr. Rhodes and I put the wagon away. Then I'll be in to fix supper."

As one, the children jerked their gazes to him as though they hoped he had the power to save them from a fate worse than death. If only he could.

Crouching before them, he clasped his hands between his spread thighs. "Remember when you told me what a brave soldier your father was?"

Johnny scrunched up his nose. "I mighta been wrong. He don't look brave."

"Bravery doesn't show on the outside of a man, lad," he said quietly. "It's tucked away on the inside. Here." He touched the tip of his finger to the center of Johnny's chest. "Being brave is doing something that you know has to be done—even though you don't want to do it."

"Are you being brave?" Micah croaked.

"I'm trying, lad." But he was so damn tempted to hoist Abbie and the children back onto the wagon and ride toward the sunset. He would have done it if he thought Abbie would never look back, but he knew her reverence for honor wouldn't allow it. "I think your mother is trying as well, so why don't you set a good example for her and show her how it's done—with your chins up."

The children set their mouths into grim lines of determination and jerked up their chins. Grayson was hard-hit with an unrelenting truth: he loved these children more than his very life.

They scuffled away, warily glancing over their shoulders from time to time. Grayson unfolded his body and took a step toward Abbie. She quickly held up a hand.

"Thank you for explaining things to the children, but please don't say anything else right now . . . or do anything." She wrapped her fingers around the lead horse's harness. "We need to get the horses un-hitched."

He fell into step beside her. Light spilled out of the house as lamps were lit inside . . . lit by her husband.

Her husband!

Good God, but he had never felt such impotent rage.

"Abbie?"

"Not yet."

Glancing over at her, he saw the tears shimmering within her eyes, the stiffness in her shoulders, the tightness in her jaw. With her head held high, she marched forward as though she was being led to the gallows.

Once inside the cavernous barn, she stumbled to a stop, her gaze darting from the stalls to the loft to the doorway as though she weren't quite sure where she was. Grayson unfurled her stiff fingers from around the harness. Her hands were as cold as a river in the dead of winter. "Abbie?"

She snapped her gaze to his. "The report said he was dead."

Wrapping his arms around her, he drew her into his embrace. He felt her fingers clutching his sides, her tears dampening his shirt, the tiny tremors coursing through her.

"He's not dead," she whispered hoarsely.

He pressed his cheek to the top of her head, unable to find any words to ease her pain or change the truth of the situation. "I know."

He ignored the pain as she dug her fingers into his ribs.

"I'm married," she rasped, as though the reality had just slapped her in the face. "Oh, dear God, I'm still married."

She broke away from him and wrapped her arms around her middle, staring at him with the tears streaming down her face. "I dishonored my vows, myself—"

"No!" he growled. "You thought he was dead. You did nothing wrong."

She squeezed her eyes shut. "Nothing wrong?" She opened her eyes to reveal her despair. "I fell in love with you—"

"Do you still love me?"

"I can't—"

"Do you love me?"

She shook her head slightly. "Do you know what I first thought when I recognized him? That I was glad . . . glad he wasn't dead."

She raced out of the barn, her words echoing around him, ripping into his heart.

The homecoming of John Westland in no way resembled that of James Morgan. Grayson sat at the table, surrounded by the deafening silence, moving his food from one side of his plate to the other, his gaze constantly drifting to Abbie who warily watched her husband. No touches. No tears of happiness. No smiles of unrestrained joy.

John Westland was so absorbed in shoveling food into his mouth that he didn't seem to notice that everyone else was eating little. The gentleman within Grayson acknowledged that the man was probably starving, if the loose clothing was any indication of how much weight he'd lost.

But the rogue inside him was tempted to announce, *Say, old man, while you were away, your wife and I fell in love. As a matter of fact, we'd planned to be married shortly. It would be rather sporting of you to step aside and let us continue with our lives.*

Abbie's gaze occasionally darted to him with an appeal that seemed to indicate she knew what he was contemplating and wanted him to keep quiet. So against his better judgment, he held his silence. He would not hurt or embarrass her for the world. Besides, holding his silence was the least he could do when it appeared he would never again *hold her.*

His chair scraped across the floor as he stood. All eyes came to bear on him. "I appreciate the meal, Mrs. Westland. It's as delicious as always, but I must beg my leave as I've decided to go into town for the evening."

"Ain't you gonna read to us tonight?" Johnny asked, desperation edging his voice.

Regretting his answer, Grayson attempted to deliver it with kindness. "No, lad, I'm not."

''We've got cotton yet to pick,'' Westland grumbled.

''I shall be here at dawn.''

Before anyone could speak another word, he strode from the house. He was in the loft, stuffing the last of his belongings into his satchel when he heard the creak of the ladder. He glanced over his shoulder and watched Abbie perch on the top rung.

''Don't leave,'' she pleaded quietly.

The thought of lying in the loft knowing she was lying in bed with her husband was unbearable. His heart felt as though it had been flayed. He much preferred not having a heart. ''I can't stay. Why in God's name didn't he write you?''

''He can't write. Working the fields was more important to him than going to school.''

''And if he can't write, then he can't read,'' Grayson murmured.

''He may have never known he was listed as dead,'' Abbie admitted.

''So in all these years, you've never heard from him?''

''Not once.''

''I would have found someone to pen a letter for me.'' He shoved the last of his clothing into the satchel, snapped it closed, and picked up his treasured book. He crossed the loft, crouched before her, and extended the book. ''For you and the children.''

She took his gift and pressed it against her breast, to the place where he dearly wanted to bury his face and forget the realities of the world.

"You aren't coming back, are you?" she asked quietly.

"I don't know. I can't stand the thought . . ." His fingers tightened their hold on the satchel. "I don't suppose you'd consider running away with me."

"I'm his wife . . . in his eyes and in the eyes of God and the law."

"And in your heart?"

Tears welled in her eyes as she touched her palm to his cheek. "Earlier I said I was glad he wasn't dead. I am, but I'm not sure that I'm glad he came home. I love you. I'll always love you."

"Then come with me."

"What of the children? I can't take his children from him."

"I am more their father than he is and you damn well know it."

She shook her head. "I can't abandon him the moment he returns home from the war. He gave me a roof over my head and food in my belly when I needed them. I can't take his family away when he needs that."

"I can't stay knowing that you are lying in his bed."

She dropped her hand to her lap. "Know that if you don't return, I understand."

She turned to go down the ladder. He snaked out his hand, grabbed the back of her head, and brought her mouth to his, the kiss a desperate, but futile attempt to hold back time, to create one last memory that he could carry with him until the day he died.

14

*G*rayson stepped through the swinging doors of the saloon. Several men turned and gave him a brusque nod of acknowledgment. Working in the fields beside them had established a bond he wasn't expecting.

Eyeing Kit and Harry sitting at a corner table, he strode across the saloon. He dropped his satchel at his feet and took the chair. Without a word, he grabbed the drink Harry poured him, tipped his head, and threw the contents of the glass to the back of his mouth.

He immediately regretted his action as the liquid fire burned its way down his throat. Coughing, with tears springing to his eyes, he dug his fingers into the edge of the table. Harry slapped his back, doing more harm than good.

"Sorry. Thought you'd remember that these Texans like their liquor strong," Harry said.

"I did. Pour me another one," Grayson commanded, his voice sounding parched.

Harry chuckled as he tipped the bottle and the amber contents splashed into the glass. "I do find a certain sense of accomplishment to withstanding the baptism by fire."

With a bit more caution, Grayson brought the glass to his lips.

"Thought you'd be with your future wife this evening," Kit said.

"She's not my future wife," Grayson ground out.

"Sorry to hear that," Harry said. "What changed her mind?"

Grayson tossed back the whiskey, this time relishing the igniting of hell within him. "Her husband."

Kit leaned forward. "I thought she was a widow."

"Yes, well, so did she until we returned home this evening and found her husband resurrected."

Harry refilled his glass. "So how did that come about? Him being thought dead when he wasn't?"

Grayson took the glass, downing the contents in one long swallow. "I don't know."

"You might want to take care with that stuff," Harry suggested. "It's not only strong, but potent. It can put you under the table in no time."

"Which is exactly where I want to be." Placing his elbows on the table, he leaned forward. "He didn't even ask her how she was. He just told her that she'd left too much cotton in the fields."

"Sounds like a caring fellow," Kit said.

"She touched his cheek, but he stood there like a stone statue. He never touched her. They never hugged or kissed—"

"Some people aren't comfortable expressing their

emotions in front of strangers,'' Kit said.

"By God, if I'd been away from her for four years, I bloody well wouldn't be able to keep my hands off her."

"How is Abbie holding up to her husband's return?" Kit asked.

"I think she's in shock. Her eyes were glazed, vacant. I probably should have stayed—'' He fought to keep the stiff upper lip for which his fellow countrymen were famous. "It's just as well he didn't touch her. I might have killed him."

"What are you going to do now?"

"He wants the rest of the cotton picked. He thinks there's at least one more wagonload left in the fields."

Harry snorted. "Good luck to him then, but I'm not picking anymore." He fanned out the cards. "I've nearly ruined my hands. Can hardly distinguish the feel of the cards."

Grayson smiled slightly. "Must make it incredibly difficult to cheat."

"I never cheat. I simply manipulate the cards so they are to my liking."

"And clean out our pockets in the process."

"Not yours. I have no need for lint."

Grayson helped himself to another shot of whiskey. The burning was less, but still satisfactory. "I'm going to take a room here."

"We've done the same," Kit said. "We thought to leave for Galveston at the end of the month."

Although the words were not spoken, Grayson

heard them echoing clearly though between them—
after your wedding.

"I suppose there's no reason to delay now," Harry
added.

"No reason," Grayson said as he stood. "Except
I'm not ready to leave." He picked up his satchel
and the half-empty bottle of whiskey. "If you gentlemen will excuse me, I'm in the mood to quietly
get drunk."

Neither said anything as Grayson walked away to
see about securing a room for the night where he
could drink himself into oblivion and drive away the
unrelenting litany that was beating through his mind:
Abbie was lying in bed with another man.

Abbie stepped into her bedroom, and the horror of
her situation slammed into her unmercifully. She
stared at the blankets piled on the floor, the rumpled
sheets on the bed, and the indention in the pillows
where two heads had rested so closely together as to
be one.

Was it only yesterday morning that she had
awoken in Grayson's arms? They had made love long
before the sun came up. Laughing and happy, she
had left this room anticipating the time when he
would lie in bed with her every night.

She rushed across the room, snatched up the pillow
where he had laid his head, and began to fluff it,
mash it, reshape it, destroying the evidence that he
had been here.

She buried her face in it, tears scalding her eyes
as his scent wafted around her—along with the

musky fragrance of their lovemaking. It was faint, like a memory that might fade over time, but would never be completely forgotten.

She tossed the pillow on the bed and began to slap her hands over the wrinkled sheets, trying to erase Grayson's presence. She jerked the sheets up to the head of the bed and grabbed the blankets, spreading them over the mattress, trying to make everything look normal when she knew in her heart that nothing would ever be normal again.

When she was finished, she changed into her nightgown. Sitting down, she brushed her hair. Faint chilly tremors cascaded through her body. She would have thought it was the dead of winter instead of the tail end of summer.

No words were spoken after Grayson walked out of the house. No one exchanged smiles or laughter. No one brought a story to life. She set her brush aside, parted her hair into thirds, and began to twine the thick strands together, wondering how she would survive this night.

Knowing what she now knew of passion, how would she endure her husband's touch? No, it was more than the passion. It was the intimacy, the intimacy that went deeper than joined bodies. A closeness that allowed them to talk during and after, to laugh, to take joy in each other.

The door opened with a resounding click, and she nearly leapt out of her skin. Favoring his right leg, John walked into the room and came to stand beside her.

Don't touch me. Please don't touch me.

A silly request when she knew he would not touch her. Not here, not outside the confines of the bed. Before Grayson, she had not realized how distant her relationship with her husband was. Four years had widened the chasm.

He trailed his blunt-tipped fingers over *Ivanhoe* before turning back the cover. "Tell me about this Englishman."

Panic clawed at her throat, and she wondered how much he had seen as they'd driven up in the wagon— before they had seen him. How much he might have guessed.

"He's a hard worker. Kind to the children."

"And to you?"

He loved me. But she held the words close to her heart because they weren't the sort of words a woman should throw at her husband to welcome him from a war. "He was kind to everyone. He read to us in the evening."

His gaze did not stray from the book. "You read."

"Yes, but his words are spoken almost as if they were a song. I reckon it's his accent. It fit the story well."

With a nod, he turned away. "I haven't slept in a bed in years."

"If you prefer, I could sleep with Lydia—"

"No. You're my wife. You sleep with me." He turned, meeting her gaze directly. "You *are* my wife, aren't you?"

She balled her hands into fists within her lap, the vows she had spoken at sixteen resounding through her head. "Yes."

The bed groaned as he lowered his weight to it. "Get into bed."

She rose slowly. She had forgotten how much she dreaded the walk from her vanity to the bed, how the apprehension would crawl up her spine like a thousand ants. "They told me you were dead," she said quietly.

He stared at his large clasped hands resting between his spread knees.

"I'm grateful you aren't dead, but I've been on my own for four years, and I'm not quite comfortable with the idea that you are home. I need time, John."

"Are you regretting the vows you took?" he asked solemnly.

Oh, God, but her heart ached—for him, for her, for Grayson. Without realizing it, they had woven a tangled web, and she feared none of them would escape unscathed.

"No, I don't regret the vows I took," she said softly. When she was sixteen, there was no Grayson Rhodes to save her. There had only been John Westland. "You were always larger than life to me. You still are."

She walked across the room and slid beneath the blankets. John turned down the flame in the lamp until darkness descended in the room. She felt the bed shift as he stretched out on his side beside her, his back to her. His silhouette had always reminded her of a mountain range, formidable, unmovable. They lay with nothing to surround them but the blackness of the night and memories gathered before the war.

"Do you regret marrying *me?*" she asked softly.

"No. I never could have made this farm prosper without you. And nature would have reclaimed it while I was away if you hadn't been here."

It always came back to the farm with them. She felt the solitary tear trail across her temple. Her husband was home . . . and she'd never felt more alone.

She rolled onto her side, stirring Grayson's scent to life. Torn between inhaling deeply and holding her breath, she hoped John didn't notice the unmistakable presence of another man.

"John," she whispered, wondering if the better part of valor wouldn't be to simply keep quiet. "What happened? Were you wounded? Captured—"

"Wounded."

She eased forward a tiny bit. She reached out for him, but stopped, her hand hovering inches from his shoulder. Slowly, she brought her hand back. "I notice you limp now. Did you get shot in the leg?"

"Yes. Head, too. Not shot there. Hit . . . Don't remember."

"Are you in pain now?"

"No. Sometimes my head hurts. Couldn't . . . couldn't remember nothing."

His voice had grown thick, raspy, and she felt a slight trembling of the mattress beneath her. Without thought, she did what she'd never done before he went to war. She scooted across the mattress, pressed her cheek to his back, and slipped her arm around him, offering her comfort and strength. He grabbed her hand and tucked it against his chest. She felt the tremors coursing through him and realized that he was crying. "It's all right, John."

"Couldn't remember nothing but the fields. Knew they'd be waiting for me."

His hand tightened painfully around hers, but she remained quiet, stoic, lost in her own grief.

How much simpler life would be if she'd waited as well.

Abbie stepped onto the porch in the gray light of dawn. This morning she would warm water so her husband could shave on the back porch. She would launder his clothes, make his bed, prepare his meals. Guilt gnawed at her because she found no joy in tending to his needs and realized with startling clarity that she never had.

She truly was grateful that he hadn't perished. She simply wished he hadn't returned home. But then at the end of the month she would have become guilty of bigamy.

She saw a movement in the fields and her heart hammered against her chest. Grayson. She had feared he would be well on his way to Galveston with his friends by now. She flew off the porch and raced across the yard, her bare feet kicking up the dirt, creating a cloud of dust around her. She stumbled to a halt in front of him, thinking she had never seen a more welcome sight.

His face in need of a shave, his eyes red-rimmed and swollen, he looked as though he had slept little the night before. She had slept not at all.

She reached out to touch his bristled cheek, but

drew her hand away just short of its destination. "You came back."

He stuffed the tuft of cotton into the sack slung over his shoulder. "It was my understanding we had not done an adequate job of clearing the fields."

"John always took pride in stripping the fields clean. He's as bad as a locust when it comes to leaving nothing behind." Throwing caution to the wind, she touched his cheek. He closed his eyes, and she watched him swallow as though he fought a battle to prevent himself from returning the gesture.

"You don't look like you slept," she said.

He opened his eyes. "I slept. Drank myself into a stupor. It was only pride that had me stumbling out of my room in the darkness before dawn. All I could think about was him reaching for you in the darkness of the night—"

"He never reached for me."

Although she had held him, John had never turned to her, had finally drifted to sleep with his back to her. She watched surprise flit across Grayson's face before relief settled in.

"I don't know what to make of him, Abbie. I would have made love to you all night if I had not been in your company for four years. I'm torn between wishing things were different between the two of you and rejoicing because he kept his hands to himself." His eyes filled with despair. "I thought I would go mad last night thinking of him—"

She watched his throat work as he swallowed. She wanted to hold him to her breast, console him, and love him. "We got married because he needed someone to tend his house and I needed to leave my parents' house. I liked to feel needed. I didn't know there was a difference between being needed and being wanted. Not until you.''

''I am a selfish bastard, Abbie, wanting you to find no pleasure in your husband's bed so you'll come back to me.''

''If it was only a matter of pleasure, I would have left with you last night. But there's more at stake. Honor, commitment, vows that bind me to John.''

''Abigail!''

She jerked her head around to see John standing on the porch, suspenders dangling at his sides.

''You need to see to breakfast!''

''I'll be there in a minute!'' She turned back to Grayson. ''Will you join us?''

He shook his head. ''No. I'm not even certain I'll be able to stay in the fields all day, to look at you, and not touch you.''

''Abigail!''

She flinched. ''I have to go.''

''If he harms you at all . . .'' he ground out.

She shook her head vigorously. ''He won't.'' At least not with physical blows. As she raced toward the house, the litany from a song she'd sang as a child rang through her mind. *Sticks and stones may break my bones, but words will never hurt me.*

Only now, as an adult, did she realize that the song was based on a lie, for words could kill a soul, strangle a heart. Her husband had remembered the fields, but he hadn't remembered her.

*   *   *

Grayson didn't know how word spread, but by mid-morning neighbors were crawling along the rows beneath John Westland's watchful eye. They all seemed genuinely glad that he'd returned home and Grayson caught snippets of conversation. Everyone was anticipating next year's crop.

Westland would know the exact day and hour when the seeds should be planted. He would know when the picking would begin, how much yield, how much loss they would have. The fields would flourish under his care.

Grayson thought it a shame that no one seemed to notice the same could be said for the man's wife. They were all here working the fields because of all she'd done during her husband's absence.

He carried his full sack to the wagon at the end of the row and snatched an empty sack from the stack on the bench. With sweat rolling down his back and gathering in the hollows of his body, he strode through the fields toward Abbie.

Her back was curved beneath the weight of a sack that was only half full. "Swap sacks with me."

Slowly she straightened and wiped the back of her hand against her brow. She gave him a soft smile that left little doubt that deep within him he had a heart and dreams, dreams she had awakened.

"Now why would I do that?" she asked.

"Because the cotton is so scattered that we're having to carry the sacks farther than we did before, and this one is lighter."

"But it'll get heavy."

"Until it does, your back won't hurt as much."

Before she could protest further, he slipped his hand between the strap and her shoulder and pulled the bag from her. He could almost see the relief wash over her face.

"I don't allow cheatin' in my fields," a deep voice rumbled.

Grayson looked past Abbie to where Westland stood, legs akimbo, eyes narrowed into an icy glare. Out of the corner of his eye, he saw other people stop their labors and stare.

"I beg your pardon?" Grayson asked, unable to prevent the haughtiness from creeping into his voice.

"I pay my workers two bits for each sack they pick. Taking a sack that's half-full is cheatin'."

"Two bits?"

"A quarter," Abbie explained.

Grayson met Westland's accusing glare. "I am not one of your workers. The only reason I'm picking your damn cotton is because I want Abbie out of the fields as quickly as possible."

"I won't pay you for the half-filled sacks you take from her."

Grayson slipped the empty sack onto Abbie's shoulder. She put her hand over his.

"Don't be a fool. If he's not going to pay you—"

"I don't want the money, Abbie. I never did."

"No one works a cotton field for nothing."

"If my working the fields gets you out of them sooner, then I didn't do it for nothing."

He felt John Westland's gaze boring into him as he headed toward a section where the cotton was a bit more abundant. The sooner he filled his sack, the sooner he could hand an empty one off to Abbie.

The day was the longest of his life. The heat was unbearable. His fingers bled, swelled, ached, and cramped, but the most painful part of all was shutting off his emotions. He was torn between confronting John Westland and honoring the man's return.

As dusk neared, the others left the fields, but Grayson continued to pluck tuft after tuft after tuft. As long as he could see the shadows, he could pick . . . and each piece he picked was one that Abbie wouldn't have to.

Abbie tucked the sheets around Micah's chin even though she knew the warmth of the night would have him kicking the sheets off his small body before he'd drifted off to sleep. A week had passed, and John had yet to say good night to his children.

"How come Gray can't read to us no more?" Micah asked.

She sat on the edge of his bed; his eyes were wide as he studied her. She brushed his hair back. "He doesn't live here anymore, and he needs to get to his place in town before night comes."

"Who's he live with?"

"He has a room at the saloon."

"Wish he lived here," Micah said.

"Me, too," Johnny piped up. "I thought maybe you'd marry him."

Abbie's heart gave a sudden lurch as she glanced at Johnny. The boys slept in one big bed—close together as though they didn't mind ramming into someone else during the night. Perhaps there was even comfort there. Unlike her and John who—after the first night—slept stiffly, each hugging their respective sides of the bed.

She shook her head. "No, no . . ." What could she say? *I was going to marry him. I want to marry him still, but Fate returned your father to me and now I must honor vows I made at sixteen.* She simply shook her head again.

"He said he's gonna move to Galveston when the damnable cotton—"

"Johnny!" she scolded, although inside a small part of her smiled. In the week since John's return, she'd never heard Grayson talk about cotton unless it was preceded by the word damnable.

"That's what he said," Johnny protested.

"I know, but that's not what we call it. It puts food on the table so we're grateful for it."

"I wanna go to Galveston with him," Johnny said. *So do I.* She would have gone anywhere with him.

"You can't. This is your home."

"But—"

"Maybe when you grow up." She rose to her feet and bent over each boy, kissing his forehead, even though she knew Johnny would prefer that she didn't. She was starving for affection and was grateful for the smallest amount.

She lowered the flame in their lamp before stepping out of their room and clicking the door quietly into place. She pressed her forehead to the door. She had never questioned the sanctity of marriage vows until now. Did one remain loyal to one's husband . . . or one's heart?

Slowly, she turned and the breath backed up within her lungs at the sight before her.

John sat at the table, turning the pages of the family Bible, brushing away the crushed flower petals until they were strewn before him on the table. Flowers that Grayson had given her.

She'd forgotten how often John would ask her to read from the Bible. Other than the almanac which she also read to him, it was the only book they'd possessed until Grayson had given her *Ivanhoe*.

As calmly as she could, she walked to the table. Cupping a hand, she started to scoop the faded petals into her hand.

"Leave them," John commanded.

"They're making such a mess—"

"He give 'em to you, didn't he?"

"H-he?" she stammered.

He lifted his hard, uncompromising gaze to hers. "Rhodes."

She sank into the chair, her heart pounding as she considered the merits of lying. But in the end, she decided he deserved the truth. "Yes."

"I figured. I'm surprised the fields don't burst into flames with the looks you two give each other."

She felt as though he'd slapped her. "I've hardly cast a glance his way all week—"

"Ah, but when you do—"

"That's not fair, John." She bolted from the chair, her breath coming in shortened spurts as though she were drowning, fighting to draw in air. She spun around and faced him, balling her hands into fists at her sides. "They told me you were dead, and I did not hold my heart as close to my breast as I should have—as I would have if I'd known you were alive."

"You love him then?"

She was unprepared for the pain she saw reflected in his brown eyes. The fight went right out of her. He didn't deserve this. None of them deserved this twist of fate.

"Yes, I love him."

Carefully he turned to the last pages of the Bible, nodding his head as he did so. With a blunt-tipped finger, he pointed to the words scrawled on the family page. "What does this say?"

She knew without looking to what he was pointing, but still she moved in closer and stared at the words she'd written at sixteen. She swallowed the lump in her throat. "John Westland married Abigail Morgan, January 14, 1856."

"You wrote them words."

"Yes, I know."

He lifted his gaze to hers. "For better or worse."

She nodded mutely. How was she to have known that better had been the years before the war and that worse would be a journey into hell?

With a brusque nod, he closed the Bible and laid his hand on top as though swearing an oath. "For better or worse, Abigail . . . until death do us part."

She knew it was risky, had the potential to cause more harm than good, but her heart gave her little choice.

She waited until she heard John snore. He had always slept hard. He never awakened when the children cried out, never stirred whenever Abbie left the bed. Tonight was no exception.

She dressed quickly, quietly, waiting until she was outside to slip on her shoes. Then she saddled the horse that the children had unanimously voted to rename Ivanhoe and rode into town.

The moon had risen high in the blackened sky, an orange orb that guided her way. Lanterns cast their glow over the wide dirt street of Fortune.

The saloon was situated in the center of town. As she neared it, she saw the stairs at the rear of the building that led to the rooms above.

What a fool she'd been. Even if she climbed those stairs and managed to get onto the second floor where the rooms were, how would she find Grayson's room? She couldn't simply knock on door after door and apologize when it was the wrong one.

A figure emerged from the shadows beside the stairway: tall, slender, familiar. Her heart tightened with an unwarranted ache. Reaching out, he grabbed the bridle, stopping the horse, before helping her dismount.

She fell into Grayson's embrace. "How did you know I'd come?"

He cradled her cheek and tilted her face up. His features were lost in the shadows of the night until a sad smile broke through the darkness. "I didn't know . . . but I hoped." He drew her back against him, and she heard him swallow. "Will you come to my room?"

She nodded. He tethered her horse a distance away from the stairs. She doubted that anyone would see it there. He walked back to her, slipped his arm around her, and nestled her snugly against his side as he guided her up the stairs and through the doorway that led into the hall on the second floor.

She had never been in the saloon, and although she could not see the main area, she still smelled the acrid odor of the cigarette smoke and the stale stench of whiskey. She heard footsteps on the stairs at the other end of the hall. Grayson moved quickly, ushering her into a room.

His room. It carried his scent. A rich fragrance that mingled with the sweat from working in the fields. A lamp burned low on a table beside the bed. Curtains billowed through the open window. She heard male laughter float up from the street. It made her feel sordid, dirty to know she was where she shouldn't be. She stepped out of his embrace, folding her arms around herself. "It's much nicer than the barn," she whispered low.

"But it's farther away from you."

He was standing beside her, so close that she could feel his warmth. "Please hold me."

His arms came around her without hesitation, strong, comforting. How she had missed this. The constant caresses, the inadvertent touches. Something as simple as holding hands.

When he stepped back, she followed, as though they were waltzing with no music except the melody from their hearts. He eased down to the bed, holding her close, rolling her over until they were both lying on their sides, facing each other. He trailed his callused fingers along her brow, her temple, her cheek, her chin.

"Tonight he asked me if I loved you," she said quietly.

He stilled his fingers. "What did you say?"

"I told him yes."

He brushed his lips over hers as lightly as a butterfly skimmed over a blossoming flower. "What did he say?"

She placed her hand on his chest, against the beating of his heart. "He showed me where I'd written our marriage date in the family Bible, and he said, 'For better or worse.'"

"Is it worse for you now?"

She pressed her face to his chest as his arms closed around her. She felt the weight of his leg over her thigh, the pressure of his body against hers.

"It hurts, Grayson, it hurts to see you in the fields. Please don't come anymore. Go to Galveston. Find your success there and forget about me."

He tucked his finger beneath her chin and tilted her head away from him. His lips came down on hers hard, demanding, his tongue sweeping through her mouth, claiming territory that it no longer possessed. Her resistance was nonexistent when he rolled her over and laid his body over hers. She felt the lines of his body, hard, unyielding, pressing against her curves. How easy it would be to forget vows and promises . . . how easy and how unbearably difficult to live with.

She tore her mouth from his, turning her face to

the side, gasping for breath even as she heard his harsh breathing.

"I have the power to seduce you," he rasped.

She shifted her gaze back to him, her heart in her eyes. "Probably. I didn't come here to be seduced, but where you are concerned, I seem to have no will-power. And yet, you promised me that with you, I would always have a choice."

He rolled off her and sat at the edge of the bed, his elbows on his knees, his face buried in his hands. "Damn it, Abbie, I don't want you to be a conquest. You're the only woman in my life that I've wanted on equal terms."

She sat up and pressed her cheek to his back, trailing her fingers along the ridge of his spine. "If you stay in Fortune, a moment will come when neither of us will have the strength to say no . . . and after that moment passes, our love will die."

He twisted around. "Nothing will destroy what I feel for you."

She cradled his cheek. "Because you don't have to look across the table at the person with whom you exchanged sacred vows of marriage . . . and you don't have to look your children in the eyes, knowing you've been unfaithful to their father. I love you, Grayson Rhodes. I will always love you. But I can no longer have you."

He surged off the bed and turned on her. "Shall I play devil's advocate here? Do you want to spend the rest of your life with a man who doesn't love you the way that I do?"

She came off the bed, her heart thundering. She

had known this would be hard, but the difficulty of sending him away was staggering. "The responsibilities you owe one person don't stop because you love another more. John was a good husband in his own way. I can't be less than a good wife. He has done nothing to deserve my abandonment." She reached out to him imploringly. "I exchanged vows with him long before you came along—"

"I am so damned tired of being second when I should have been first. The duke was betrothed when my mother sprang her little surprise on him, but he wouldn't put aside his betrothal to marry an actress. So here I am, his firstborn son treated as though I am his last.

"And now here you are telling me that because I was not here when you exchanged vows with Westland, it matters not that I love you more than my very life. I am relinquished to the dung heap . . . even though I am the first man to love you."

She sank onto the bed, tears burning her eyes and throat. "You're more than that. You're the first man I've ever loved. But is our love enough to justify destroying a life? Because we will destroy him. He's a proud man, Grayson. If he were cruel or hateful . . . if he beat me . . . if he did anything that made my life unbearable, then I would leave him. But I knew he didn't love me when I married him. I knew he only needed me. How do I tell him now that need isn't enough?"

He dropped to his knees before her and cradled her face between his palms. "Do you know what I love most about you? That you never put yourself first. I had hoped this time that you would.''

She combed her fingers up into his thick, golden hair. ''I feel as though I'm being stretched out on a rack in the dungeon, but I know if I turn my back on John, something inside me will shrivel up and die . . . and I will become a woman you will grow to hate.''

''I would never hate you, and damn me, I don't know why but I love you more at this moment than I've ever loved you before.''

''Then be kind to us both and leave Fortune.''

Within his eyes, she watched dreams war with reality—battles she had constantly fought herself within the last week.

At long last, he stood, took her hand, and pulled her from the bed. ''I think I much prefer being a rogue to being a gentlemen. The pain is so much less.'' The kiss he bestowed upon her was bittersweet and carried the salt of her tears.

When he drew away, he grazed his knuckles over her cheeks. ''I shall escort you home.''

''No. We'll just have to say good-bye all over again. I can't—''

He touched his finger to her lips. ''Enough said.''

He strolled across the room, quietly opened the door, and glanced into the hallway. ''All clear,'' he whispered.

She walked from the room into the hall. His arm came around her, shielding her as he led her outside and down the stairs. He retrieved her horse and helped her mount up. She gave him a smile that she feared might look as cracked as her shattered heart. "Be happy, Grayson."

"Impossible, sweetheart, without you by my side."

She urged her horse into a gallop, his words echoing through her heart. Impossible for both of them.

Grayson watched her ride into the night, the pain within his chest growing worse as she receded into the distance.

"So your waiting finally paid off," Kit said as he stepped out of the shadows.

"Spying?"

"No, just taking a late-night stroll. Ironic, isn't it? You always preferred married women—and just when you think you've changed your ways, you're bedding a married woman again."

"I did not bed her."

"You don't have to lie to me—"

He spun around. "I'm not lying, dammit. She came to say good-bye. That's all. How soon can we leave for Galveston?"

"A day or so. What about the cotton in her husband's fields?"

"It can rot for all I care. Just do whatever it takes to get us out of this hellhole quickly." He tromped up the stairs, wishing he'd sent his conscience to purgatory and made love to Abbie one last time.

15

*G*rayson waited until he was certain everyone had left the fields before he brought his horse to a halt and tethered it near the barn. He had stayed away three days while Kit made the arrangements to travel to Galveston. He thought it had taken his friend an exceedingly long time, and he had wondered more than once if perhaps Kit had no desire to leave.

He walked along the furrows. Hardly a tuft of cotton in sight. Abbie was right. John Westland liked his fields clean.

"Hey, Gray."

Grayson turned slightly at the sound of the youthful voice. "Evening, Sir Johnny."

Johnny smiled brightly. "When are we gonna have another tournament?"

He had come to say farewell, and suddenly the word became lodged in his throat, too damnably hard to say. "I don't know."

"The last one sure was fun."

"Yes, it was," he admitted, remembering every

smile that Abbie had graced him with that day.

Johnny plucked a bit of cotton free and stuffed it into his trousers pocket. "It's funny having . . . Pa home." He glanced up. "I reckon he's my pa since Ma says he is, but I don't 'member him none."

"I imagine it's hard, but in time . . . well, it'll be as though he never left, won't it?"

Johnny wrinkled his nose. "I reckon." He rolled his shoulders forward and dug his big toe into the dirt before peering up at Grayson. "What's a whore?"

Grayson snapped his head back, the shock of the word coming from a young boy's mouth rippling through him. "Well, it's a woman . . . Where did you hear that word?"

"I heard Pa call Ma a whore just now when he come in from the fields. She started crying. That's how come I come out here."

Rage—white, blinding, and hot—surged through Grayson. "Your mother is not a whore," he ground out through clenched teeth, "and never under any circumstances are you to think of her as such."

He spun on his heel, in his anger crushing plants as he stalked toward the house. If John Westland thought Abbie was a whore, he was about to discover what a true bastard Grayson Rhodes really was.

He stomped up the steps and flung open the door, not bothering to hide the sounds of his arrival. He caught a glimpse of Westland pacing before he staggered to a stop and glared at Grayson. Abbie stood behind a chair at the table, her hands gripping the back until her knuckles turned white. Lydia and Micah stood nearby, eyes wide, mouths agape.

"Lydia, Micah, go outside and see if you can find some fresh grass for my horse," Grayson said, surprised his voice wasn't shaking as much as his body was trembling.

Westland took a menacing step forward, his hands balled into fists at his side. "You will not, by God, give orders to my children."

"Trust me on this, Westland. What I am about to say, you do not want them to hear."

Westland looked at his children and jerked his head toward the door. "Go on."

Holding hands as though at last having a common cause, Lydia and Micah scurried out. Once they were well on their way to the fields, Grayson slammed the door in their wake, the harsh sound reverberating around the room.

Breathing heavily, his fists clenched, he spun around to face a man he loathed.

"Don't say anything," Abbie said quietly.

Grayson snapped his gaze to hers. Releasing her stranglehold on the chair, she licked her lips. She looked so damned young, so vulnerable, and yet strength was visible in the way she held herself, a strength he knew had been forged from the ashes of war.

She turned to her husband. "I'd like a few minutes alone to talk with Grayson."

"I'd say the two of you had enough minutes *alone*," Westland growled.

Abbie jerked her head back as though he'd slapped

her. Grayson took an ominous step forward. "I'll not have you speak to her like that."

"I'll talk to her any way I like. She's my wife, by God!" He glowered. "And I have no doubt she's your whore since she's carrying your *bastard* in her belly."

The word, the implication almost had Grayson doubling over in pain, as though someone had pole-axed him.

"You will *not* use *that* word in reference to this child," Abbie ground out, her violet eyes blazing.

Westland looked as though she'd punched him. Grayson dropped his gaze to her stomach. "Is it true? Are you carrying my child?"

Tears welled in her eyes.

"Hell, yes, it's true," Westland snarled. "She's been puking most of the day."

"It could be something I ate," she said softly.

"You know it ain't," Westland said. "And it damn sure ain't mine 'cuz I ain't touched you since I been home."

She turned to her husband, a plea in her eyes that Grayson thought would have made Satan himself relent. "Please let me talk to Grayson alone for a few minutes."

His hardened glare darted between Grayson and Abbie. "Reckon the harm's already been done. Just remember that you are my wife."

He stormed out the front door. The blood drained from Abbie's face as she sank onto a chair and pressed a hand to her mouth.

"Are you all right?" he asked.

She nodded. "I'm so sorry."

He knelt before her. "Is this why you came to see me, why you asked me to leave? So I would never know that I had a child?"

"No, I only began to suspect yesterday."

He furrowed his brow. "It seems too soon—"

"It had to have happened before . . . before the night you shared my bed."

His stomach tightened. "So much for my thinking that withdrawing from you was adequate." He shoved himself to his feet. "A bastard—"

"This child will *not* be a bastard. He will be born within the sanctity of a marriage."

Rage surged through him. "And you think that's enough? Do you honestly believe *that* man will accept my leavings as his own? Do you honestly think I will allow it, that I will not claim—"

Abbie came out of the chair like an avenging angel. "If you care for this child at all, you will allow it. If you love me as you claim, you will hold your tongue. John will accept this child as his. To do otherwise will bring him shame, and he has too much pride for that."

"Were you going to let me leave without telling me?"

"I don't know. It's as much a shock to me as it is to you. I want what is best for this child, but the laws of God and man will not allow me to marry his father." Her eyes reflected a tapestry of acceptance. "But they will allow my husband to accept the child as his own."

"You can't expect me to walk away."

"What good will come of you staying?"

He turned away, feeling as though his heart had been flayed. "I never wanted this for you . . . or for our child. There has to be another way."

"We've all been caught in an unfortunate circumstance. It can't be undone so we have to make the best of it."

He felt a strong need to erupt into harsh laughter. Why couldn't John Westland have died in battle as reported?

He met and held her gaze. "I don't know that I have the strength to walk away, Abbie. Not now."

Tears shimmered in her eyes. "You do," she said quietly, with so much conviction that he had no choice but to believe her.

He gave a brisk nod. "I shall let you know where I am . . . and if you ever need *anything* . . ."

She nodded quickly. "Please go."

He jerked open the door and stepped onto the porch. Leaning against the pillar, Westland stared at the fields.

"Did you finish talking to your whore about your bastard?" he asked.

To his great surprise, a calmness settled over Grayson, and he wondered why the simple answer to their dilemma had not occurred to him before. "I told you that I would not tolerate your speaking of Abbie in those terms. For the lady's honor, I challenge you to a duel. Pistols at dawn two days from now." He leapt from the porch and stormed toward his horse.

He didn't wait for Westland's acceptance of the terms for his acceptance was of no consequence. One way or another Grayson would meet him, and one way or another—

He heard the patter of feet hitting the dirt and then felt the slender hand close around his arm. He staggered to a halt and met Abbie's tear-filled gaze.

"I don't understand what you just did," she said.

"My intention, sweetheart, is to make certain that you are well and truly a widow."

The moon was nothing but a sliver, a mocking smile in the night sky when Grayson arrived in Fortune. After securing his horse at the only stable in town, he headed for the saloon.

It was a dreary place. The smoke thick, the stench of whiskey filling the air. A few men looked his way. Most just continued to drown their sorrows, worries, or fears. He cared about none of their troubles for none of theirs could equal his.

He stalked across the room to the corner table where Harry sat with a young woman. Both held several cards fanned out in their hands.

Harry smiled as he approached. "Gray! Meet Jessye. She's teaching me the finer points of poker."

"I'm not teaching you anything. I'm trying to figure out how you cheat," she said in a voice as thick as the smoke in the room.

"Now, love, I never cheat."

She narrowed eyes the green of the first leaf of spring. "You not only cheat, but you lie."

Harry laughed, a sound that broke the last of Grayson's restraint. "Have you any dueling pistols?"

Harry sobered as though Grayson had shoved one

of the requested pistols into his face. "I beg your pardon?"

"Did you happen to bring dueling pistols?"

"Yes, as a matter of fact, I brought a pair I inherited from my grandfather. Why?"

"I've challenged Abbie's husband to a duel."

Jessye's eyes widened, and she laid her cards down to reveal all hearts. "Are you talking about John Westland? You challenged him?"

"I intend to defend the lady's honor."

Harry shoved his chair back. "I'll get them."

Grayson took the chair Harry vacated and poured himself a drink, surprised to see his hand tremble. He'd never known such anger. He felt Jessye's gaze on him. He peered at her over the rim of his glass as he took a long swallow.

She met his gaze with absolutely no coyness. "He'll kill you."

He shrugged carelessly. "We'll see."

"Abbie won't forgive you."

He thought the whiskey must have finally made its way to his stomach because the burning intensified. "She was happier when she thought he was dead."

"She's not one to put her own happiness before another's."

"Which is why I shall do it for her."

"Even if it costs you her love?"

Involuntarily, his hand tightened on the glass. "I want her to carry the sunshine in her eyes, the sunrise in her smile." He downed the last of the whiskey and slammed the glass on the table. "Regardless of the personal cost to myself." Eager to change the dismal subject, he raised a brow. "Harry does cheat, you know."

She scrunched up a face that was blanketed with far too many freckles to be alluring. She gathered up the scattered cards and began to shuffle. "I know. I just can't figure out how he does it."

He didn't know what possessed him to add, "I suppose you also know Harry is a scoundrel."

She gave him a gamine smile, and he realized it was probably that smile that had Harry sitting at this table with her.

"Are you the protector of all women?"

"Hardly. But I wouldn't like to see you hurt."

"I was raised in a saloon. I know Harry is a man who enjoys the chase, but I reckon he's one to let the rabbit go once he's played with it a couple of times."

"So you don't intend to ever let him catch the rabbit?"

She smiled brightly, a false smile that took the light from her eyes, and turned them into flawed emeralds. "Learned the hard way that I ain't the type of woman a man wants for keeps."

"Then I would wager that you've only known men who were fools."

The sparkle returned to her eyes. "Lordy, you Englishmen are charmers, aren't you?"

He smiled warmly. "I have been known to charm a woman or two."

"Abbie?"

He felt as though he'd been punched in the gut and his smile dwindled. "No. Never Abbie."

He shoved the chair back and stood as Harry approached. Harry set an intricately carved wooden box on the table.

"My grandfather's," he announced with a measure of pride.

Carefully he lifted the lid to reveal two shining dueling pistols. Reverently he wrapped his hand around one, withdrew it, and extended it toward Grayson. Grayson took the gun and aimed it at a bottle resting on a shelf above the bar. "How are the sights?"

"Excellent."

"I thought I might need a bit of practice so I set the duel for two days from now."

"Wise decision," Harry said.

"Where's the holster?" Jessye asked.

Grayson glanced over his shoulder. "The holster?"

She nodded. "You know. The thing you carry the gun in."

Harry gave her an indulgent smile. "We carry the pistols in the box."

"He'll be dead before he ever gets the gun in his hand."

Harry leaned toward her. "Love, the rules prohibit that."

She rolled her eyes. "Sweet Lord, spare me from the ignorance of fools." She met Grayson's gaze. "You challenged him to a gunfight?"

"A duel."

"We don't duel here. You strap a gun onto your thigh and face each other. The last man to draw his gun from the holster is the man to die.''

Grayson looked at Harry who was staring at Jessye. ''Are you talking about these guns that the men around here wear against their thighs as though they're always expecting trouble?'' Harry asked.

''Yep.''

''They withdraw the gun from its holder—''

''They draw it out fast.'' She turned her attention to Grayson. ''You've gotta pull your gun from the holster faster than John Westland can get his gun out. You gotta aim it and fire before he does.''

''Sounds absolutely uncivilized,'' Harry said.

''It's worse than that, English,'' Jessye said. ''It's downright deadly.'' She met Grayson's gaze. ''Do you know how to use a Colt?''

Confusion swamped him. ''I know how to ride, but I wouldn't use a horse before he had matured—''

''A Colt revolver,'' she snapped. ''If you were a smart man, you'd call off this *duel*.''

Grayson brought his shoulders back, and she quickly held up a hand. ''Don't bother to protest. I ain't never met a smart man yet. I'll teach you what you need to know . . . and then I'll weep at your funeral.''

Abbie felt ill, a sickness that had little to do with the child growing within her. Grayson's child. The thought filled her with incredible joy—and fear. How would John treat the child once he was actually born? If John survived tomorrow.

Standing at the edge of the field, she watched her husband pluck the cotton as though it might not be his last evening to do so. Neighbors had stopped coming. What remained was hardly worth the effort, but John continued on as he always had in the years before the war—as though he fought a private battle against nature. The bolls didn't mature at the same rate and sometimes the late bloomers would be bursting forth a month or so after picking time . . . and John would snatch them from the vines.

She remembered when they'd first gotten married. She'd followed him through the fields, her back aching, her legs hurting, her fingers swollen, trying to understand what made him continue. "You don't have to pick no more," he'd said. "Just keep me company."

In silence, she had shuffled along the rows behind him. It had seemed to be enough for him, just to have her there. Perhaps that was all he'd ever wanted of her. Someone to walk beside him. She had been amazed to see that he never seemed to tire, to grow weary of the task.

And now he felt betrayed. Why couldn't he understand that she'd thought he was dead? That she had lived her life with false knowledge.

She pressed her hand to her stomach, to the place where Grayson's child had taken root. She was married. She would find a way to make John understand that he had to claim the child as his. She would not have her child suffer for her sins.

If John survived tomorrow morning.

She slammed her eyes closed. What a stupid thing—a duel. What would it accomplish except to leave one man dead? She loved Grayson, but even so she didn't want to see John killed. He had been there when she needed someone. In his own way, he had been good to her . . . and she would have spent her life content if she'd known nothing better.

She heard the thunder of an approaching horse and turned in time to see Jessye Kane draw her horse to a halt. She had always liked Jessye even though she worked in a saloon. The women were always speculating as to exactly what a woman did in a saloon. Abbie had never gotten up the courage to ask her.

Jessye dismounted and tethered the horse to a cotton plant. Abbie wondered why she'd even bothered. If the horse wanted to bolt, the stalk wouldn't stop it. She walked toward her visitor. "Hi, Jessye."

Jessye wore trousers and a faded flannel shirt. Another reason the women gossiped about her. She rode a horse astride instead of sidesaddle. "What brings you out here?" Abbie asked.

"Probably something that ain't none of my business." Her gaze dropped to Abbie's stomach.

Protectively Abbie placed her palm over her stomach. Jessye lifted her gaze, her eyes filled with sympathy and understanding.

"I was playing cards with Harry last night. The whiskey loosens his tongue something fierce. Loosens his hands, too—" She blushed. "—but that ain't your concern. Anyway, he was saying how he thought Gray was a fool to get into a gunfight just to get land. I asked him what he was on about . . ." She dropped her gaze and began jerking leaves from the plants.

"What did he say?"

She heaved a deep sigh. "He said . . . Gray wanted your land. Said he'd been courting you, trying to make you fall in love with him so he could marry you and be a landowner."

Abbie took a step back, her heart thundering, her chest aching. "I don't believe that."

"He had no reason to lie to me. It's God's honest truth that he's a scoundrel and he cheats at cards. I ain't caught him yet, but I know he does . . . but I don't think he lies . . . well, except about cheatin.' "

Abbie spun around and pressed her fingers to her mouth. "But why would he do that? There's plenty of land for the taking."

"Reckon he didn't know that." With the toe of her boot, Jessye kicked away a rock. "And that ain't all."

"What else could there possibly be, Jessye?" she asked, the pain in her heart reflected in her voice.

"I done something awful. I taught that rogue how to use a gun yesterday. How to draw it from a holster. I swear he took to that gun the way a bird takes to the air. I ain't never seen nothing like it."

Abbie jerked around and watched John walking through the fields. "John grew up with a gun in his hand."

"Yeah, I know. And if you'd asked me two days ago, I woulda said the Englishman didn't stand a chance. Hell, I *did* tell the Englishman he didn't have a chance of winning. But now I ain't so sure. He's not only fast—he's damn accurate."

"Then he stands a good chance of killing John."

"That's what I'm thinking—and that's where Harry is putting his money."

Horrified, Abbie looked at Jessye who nodded solemnly. "Yep. That's right. They're wagering on the outcome like it was a game or something. I'm thinking these Englishmen ain't got a heart among 'em."

He'd known she'd come. Or at least he'd hoped desperately that she would. But then he'd hoped last night and the night before, ever since he'd been hit with the discovery that she carried his child.

His child. His *bastard*, Westland had called it, and it had taken every ounce of willpower he possessed not to kill the man then and there. If he had any control over it at all, his child would never hear that despicable word directed his way.

He stepped out of the shadows as she pulled the horse to a halt and dismounted. He drew her into his embrace. "Abbie—"

She pounded her fists into his chest, and he staggered back. The light from the lantern hanging at the side of the saloon sent an eerie glow over her face. He saw the anger burning in her eyes, almost as brightly as the flames in a fire.

"I realize that you are no doubt upset about tomorrow's confrontation—"

Tears shimmered in her eyes, caught by the lantern's glow. "Tell me that you don't want the land."

Confused, he could only stare at her. "Of course I want land. What man of ambition wouldn't?"

"Enough to tell me you love me? Enough to kill my husband to obtain it?"

"Where did you get such an absurd notion?"

"From a scoundrel," she spat. "Didn't you tell your friends that you'd always fancied yourself a landowner?"

He slammed his eyes closed. Ah, Christ, Harry. He'd seen him drinking last night, drinking and playing cards with Jessye. His tongue loosened to excess when he was in his cups. He opened his eyes. Imploringly, he held out his hand. "Abbie—"

She slapped it away. "Deny it!" she ground out through clenched teeth. "Tell me you don't want the land."

"My wanting land has nothing to do with my wanting you."

She backed up a step. "Prove it."

"How? Tell me what to do and I'll do it."

"Leave Fortune and never look back."

"That, sweetheart, is the one thing I cannot do. I am not going to leave my child to suffer the degradation of being unwanted nor am I going to leave you in the hands of a man who obviously has no affection for you."

"John is my husband and I will honor the vows I exchanged with him until the day I die."

"And what of the child? Will you hand him over to me when he is born?"

He saw her visibly pale as she backed up another step. "No!" Her hands formed a protective barrier over her stomach.

"Don't demand that I give up you *and* my child."

She thrust up her chin. "If you kill John, I will

not marry you—and this child will be well and truly born a bastard.''

"Abbie, you don't know the life to which you are condemning this child."

"You condemned this child with your lies." She spun on her heel, strode to the horse, and mounted.

"Abbie!"

Ignoring him, she jerked on the reins and sent the horse into a gallop. He staggered back, dropped to the steps, and buried his face in his hands. How in the bloody hell had the potential for happiness turned into anguish?

16

With her arms wrapped around her knees, Abbie rocked back and forth in the corner of the loft. The moonlight spilled through the opening, casting its pale glow over the pallet she'd sewn for Grayson, the place where she'd first learned the true wonders of love. Or so she'd thought.

Damn the rogue.

She wanted to hate him, but she only felt bereft. John had never told her that he loved her, but he'd always been honest about his feelings. The land was his mistress. Guilt allowed Abbie to tolerate his love of the land. Guilt because she cared for him, but didn't love him.

She heard the ladder creak and moan, the sound too loud to be created by one of the children. She held her breath, her heart hammering. Had Grayson followed her home?

"Abigail? You up here?" John called out.

She considered holding her silence, hoping he'd leave without ever seeing her hidden within the shadows, but nothing was to be gained by making him fret and sending him on a wild goose chase looking for her.

"I'll come into the house directly, John," she said quietly.

She felt the loft quiver beneath her and saw his shadowed form moving toward her. He hunkered down, just inside the loft opening, the moon framing a portion of his face in light.

"What are you doing out here?" he asked.

"Just . . ." She swiped the tears from her cheeks. "Just needed to be alone for a minute."

"Thought you took a bath outside when you needed that."

Unblinking, she stared at him. Before the war, she'd always taken her baths after he'd fallen asleep. Since his return, she'd taken none outside. "How did you know about the baths I took outside?"

"I always feel you leaving the bed."

"Why didn't you tell me?"

She saw him shrug in the moonlight, pick up a piece of straw, and slip it into his mouth. "Figured if you'd wanted me to know, you woulda told me. So I just pretended to sleep. Figured it was a secret you wanted to keep for yourself. No harm in it."

"And if you had thought there was some harm in it?"

"Reckon I woulda said something."

Or come searching for her. He'd been asleep when she'd left to confront Grayson. At least she thought he'd been asleep. "Do you *always* feel me leave the bed?"

"Always." He jerked the straw from his mouth and tossed it out the opening. "You go see him tonight like you did the other night?"

Him. He didn't have to speak the name for her to know to whom he referred. Guilt swamped her. He knew she'd left his bed, knew she'd gone to see Grayson. "Not quite. The other night I asked him to leave Fortune. Tonight I told him."

"Is he gonna leave?"

She released a quick burst of harsh laughter. "I don't know. I only know that he doesn't love me . . . and it hurts."

She rasped the last phrase, her throat tightening against the anguish.

"Ah, Abigail, don't go to crying."

"I can't help it." She felt the tears burn her eyes and spill over onto her cheeks. "John, will you . . . will you please hold me?"

He hesitated a moment before scooting across the loft and awkwardly putting his arms around her. She didn't fit against him as snugly as she did Grayson, but she took comfort where she could. He patted her shoulder as though she were a horse who had given him a good day's work in the fields.

"John, I'm not only sad about Grayson, I'm sad about this baby."

"You don't want it?"

She was surprised to hear the disbelief mirrored in his voice. "I do want it, with all my heart, but I'm afraid he'll grow up feeling unloved."

"You'll love him."

"Yes, but he'll think you're his father."

"You're not going to tell him about Rhodes?"

She took a deep sigh. "Not until he's old enough to understand and accept the sins of his mother."

She had hoped John would deny that she'd sinned, but he was too God-fearing for that. Yet the question he asked her went straight to the heart of her sadness.

"You're wanting me to love the baby?"

"No, I'm only asking you not to hate him."

"Only a cruel man would hate a child for things that weren't his doing. You think I'm a cruel man?"

She tightened her arms around him. "I know you're not a cruel man, John."

" 'Sides. He'll give us another pair of hands in the fields."

Abbie pressed her cheek against his chest, not certain if she should laugh or cry.

While dawn waited at the edge of the horizon to make its appearance, Abbie sat in a chair beside a hearth as empty as her heart. She watched her husband disassemble his gun, clean and oil the various parts, and put it back together with calm precision. Black dots swam before her eyes, and she thought she might swoon from what his actions served as evidence for. She swallowed the bile rising in her throat. "John, surely you're not going through with this."

"He give me no choice, Abigail," he said, his gaze never leaving the gun.

Abbie rose onto trembling legs, crossed the space separating them, and knelt before him, placing her hand on his thigh. His movements stopped, but he didn't look at her.

"He doesn't love me," she said softly. "He never did. He wanted the land. All along, he only wanted the land."

He shifted his gaze to her. His fingers, scarred and roughened from years of picking cotton, lightly grazed her cheek. "That day you learned I was alive, you were comin' back from the cotton gin."

She nodded slightly. "Yes."

"I was walking through the fields, listening to the wind rustling the leaves, and then I heard the sweetest sound . . . It was you . . . laughing. In all the years we was married, I never heard you laugh." He turned back to the weapon and began putting the pieces into place with audible clicks. "I gotta do this, Abigail. I just got to."

She pressed her forehead against his thigh. "Please don't do this. I won't stray from my vows."

"I got no choice."

She surged to her feet. "If you kill him, I'll hate you until the day I die."

"Do you love me now?" he asked, slamming the gun onto the table.

Reaching out, she wrapped her hands around his, stilling his actions. "I care for you, John. You gave me a roof over my head, food in my belly, and children. You gave me everything I needed when I had nothing."

"But I never gave you the one thing you wanted. I never gave you love. Well, now I aim to give it to you."

He shoved to his feet and stalked across the room toward the door.

"Killing him will not show me that you love me!" she cried out after him.

He staggered to a stop. "You've changed, Abigail."

"I think the war changed all of us."

"Made you stronger. Made me weaker. Now I gotta be strong."

"You're not weak, John."

His only response was to slam the door behind him. A few minutes later she heard the sound of galloping hooves and knew a terror greater than any she'd ever known.

Abbie stood on the front porch, watching the sun ease over the horizon. Was it over yet? Was one man dead, another alive? She hadn't been able to bring herself to go, to watch men die uselessly.

What did they hope to gain? To prove? Damn male pride.

Lydia came around the corner, dragging her feet in the dirt, her basket filled with eggs.

"You did a fine job gathering the eggs this morning," Abbie said as she stepped off the porch and ran her fingers along Lydia's braid. The child simply looked toward the barn. "Your brothers seem to be working a bit slow this morning. Why don't you tell Johnny to hurry up with the milking and then you help Micah with the kindling. Maybe we'll go on a picnic—"

"The boys ain't here," Lydia said.

"What do you mean, they aren't here?"

Her daughter pursed her lips and studied her toes

with great interest. A sense of foreboding ricocheted through Abbie. She wrapped her hands around Lydia's arms. "Where are your brothers?"

Lydia didn't lift her gaze as she answered, "They wanted to see the gunfight so they went to town."

"Oh, God." She cupped Lydia's chin, forcing the child to look at her. "I have to go to town. I want you to go into the house. *Ivanhoe* is in my room. I want you to sit on my bed and look at the book while I'm gone."

Lydia's eyes brightened. Even though her daughter couldn't read, Abbie knew she took pleasure in turning the pages of a book.

After Lydia disappeared into the house, Abbie straightened and raced for the corral, knowing even as she did so, she'd be too late. She saddled a horse, mounted, and galloped toward Fortune.

As she neared the edge of town, she saw the two men standing in the street. For a single heartbeat, she thought perhaps she'd arrived in time to stop them, to return sanity to an insane situation.

But then she watched in horror as both men slid guns from holsters.

"No!" she cried.

She heard the solitary gunshot echo through the stillness of dawn. As her horse reared up, she saw Grayson stagger back, bright red blood bursting forth over his white shirt like cotton exploding from the boll. Her heart plummeted as she lost her balance and tumbled from the horse. She felt a sharp pain at the back of her head before the darkness engulfed her.

*   *   *

John studied his wife, who was lying so still on the bed at the doctor's house. For one horrifying moment as the horse had reared up and he'd watched her topple, he had known a fear far worse than anything he'd experienced in battle: his sweet Abigail might die.

But the doctor had assured him that she would be all right. "Just a bump on the head," he'd said.

The baby wasn't in danger either, and if John were honest with himself, he had mixed feelings about that. He knew it would break Abigail's heart to lose the child. She so loved children. They were the only thing he knew how to give her, the one way he could show her that he cared for her.

"I want lots of children," she'd told him after he asked her to marry him. He wasn't quite sure how many *lots* were, but he figured she'd tell him when she had enough.

"For God's sake, man, at least hold her hand."

John snapped his head around. Pale, his lips pressed into a straight line as though he were fighting the pain, the Englishman leaned against the door frame. His left arm was in a sling and through the hole the bullet had created in his shirt, John could see the white of a bandage that stood out in direct contrast to the red streaks staining his shirt.

John turned his attention back to Abbie. She had yet to wake up; her face was almost as pale as the Englishman's. Tentatively, as though afraid she might jerk away, he wrapped his hand around hers. Her hand was so small that it made his look like a giant's.

"Why didn't you shoot?" he asked quietly. "Your

gun was out of the holster long before mine was. You had a clear shot—''

"It dawned on me with startling clarity that I would prefer to live the remainder of my life with Abbie's dislike rather than her hatred. And she would have no doubt hated me had I killed you.''

"She said you wanted the land.''

"In the beginning, yes.''

He glanced over his shoulder. "And now?''

"I want her happy, and I want the child—her child—never to carry the label of bastard.'' Rhodes shifted his gaze to Abbie, his eyes roaming over her as though he were painting a portrait of her. "I shall walk from this room, from your life and hers—never to return—if you will promise to honor two conditions.''

"What would those be?''

"Accept the child as your own. For the child's sake and Abbie's. I will send you funds periodically so nothing is taken from your own children—but this child must never doubt his place in the world.''

"And the other condition?''

"Have some tender regard for Abbie's heart. Her loyalty to you was commendable. Had she known you were alive, she would have never turned to me, regardless of what her heart wanted.''

John slammed his eyes closed, his throat tightening until he thought he might choke. "I'll see to takin' proper care of the child and Abigail.''

"I prefer to keep this bargain between us.''

John opened his eyes, met Rhodes' gaze, and gave a brusque nod. "What do you want me to tell her?''

"I think my leaving will say it all.''

He thought Rhodes looked unsteady as he shoved away from the door and walked from the room.

Grayson thought it might have brought his father a measure of pride to see the way his son walked, albeit a bit crookedly, out of the physician's house. Kit and Harry had their horses nearby, saddled and waiting. He wasted no time in joining his friends.

"Shall we be off?"

"The doctor said you shouldn't travel for a few days," Kit said.

"Yes, well—" With a low moan, he pulled himself into the saddle. "—he doesn't know what's best for my health."

"How's Abbie?"

"She hasn't woken up yet, but the physician assures me that she will."

"And the baby?"

"No harm done there."

"How far shall we ride today?" Harry asked.

"At least until the town is out of sight," Grayson suggested. At which point, he thought he might be able to give into the pain and allow unconsciousness to claim him.

Abbie was vaguely aware of her surroundings. A soft bed. Deep voices, male voices, rumbling in and out, causing the pain in her head to increase. Then the blessed silence.

A man's hand wrapped around hers. At first, she thought it was Grayson's. Had he died? Was he taking her to heaven? She remembered the thunder of a gun, remembered the sight of him staggering back, the blood just before the blackness.

But this hand was warm. Wasn't his. It was too large. The fingers weren't as long and they were thicker. She forced her eyes open to find John sitting beside her, his face anxious. "Grayson?" she croaked.

"He left."

"He's not dead, then?"

Understanding dawned in his eyes, and he shook his craggy head forcefully. "No, no. Took a bullet in the shoulder, but it'll heal."

"You said he left?"

"Went to Galveston with his friends."

The pain streaked across her chest like lightning in the midst of a storm, even though she knew it was for the best. She turned her face toward the window, away from John. "The boys?"

"They come running out of hiding when you fell. I didn't know they were here, Abigail. They're sitting in the front parlor now—if they know what's good for them."

She felt his heavy hand come to rest on her stomach. She turned her head slightly.

"I know how much you love children," he said, his eyes on his hand instead of her. "This one . . . I'll claim it as mine if you'll stay with me."

With tears in her eyes, she laid her hand over his. He turned his palm up and did what he'd never before done: wove their fingers together.

17

*"T*he responsibilities you owe one person don't stop because you love another more. John was a good husband in his own way. I can't be less than a good wife.''

Grayson pondered Abbie's words as he walked along the beach at Galveston, the waves washing upon the shore. He found it disconcerting to discover that he was beginning to view his father and the choices he'd made a little differently, perhaps with a bit more tolerance. Perhaps love was not determined by the measure of *things* but rather the measure of *sacrifice*.

What had it cost his father to openly accept and raise his bastard son? His father had never hinted at any personal detriment—yet Grayson knew Abbie would hide the cost to herself from those she loved, would lock it away inside her heart, and never dwell on what might have been.

Had his father done the same? Until a woman with violet eyes had shown him, Grayson hadn't understood that love was greater than obligation because it could step aside and never lose its importance.

He could not help but think that he had done a disservice to his father.

He listened as the seagulls screeched around him. He decided that he had lied to Abbie when he said he wasn't fond of salt air because in the two days since their arrival, he had found himself walking the docks and staring out to sea more often than not, and breathing in the warm salt air.

He had no desire to do anything else.

"Of course you don't feel like doing anything," Kit had assured him. "You're healing."

But it was more than that. Where before his life had seemed to have little meaning—now it had none whatsoever. Without Abbie to brighten his days, they possessed a bleakness that made him wonder how he managed to get out of bed.

But he did. Long before dawn. It was ironic really. He had nothing to do, and yet he walked the wharves, watching the sun come up and the fishermen head out to sea. He had seen the enormous fish the men caught when they took their boats out, and he thought how much he'd enjoy taking Johnny and Micah fishing on the gulf waters. He could almost envision their excitement as they climbed aboard a boat—and Abbie's worry as he took them away from shore.

He rubbed his aching shoulder. The wound was healing, but it seemed particularly sensitive today.

The sun hovered at the edge of the water, a red and orange orb slowly sinking away. He wondered what the day had wrought for his friends.

He saw the weathered *Anne Marie* making its way toward the dock. He ambled to the slip where he knew the old sailor would moor his boat. He had met the man upon first arriving at Galveston. Jack was a colorful sort whose personal habits left a bit to be desired. Grayson doubted the man ever bathed, but his jovial laughter echoed along the island coast.

"Hey, boyo!" Jack called out as he tossed a rope onto the dock.

Grayson secured the line. "How was the fishing today?"

"I told you, boyo, I don't fish, I crab." He sent a stream of spittle into the water. "And today the catch was lousy. There's a storm comin' in."

He rocked with the boat. Grayson was amazed the man never seemed to lose his balance and topple into the water. He looked toward the dark blue sky. "How do you know there's a storm coming?"

"Lookit here," Jack said as he grabbed the large claws of a crab and held the creature over his head. The normally silver and blue back was barely visible through the mud coating it.

"Looks as though he could use a bath," Grayson admitted.

Jack snorted. "He was hiding in the mud, afeared of the storm." He tossed the hapless crab back into the water. "Bad storm comin'. You and your mates had best head inland."

Grayson crouched on the edge of the dock. "Because a crab got a bit dirty?"

Jack squinted his one good eye. A white cloud covered the other and Grayson thought the old man might have more luck with the ladies if he wore an eye patch.

"I know because I didn't catch no crabs today, except for that bugger. They go deep when there's a storm brewing. Bury themselves in the mud. That's how I know. 'Cuz I know crabs." He wagged his finger. "Go inland, boyo."

"Scurry away from a little rain and wind?"

Jack scrambled onto the dock, the wiry white hair on his chest visible because he didn't seem to realize buttons had a purpose. "A tempest. A hurricane. It destroys everything in its path." He wrapped his gnarled, bony fingers around Grayson's arm and pulled him down until they were eye level. "I was here in thirty-seven when the sea's fury was unleashed like the wrath of God. October it was. For three days and three nights, the heavens battled the earth. The mighty hand of God threw eight ships onto dry land. Broken masts and rigging were strewn about everywhere." His fingers tightened their hold. "Only one house survived the onslaught."

"You think that sort of storm is headed this way?"

"Aye, boyo. Mark my words on it. You can see it gathering its strength on the horizon. Might not hit Galveston, but it'll hit somewhere along the coast."

Grayson looked toward the distance where the sky met the sea in a calm straight line. He could barely discern the dark clouds. He thought of Abbie and her comment about storms. Was this what she feared? A hurricane? He didn't think enough cotton remained to worry over, but it sounded as though the storm could harm far more than the white bolls. "How far inland does it travel?"

"One, two, three hundred miles. Just depends on its power, its anger. Nature ain't a kind mistress when she's been scorned." He released his death grip and smiled, revealing a grin that had few teeth. "Have I ever showed ya how I can lift a schooner over me head?"

Grayson had always thought a schooner was a ship—so did Harry when he accepted Jack's wager, certain the old man couldn't lift a boat with his scrawny arms. With a lustful laugh, Jack had ordered a schooner of beer, lifted it over his head, and taken Harry's money. "Yes, you showed me."

With a nod, he patted Grayson's shoulder. "Head inland."

Grayson found Kit in the saloon where they had taken rooms. He was sitting at a table in the corner, papers strewn before him as he made meticulous notes. He barely looked up when Grayson took a chair. "Where's Harry?"

"Haven't a clue. Off gambling somewhere, I imagine," Kit mumbled.

"In that disreputable part of town?"

"Probably."

"Jack says we should head inland. There's a storm coming."

"What's a little rain and wind?"

"Apparently these are more than that. I know storms coming up from the coast were a concern to Abbie."

Kit ceased his writing and looked at Grayson. He hated seeing the sympathy in his friend's eyes.

"Were you thinking of warning her?"

"If we happened to be in the area . . . I thought I might just look in, make sure she's all right—" He placed his elbows on the table and rubbed his hands up and down his face. "Christ, I can't stop thinking about her, wondering if my leaving was the best thing to do." He peered over his fingers at Kit. "I feel as though I did what I've done all my life—shirked my responsibilities."

"It was a difficult situation, Gray. Westland said he would accept the child as his. Although I'm not totally unbiased, in the long run I think you made the best of a poor situation."

Grayson nodded. Christ, he hoped so. He nudged a sheet of paper toward Kit. "What's all this?"

A gleam came into Kit's eyes. "Our future." He eased up in his chair and folded his arms on the table. "I think cattle is the way to go. I was talking with a couple of gents earlier—they were ranchers before the war. Most ranchers who joined the Confederacy simply set their cattle free—to roam the wilds as it were. They say to the west of here the cattle have been reproducing like rabbits—and they belong to no one."

"So you just take them?"

"Exactly."

"Then why isn't everyone doing it?"

"I think everyone will do it—eventually." Kit moved some papers aside and spread a copy of the

New York Daily Tribune across the table. He pointed to an article. "They are desperate for beef up north. One of those cows we saw wandering near Fortune is worth four dollars here. But if we can get it to a northern market, we can get forty dollars for it."

"So you take a few cattle—"

"A thousand. At least a thousand. We gather them up. We burn our brands into their hides and guide them to market." He shuffled the papers around. "Of course, with that many cattle, we'll need more than the three of us but since it will be our enterprise, we will receive the bulk of the profits. We'll need supplies . . ." He looked up a little sheepishly. "I've got most of it worked out. Our expenses, maps, the routes we can take to get through Kansas." He grazed his thumb over the scar beneath his chin. "But to truly make a fortune, we must be the first."

Grayson studied the notes spread before him. Kit's penchant for detail was incredible. "It sounds risky."

"It is. So I know Harry will go for it . . . which is good since we'll be using his funds to purchase our supplies."

"Sounds as though it might be easier than cotton farming."

"Definitely. All we have to do is prod a few cattle and the herding instinct will have the rest following. Nothing could be simpler."

Grayson narrowed his gaze. He couldn't help but believe there was more to it than Kit either knew or was revealing. "When were you thinking of pursuing this undertaking?"

"The sooner the better. I'd like to leave in the morning."

Grayson chuckled. "Not excited about this, are you?"

"It's like making love to a woman for the first time. You aren't exactly sure what to expect, but you know you'll experience a great deal of satisfaction."

The area around Market Street raised the hairs on the back of Grayson's neck and arms. Prostitution, gambling, and drunkenness ran rampant, blatantly ignored by the city marshal and his minions. The opportunity for vices and the tolerance of them was supposedly the legacy of a pirate named Jean Lafitte.

Grayson followed Kit into a shadowy saloon that made the one in Fortune look downright grand. He couldn't stop his gaze from darting warily around the room while they ambled to the bar.

Kit signaled for the bartender. "We're looking for a friend of ours. Tall chap, black hair, black beard, likes to play cards—"

"Red vest, black jacket?"

"Yes, that's the one."

Harry had purchased new clothes as soon as they'd arrived in Galveston. A need to cast off the image of cotton farming, he'd said.

With a quick flick of his wrist, the bartender slapped his towel on the bar, killing a fly. "Some fellas took him out back."

Grayson didn't like the sound of that, or the sneer on the man's face and the triumph in his eyes.

Kit leaned forward slightly. "I beg your pardon? Out back?"

The bartender gave a nod. "Behind the saloon. Caught him cheatin'. It'll be a cold day in hell before he cheats 'round here again."

They found him huddled in a corner, cradling his right hand.

"Good God, Harry, are you all right?" Kit asked as he crouched beside him.

Grayson knelt as well, holding his breath against the surrounding stench.

"They broke my hand," Harry said quietly, his voice strained as though fighting the pain.

"Ah, God," Grayson said, slipping his arm around Harry's shoulders. "Let's get you up and to a physician."

"It was a damn physician that broke my hand. Said he could do it so it'd never heal properly. Damn bastard." Harry flinched. "Sorry, Gray. No offense meant."

"None taken."

"We'll get you to a physician in the better part of town," Kit assured him, helping Grayson get Harry to his feet. "Once we're done there, we're going to take your money and invest in cattle—"

"There is no money."

Grayson and Kit exchanged bewildered glances, before returning their attention to Harry. Grayson knew they should concern themselves with Harry's injury and not his money—

"You mean the men who attacked you stole your money—"

"No."

"You gambled some of it away—" Kit began.

"No!" Harry lunged out of their grasp. "There is no money. There never was any money. How in the bloody hell do you think my father forced me to come here?"

Breathing heavily, he slumped against the wall. "I wagered it away in England. A bloody fortune. Creditors were breathing down my neck. My father said he would pay my debts if I agreed to come here."

"Why didn't you tell us the truth?" Kit asked. "Why did you allow us to believe—"

"Because I thought my luck would change . . . that I'd win enough back that you need never know what a fool I'd been."

A heavy silence descended until all Grayson could hear was the distant roar of the surf. "How did you manage to play games of chance without money?"

Harry sighed deeply. "The myth of English nobility. I convinced them that as the son of an earl, I was good for it."

"And when they discover differently?" Kit prodded.

Harry released a mirthless laugh. "Then I shall probably find myself at the bottom of the sea."

Grayson stepped forward and extended his hand toward his friend. "Come on. Let's get your hand tended. There's supposedly a storm brewing. I think it would serve us well to leave before its arrival."

Harry staggered forward. "All is not lost. If you're willing to return to Fortune, I think I might know where we can get the funds."

"I ain't never been fishin' in a boat before!"

Abbie smiled at Johnny, trying not to let her apprehension show. On the ground, the thing John called a boat rocked from side to side when Johnny clambered into it. She didn't want to think what it would do on the water.

John must have had some doubts himself since he'd forbidden Micah to go until he'd learned to swim. He was explaining to Johnny how to use the paddles to maneuver the boat. Johnny's head was bobbing so fast and hard that she was surprised it didn't go flying off his shoulders.

John unfolded his body and Johnny climbed out of the boat. "We're gonna be real fishermen, Ma."

"You sure are."

John stepped around the boat, took her hand, and gave her a small kiss on the cheek. "You try and rest while we're gone."

"Are you sure that thing is safe?"

He gave her a hesitant smile. "My pa took me fishing in it."

"I thought old boats rotted."

"If you got 'em sitting in water. We kept this one in the shed. 'Sides, Johnny can swim."

"And what about you?"

She saw the red creep up his face. She was slowly realizing that he wasn't the only one who hadn't been giving affection. Awkward moments still existed between them, but they were both working to make better out of worse. She didn't think a woman could ask more of her man than that.

"Yeah, I know how to swim, too."

Lifting a hand, she shielded her gaze from the sun and looked in the distance. She saw dark clouds forming. "It looks like a storm might be coming in."

John squinted. "Ah, it's been lookin' like that for days now. Nothing will come of it."

"You'll lose what's left of the cotton in the field if it is a storm."

She saw him hesitate and wished she'd kept her mouth shut. Johnny had done nothing for days but talk about the fishing trip he was going to take with his father. She just wished the chills would stop racing along her spine whenever she thought of Johnny in a boat on the water. It was ridiculous really. John was a strong man, a good swimmer. He wouldn't do anything to endanger his son.

She released a dry laugh. "I'm just being silly. Take Johnny fishing. Lydia, Micah, and I will stroll through the fields—"

"I want you resting."

She smiled, wondering if she'd ever grow accustomed to his concern. She patted his shoulder. "Go on. Get on with your fishing."

He lifted the heavy end of the boat while Johnny lifted the lighter end. She watched them trudge toward the woods, father and son.

"Come back if it starts to rain!" she called after them.

John waved a hand in the air just before they disappeared into the woods.

She looked toward the south, hoping those dark clouds would go back the way they'd come.

"Well, English, I never expected to see your shadow crossing our threshold again."

Grayson had never in his life seen Harry blush. He found it rather amusing as Harry approached Jessye.

"They say absence makes the heart grow fonder. Jessye love, I never knew what those words meant until I left—"

She held up a hand. "I ain't buying it, Harry." She gave a curt nod. "What happened to your hand?"

Harry turned his hand one way, then the other as though only just noticing the heavy bandage that kept the bones in place. "I was playing a bit of poker in Galveston, having quite a bit of luck actually, and some fellows—"

"Figured out you were cheating."

Harry's shoulders slumped forward. "Yes."

"I warned you about cheating. You're damn lucky they left your hand attached to your arm."

"I'm not so sure. It hurts like bloody hell."

"You and your friends find a table. I'll bring you some whiskey." She winked conspiratorially. "For medicinal purposes."

Grayson fell into step beside Kit as they followed Harry to a corner table. Harry took a chair. "I thought here would be best. Away from prying ears."

Grayson dropped into the chair and leaned forward. "You aren't thinking to play poker with her and win—"

Harry grinned. "Of course not. I'm almost certain she cheats. But she's a risk taker and I know she has funds."

"She is to be the source of our money?" Grayson asked, incredulously. "She can barely tolerate the sight of you!"

"I once thought the same of the Widow Westland in regards to you. I was wrong and so are you." Harry came out of his chair, giving Grayson no opportunity to thrash him. "Jessye love, join us for a moment."

She set three glasses and a bottle of whiskey on the table. "I've got paying customers that I need to see to."

"Just for a moment. I want to make you a proposition."

Grayson was astounded to see the good humor completely disappear from her face.

"I told you, Harry, I don't do that sort of thing."

Harry shook his head briskly. "No, not that kind of proposition. A business venture. Cattle."

She angled her head thoughtfully. "Cattle?"

"Yes, just give us five minutes. Kit can explain it to you."

Kit removed sheaves of paper from inside his jacket. "Yes, it's really quite an exciting and bold venture."

She cast a suspicious glance at Harry before cautiously lowering herself into a chair. "All right. Explain it."

Grayson leaned back in his chair. He had no need to hear the explanation as Kit had talked of nothing else during their journey. Grayson heard the wind howl, a low ominous shriek. They had come up from the south and he'd almost taken a detour by Abbie's . . . even if it entailed no more than catching a glimpse of her from a distance. But in the end, he'd decided against it. It was bad enough that he was in the town—just for one night, Harry had promised. Then they would be on their way—

"Are you out of your mind?" Harry snapped.

Grayson jerked his attention to those sitting at the table. Harry looked like a cotton boll on the verge of bursting.

Jessye crossed her arms over her chest. "It's my money."

"But you can't go on a cattle drive with men."

"Why not?"

"Because you're a woman. Your reputation—"

"I've worked in a saloon since I was twelve. I've got no reputation."

Harry waved his uninjured hand in the air. "Kit, Gray, explain to her why she can't go with us."

She barked out her throaty laughter. "I don't trust your friends any more than I trust you. For all I know this *venture* is no different than you skimming a card from the bottom of the deck. If I invest my money, then I will dog your every step—closer than your shadow." She scraped her chair back and stood. "So think on that, English. If my money goes, so do I."

She stormed back to the bar, her balled fists swinging at her sides.

Kit began to gather up his papers. "Well, so much for that brilliant idea."

Harry simply leaned back in his chair and grinned. "Where does a man's shadow rest when he sleeps?"

Staring at his friend, Grayson clenched his teeth to stop his mouth from dropping open. "You aren't seriously considering allowing her to go with us."

Harry shrugged. "Why not? She knows the state. She's good enough with a gun to be able to teach you how to use it. She's not squeamish."

"She could get hurt."

"She could also get wealthy enough to leave this life behind."

Grayson turned to Kit for support. "What do you think?"

He narrowed his eyes and pursed his lips. "I think if we combined the money we received from the cotton—"

"Mine's gone," Harry said quietly.

Grayson shifted in his chair. "I . . . I sent mine to Westland . . . to cover expenses—"

Kit raised his hand. "Enough said. Then I don't see that we have much choice. We've seldom painted ourselves as responsible." He cut his gaze to Harry. "Your latest debacle—"

"I can't stand it when you get so intolerably righteous. I suppose you're going to tell us that you still have your money," Harry said.

"No, but what I did with it is my business, not yours. Suffice it to say that it was needed elsewhere, so elsewhere it went."

Harry grimaced. "Sorry. If I'd been honest and

told you I had no money, you no doubt would have held onto it—''

''Keeping it was never a consideration. So—'' He slapped his hands on the table. ''Gentlemen, I don't see that we have a choice. The woman goes with us.''

Reluctantly Grayson nodded. He didn't like the idea of exposing a woman to danger—even if she seemed capable of taking care of herself.

Harry leaned back in his chair, raised an arm, and snapped his fingers. Jessye looked toward him and gave him a look that said, *You can do that until hell freezes over; I ain't no dog.*

Harry groaned. ''God, she is stubborn.'' He stood. ''Jessye love, come here. Please.''

She sauntered over as though she already knew how their private discussion had ended. She came to a stop, threw out her hip, and planted her hand on it. ''Yes?''

As gentlemen, Kit and Grayson both stood.

''You may come with us,'' Harry said.

She smiled brightly. ''You won't regret it.''

Kit cleared his throat. ''We do have some details to work out, but we'd like to leave—''

A loud bang had them all glancing around. A gust of wind made the doors of the saloon swing open.

''Lord, we got us a thunderstorm kicking up,'' Jessye said.

Grayson realized now that the howling had grown louder. Outside, it looked like night had fallen. He pulled his watch from his pocket. It was only three in the afternoon. Dread pierced him. ''When we were in Galveston, an old fisherman said that a storm was coming, a hurricane—"

"Good Lord!" Jessye rushed to the window and looked out. "We gotta let people know so they can board up their windows." She turned to address the room. "Fellas! Listen up. We might have us a hurricane coming. We need to get the word out."

Grayson watched in amazement as men scrambled from the tables, knocking over chairs in their haste to get out the door. He had no idea how many families those few men could warn.

"I'm gonna ride south and warn the Westlands," Jessye said. "They'll be hit first."

"I'm going with you," Grayson said.

Jessye's wide eyes and trembling voice told him more than he wanted to know about this storm. He only hoped they wouldn't be too late.

18

Why today? Why today? Why today?

The wind whipping around her, Abbie stood on the front porch, wondering why John couldn't have taken Johnny fishing yesterday or tomorrow. She felt the big fat raindrops hit her as the black ominous clouds rolled in, one over the other as though they were trying to win a race.

"Ma?"

"Go back inside, Lydia."

"Where's Johnny?"

"They'll be here. Now go inside."

"Will you come inside, too?"

"In a minute."

Her heart was thundering louder than nature's roar. Then she saw the riders galloping through the storm while the wind lashed at them. They grew nearer and Abbie's breath caught. It couldn't be—?

But dear God, it was!

She flew off the steps, straight into Grayson's comforting arms. He nudged her toward the house, yelling over the wind. "Get into the house, Abbie."

She dug in her heels and drew back, shaking her head fiercely. "John took Johnny fishing. They haven't come back." She looked at Jessye, a plea in her eyes. "They haven't come back."

"I'll watch the young 'uns. You take my horse." Jessye handed her the reins and raced to the house.

Abbie took a step toward the skittish mare and felt someone jerk her back. She looked up into Grayson's angry face.

"What do you think you're doing?" he roared.

"I've got to find John and Johnny."

"I'll find them. You get in the house."

"You don't know where they might be. I do."

He spread his hand over her stomach. "Sweetheart, you're going to get yourself killed."

Tears stung her eyes because she knew he wasn't only thinking of her. Dear God, how could a mother choose? She couldn't, not consciously. She only knew that she had to find Johnny. "They should have been home by now. John promised if it rained—"

"Bloody damned hell!" He hoisted her into the saddle. "You stay near me!" he ordered before mounting his own horse.

But she knew where they needed to go. She urged the horse forward, taking one last look at the house, and the two small faces pressed to the window. She saw Jessye running around the house, slamming shutters closed, barring them against the storm, and she knew at least two of her children would be safe.

The copse of trees offered them some protection from the storm, the thick tree trunks forming a barrier against the wind, but above them the branches danced wildly. They journeyed until they reached the bank of the river, the spot where Grayson had gone fishing with the boys so long ago. The water slapped unmercifully against the shore, rising over the bank. She knew it was only a prelude . . . the black heart of the storm had not yet arrived.

She followed the course of the river north as it fought its own battle against the storm, the water cresting, lifted by the wind, pounded back down by the rain. And then she saw it—what she had dreaded, what she had feared.

The wreck of a boat, splintered boards beating against the shore, seeking refuge they would never again find. Tears sprang to her eyes, her throat tightened. Without thought, without care, she dismounted. Grayson was beside her before she'd taken a step.

"It's their boat!" she cried.

He gave a nod and turned back to the horses, securing the slippery reins to a wet branch. She sloshed through the mud, slipping, losing her balance until she reached the water's edge. "Johnny!"

The water was black, as black as death, the sky an ominous gray.

"Johnny!" she cried again, the tears clogging her throat.

"Johnny!" she heard Grayson shout. "Westland!"

His voice was so much deeper, carried so much farther but the unforgiving wind caught the sound and swallowed it whole.

He wrapped his arm around her, drawing her into

the curve of his body, sheltering her from the storm as much as he was able. She searched his face for the answer she didn't want.

"The current could have carried the boat here," he said in a low, strained voice, close enough to her face that she could hear. "They might have made it to safety farther upstream."

She looked past him to the turbulent river. What if they were going in the wrong direction? What if they had floated with the boat, floated downstream?

"Maybe we should split up—"

He shook his head.

"But what if they aren't up there?"

He voiced no answer for there was no need. The bleakness in his blue eyes told her that their only hope lay farther up the river. She fought back the tears, set her mouth into a determined line, and nodded.

For the barest of moments, before he turned, she thought she saw a tear glisten within his eyes.

Holding the reins to both horses, Grayson followed behind Abbie, reaching for her whenever she slipped.

"Johnny!"

He didn't have the heart to tell her that her son would never hear her voice over the wind. Then she stumbled to a stop and clutched his shirt.

"There!" she cried, pointing toward a huge boulder in the middle of the river.

Trees had somehow sprouted out of it. John seemed to be tangled in the brush while Johnny was desperately clinging to a branch.

Abbie took a step toward the river, and Grayson's

heart rammed against his chest. He jerked her back.

"We've got to help them!" she cried.

"I'll help them. You stay here."

"What are you going to do?"

He glanced over his shoulder at the horses and breathed a sigh of relief. Jessye had mounted a rope to her saddle. Bless the woman.

"I'm going farther upstream—"

"But we found them."

"I know, but I can't swim against the current. I'll go farther up and let the current carry me down to them."

"I should go."

He led her away from the bank, to a tree that offered only the slightest protection. He tethered the horses before turning to her and cradling her face, wishing that his hand wasn't trembling. "You need to wait here for Johnny . . . and John."

She started to speak and he touched his finger to her lips. He reached into his trousers pocket, removed his watch, and pressed it into the palm of her hand. "Just in case . . . it was my father's. Give it to my child."

Reaching behind her, he grabbed the rope from the saddle and stalked along the river's edge, trying to judge the river's flow and how much room he needed to give himself. He began to unwind the rope. It wasn't as long as he'd hoped. He staggered to a stop, judging the distance.

He stripped out of his clothes, completely, absolutely, fearing the boy or man might weigh him down enough. He wanted no soggy clothes to add to his burden. Lightning streaked across the sky and thunder roared. He tied one end of the rope to a sturdy tree, the other around himself and dove into the river.

The current was stronger than he'd anticipated, and he'd given no thought to the fact that his shoulder wasn't fully recovered. He fought the pain, fought the driving current, swimming toward the boulder while the river carried him downstream.

He saw the huge slab of stone and made a Herculean effort to reach it, bumping along the branches until he was able to grab one to stop himself.

"Gray!"

He pulled himself onto the boulder, clinging to the branches until he was able to reach Johnny. "It's all right, lad!" he yelled over the roar of the wind.

"My arms . . . getting tired."

"Hang on just a bit longer, all right?"

Johnny nodded. Grayson untied the rope from around his waist and tied it beneath Johnny's arms. "Let go!" he ordered, pulling Johnny onto the boulder.

"I think Pa's dead!"

"Hold onto this branch."

When the boy had a firm grip on the branch, Grayson leaned toward John Westland. The man had a bloodied gash on the side of his head, and he was staring at the sky. Grayson slipped his hand beneath the man's throat and found a weak pulse. Westland was caught in the trees, high enough that the lapping water didn't drown him.

Grayson turned back to Johnny. "He's not dead." He watched relief wash over Johnny's face. "I'll come back for him. Right now, let's get you to your mother. The rope will keep you from going downstream. Just swim!''

Johnny nodded.

Grayson grabbed the rope, hoping that would be enough to keep him from going downstream, enough to help him push Johnny across the river. They slid from the boulder into the water. Kicking, stroking, swimming toward shore while the rope held them at bay. Gasping for breath, they reached the bank. Abbie slid in the mud, taking Johnny into her arms.

''Oh, God, oh, God.'' She looked at Grayson with tears in her eyes. ''Thank you.''

He nodded, untying the rope from around Johnny.

''John?'' he heard her ask.

''Hurt but alive.''

He wrapped the rope around himself and trudged back to his jumping-off point. How much simpler it would have been to have said that the man were dead. Grayson would have had all that he wanted, all that he needed, everyone that he loved.

Honor was a damnable nuisance.

Abbie remembered little of the journey home. Johnny had ridden on the horse with her, his arms wrapped tightly around her. Grayson had slung John over the other horse and walked.

She remembered that Jessye had taken Johnny aside when they walked through the house. Warming him with cocoa, she'd gone about drying him and getting him into fresh clothes.

Grayson had helped her tend to John. John. He was

lying in bed now, his eyes staring blankly at the ceiling while she dried the ends of his hair.

"Johnny says you caught a really big fish, but it got away." She pressed her lips to his forehead. "Wake up, John. Don't keep staring like that. It frightens me."

She glanced over her shoulder at Grayson, who was soaked to the bone, his gaze weary. Tears burned her eyes. "There was cotton in the field. We always have cotton bolls bursting open late in the season. I told him I thought there was a storm coming. He said he'd pick the cotton tomorrow. Now it's ruined."

In four long strides, Grayson crossed the room and took her into his arms. He sank to the floor with her nestled in his lap. She buried her face against his shoulder and let the painful sobs wrack her body. "Oh, God, I would have lost them both if you hadn't come."

He rocked her back and forth, his hands stroking her back. "Shhh, Abbie. It's all right now."

"I was terrified. Afraid I'd lose them. Afraid I'd lose you. It was like having to choose, a hundred times, over and over—"

"Shhh. No more choices have to be made. It's over."

But it wasn't. She heard the wind shrieking, the thunder rumble, and the rain pounding on the roof. Inside she was cold, but outside, she was sheltered by his warmth.

"You need to get into some dry clothes," he said.

"Hold me just a minute longer."

His arms tightened around her.

"Why are you here?"

"Cattle. We're going to try our hand at cattle, and we needed someone . . . to fund our enterprise."

"Jessye?"

"Yes, she plans to go with us."

She smiled softly. If anyone could keep these disreputable men in line, it would be Jessye.

"Now, come on. You're going to get sick if you don't get out of these wet things," he said.

She drew back. He gave her a halfhearted smile. "I'll send Jessye in to help you."

"Those are hardly the words of a rogue."

"They are when the lady's husband is in the room."

His arms tightened around her, and he pressed his mouth to the pulse fluttering at her throat. She heard him swallow before moving back. "Come on. Up with you now," he said, his voice strained.

She scrambled out of his lap. "Let me get you some of John's clothes to wear."

He nodded, but his gaze wandered to her husband, lying so still on the bed. She walked to the wardrobe and opened the door. She heard the low rumble of Grayson's voice.

"You know, Westland, it would make things a great deal simpler if you would wake up. This storm is creating a bloody mess. I won't have a clue as to where I should begin. Are you listening to me? I thought you and I had agreed to make Abbie happy. Well, you're doing a poor job of it, lying there, staring at the ceiling. I can't stay forever. My friends and I are going to gather cattle. I don't want to miss this opportunity—'' He glanced over his shoulder as Abbie strolled to the bed, John's folded clothes within her hands. "I'm rambling," Grayson said.

"Probably helps for him to hear a voice. When I hit my head, I heard the rumble of voices. I just sorta moved toward that sound and woke up. Think I'll try reading the almanac to him."

"Hmmm. Sounds like an intriguing tale."

Shaking her head, she smiled with a memory. "He was so happy when he learned I could read. He'd been depending on his ability to judge nature's signs to determine when to plant his seeds. The first time I read to him from the almanac, you would have thought he was the richest of men."

"He *was* the richest of men, Abbie. He had you. And his wealth has not dwindled."

Then, taking the clothes she offered, he walked quietly from the room.

The wailing rose in tempo. Grayson decided he might be able to relax if he thought the house could withstand the force of the gale. The winds might have had a calming effect if it weren't for the occasional jarring crash of something outside banging into something else. The shutters on the windows rattled. The wind whistled through the chimney, down through the hearth—even after Grayson had closed the damper. Jessye had doused the fire and cleaned out the hearth. "Just in case we need a place," was all she'd said when Grayson had asked her about it.

His mouth dry, he sat in the worn wing-backed chair, Micah snuggled against his side, his tiny body rife with tremors as Grayson haltingly read *Ivanhoe*.

Jessye sat on the floor, her legs folded beneath her, her arms around Lydia and Johnny. Despite the bruises and scratches on his face, Johnny seemed to have recovered remarkably well from his ordeal although he did jump every time they heard a clap of thunder.

But then Grayson jumped, too.

The door to the bedroom opened and Abbie ambled out, a weariness to her step, a droop to her shoulders.

Johnny jerked his head around. "How's Pa?"

Abbie knelt beside him and hugged him fiercely. "He's . . . I don't know what he is. Sleeping, I guess."

"A big 'ol limb from a tree hit him when he was getting me to the rock," Johnny explained. "I thought he was a goner."

"Maybe I oughta go for the doctor," Jessye said.

Incredulously Grayson stared at the woman, trying to determine if she was courageous or foolish.

Abbie shook her head. "No, Jessye, we've risked enough lives today. I don't think the doctor will be able to do anything for him now that he won't be able to do once the storm passes."

"Grayson was a hero," Johnny announced.

"Hardly, lad," he said, much more comfortable when he was described as disreputable.

Holding his gaze, Abbie smiled softly. "Yes, he was."

The gratitude in her eyes, directed his way, was almost a painful thing to behold. Gratitude because he'd not only saved her son, but her husband.

The wind quieted, the rain lessened, the silence echoed more loudly than a storm. Grayson felt the knots in his muscles unwind as he slumped back in the chair. "Thank God, it's over."

"No," Abbie said quietly. "Not yet." She rose to her feet. "Come outside with me for a minute."

He shifted Micah off his lap and handed the book to him. "Hold my place."

The lad beamed as though he'd just been given the responsibility of saving the world.

Outside the world was an ominous gray. Debris seemed to move with no wind to push it. The silence became oppressive.

"There's always an eerie lull like this," Abbie explained. "It's like the storm is sitting up there, waiting and watching."

"While it's quiet, I should fetch a physician—"

"No. You don't know how long it'll be before the rest of the storm hits and I don't want you caught in it."

"So we just wait."

She nodded.

She was standing close enough that with the slightest movement, he could have her in his arms. "How have you been feeling?"

"The sickness isn't as bad."

"Good. I'm glad to hear that. I didn't like the thought of you being ill . . ." He allowed his voice to trail off, suddenly at a loss for words. So much remained unsettled between them. She had asked him not to kill her husband—he hadn't. She'd asked him to leave—he had.

She turned her gaze toward the damaged land. "You could have left John where he was. He wouldn't have survived the storm. You could have come back to shore and told me he was dead and I never would have known differently." She looked at him then, tears shimmering within her violet eyes. "I think you lied to me, Grayson Rhodes. I don't think you're a rogue at all."

"Unfortunately, sweetheart, I'm afraid there will be many a lonely night when I shall regret that I wasn't."

Inwardly, Abbie sighed. She'd adopted some of his bad habits, torn between wanting him to be happy and never wanting anyone to replace her within his heart.

She stood for long moments, simply gazing out, waiting for the storm, waiting for words that would unburden her heart. The words wouldn't come. But the storm did. She heard its roaring, its anger. "We need to get back inside."

She jerked around. Lydia stood within the doorway, pale as death. "Lydia, you need to go inside."

"But Mama—"

She nudged her daughter's shoulder. "No buts. The storm is coming—"

"Pa went out the back door."

"What?" She spun around, a movement catching her attention. A shadow in the fields. "John!"

She turned back to Lydia and pushed her through the doorway. "Do not leave this house. Do you understand me?'' She looked at Jessye. ''John is in the fields. I have to get him. Keep the children.''

''Abbie, let him go,'' Jessye called after her as she slammed the door shut.

She saw Grayson running toward the fields, his shirt billowing in the wind like a flag of truce. She leapt off the porch. The wind slapped her and she staggered back. Dear God, the storm had returned so quickly, with such ferocity. ''John!''

She raced to the fields. She saw Grayson grab John's shoulder. John shrugged him off. She watched John snatching up bits of muddied cotton. It was ruined. It was all ruined. Why couldn't he leave it now?

By the time she neared them, Grayson and John were yelling at each other, their words tossed about on the wind, indecipherable. She grabbed John's arm. ''John, you have to get back into the house.'' She tried to pull him, but he jerked free.

''I've got to finish cleaning the fields,'' he yelled, looking at the soggy, muddy tufts in his hand. ''There's too much left.''

''John, whatever is left is ruined. The picking season is over—''

''No! It's not over until I say it's over.''

In horror, Abbie watched him turn away, searching for remnants from a dead field. She felt Grayson's arm come around her. ''Let's get you to the house and I'll come back for him.''

With his body as a flimsy shield against the wind and driving rain, he guided her back to the house. The children rushed to her, wrapping their arms around her, their small bodies trembling against hers.

She heard the wind howl its rage, the house tremble. A shutter tore from a window. Lydia shrieked.

"Abbie, you and the children get in the hearth," Jessye ordered.

"What about you?"

"The one in the bedroom will only hold one. I'll take it." She jerked her gaze to Grayson. "Lessen you want it."

"No, no, not at all," Grayson said.

Abbie gathered the children and ushered them toward the hearth while Jessye rushed into the bedroom.

"Children, crawl into the hearth," she ordered.

"Why are you putting them in the hearth?" Grayson asked.

"We've seen many a house fall and the chimney stand."

"Thank God, it's huge."

But not huge enough. The children crowded inside and Abbie was able to make her way into the alcove—barely. No room remained for anyone else. When she was tucked inside, Grayson took her hand. "I'll get Westland."

She wrapped her hand around his. "No, I won't take a chance on losing both of you."

She saw doubt in his eyes, and her love for him increased tenfold. She squeezed his hand. "He's bigger. He'll struggle and you might both get caught out there. Hopefully, he'll take shelter in the barn."

He nodded, as though better able to accept leaving John. He used his body to form a protective barrier over the opening to the hearth.

The pitch of the wind grew to an ear-splitting shriek. Abbie drew her children around her as much as she was able in the small confines. She felt the ground shaking, the earth trembling, Grayson's hand seeking hers. She intertwined their fingers just as she heard the deafening crack and the incredible roar that signaled the unleashing of hell's fury.

19

"**A**bbie, don't move."

She didn't think she could have if she wanted. She ached everywhere. She struggled to open her eyes and tried to smile at her sister. "Elizabeth?"

"Shhh. You just lie still until I've made sure nothing is broken."

Broken. Broken. Images flashed through her mind. The blackness of the hearth, the sound of splintering wood, the rumble, Grayson's groan, the children's screams.

She bolted upright.

"Abbie," Elizabeth scolded.

"Where are the children?" Her gaze fell on the remains of her house, wood strewn about and scattered.

"The children are fine. Jessye's fine."

She clutched her sister's hand. "Grayson?"

"You need to stay calm—"

"Oh, God."

338

Elizabeth pulled her close. "He wasn't as sheltered as you were."

"Dear God." She broke free of Elizabeth's hold and scrambled to her knees. "Where is he? Where's John?" She felt as though a hurricane was spinning inside her head, throwing out questions, demanding answers. She worked her way to her feet. "Where are they?" Her voice sounded like the shrieking wind. She turned to her sister. "Elizabeth, where are my children? I need to see my children."

With Elizabeth to support her, her legs shaking badly, she stepped over the rubble. Her gaze darted over the area, looking for Grayson, for John, for evidence that the unspoken truth she heard in her sister's voice was a lie.

She found the children with blankets wrapped around them, huddled in the back of a wagon, eating cookies taken from a plate that Amy was holding. She hugged each one fiercely, the tears streaming down her face. They were safe. Her babies were safe.

She walked a distance away from the wagon before she dared to ask, "Where's John?"

Silence . . .

She stumbled to a stop and glared at her sister. "Elizabeth, not telling me is not going to change the truth."

She pointed toward the fields. "He's over there."

Abbie was surprised by the calmness that settled over her as she walked toward the ruined, beaten fields because her heart knew—*knew*— what she would find in the middle of the group of kneeling men.

James stood and held out his hands imploringly. "You don't want to see this, Abbie."

"Don't tell me what I want, James. If that's my husband lying there, then I, by God, want to see him."

With a brusque nod, James stepped aside. When she knelt beside John, the other men quietly moved away, leaving her alone with a man who had given her as much as he could. She took his hand, fisted around bolls of cotton, and brought it to her lips. "You were a good husband, John Westland, a good man." The tears welled in her eyes, rolled over onto her cheeks. "I couldn't cry before, but I am now. This time, John, you died with someone loving you, not as powerful a love as you probably deserved, but love all the same." With a deep sigh, she gently placed his hand on his chest, tucking the cotton more securely into his grasp. "You and your cotton."

Rising unsteadily, she faced her brother and sister. "Where's Grayson?"

"Other side of the house," Elizabeth said. "We thought it best that the children not see—"

She didn't wait for her sister to finish. With a purpose, she strode across the yard. She saw Harry and Jessye standing a short distance away, each scolding the other. They were alive. What was there to argue about?

Just beyond the rubble that surrounded her chimney, she saw the amber gold of Kit's hair. Dear God, but she wanted to see wheat. She rounded the corner of the crumpled building that had once been her home. With her heart curling into an aching ball, she approached the man sitting on the ground, his back against one of the chimneys that had stood intact during the ordeal.

Heavy bandages were wrapped around his bare chest. His shockingly white bone was protruding through the torn and ragged flesh of his right arm. She had held his right hand during the tempest. Why hadn't he released his hold on her? Would it have made a difference?

He gave her an achingly sweet smile that nearly ripped her heart in two.

"Hello, sweetheart."

She dropped to her knees beside him, the tears swimming within her eyes. "You're all broken."

"The body is. The spirit might be all right. The doctor's gone in search of something he can use as a splint. I don't think he'll have any trouble finding something." With his good hand, he cradled her face and brought her head into the nook of his shoulder. "Dear God, Abbie, I've never been so terrified. Are you truly all right?"

"Yes. And the children. They're shaken, but fine. John . . . John—"

"I know, sweetheart. I heard. I'm sorry."

His voice carried the true measure of his sorrow, and she thought she might never love him more than she did at this moment. She moved around him so she could have his whole arm holding her instead of only his hand.

"The land always came first with him," she said

softly. "It's only fitting, I guess, that he should die within its arms."

She pressed her face against his shoulder, not caring who saw her weep as he held her close.

"Snakes! You gotta watch out for the snakes," Johnny warned.

Grayson glanced around, not liking the sound of that at all. "Snakes?" he repeated, wanting verification that the fanged serpents existed.

"They was here before, but usually they're afraid of us so they stay hidden. But the ground shakes during a storm and out they come."

"Wonderful."

"And the ants, too. It's the craziest thing. There'll be hordes of 'em in the water so you don't want to stand in water long."

"Ants."

"Yep. Come next summer, the mosquitoes will be awful on account of they'll be laying their eggs on all this water."

"How do you know all this?"

"Ezra Jones told me."

"Ah, yes, the lad with the weapons."

"Yep."

"Maybe he could take his gun and kill the snakes."

Johnny laughed as only a child could. Grayson was grateful someone found humor in this dreadful situation. The house was gone. Somehow the barn had remained intact—for the most part. It had a board missing here or there, but still it stood. He supposed

the wind had simply whistled through the structure
that was open at each end. The rain had beat the crops
into the ground which probably wasn't a bad thing
since most of the cotton had been picked. And Grayson couldn't help but feel that the soil would be
richer for all the water the tempest had dumped on
the land.

But still—snakes?

They had laid John Westland out at Elizabeth's.
Abbie was there now, sleeping. Grayson had come to
see what, if anything, could be salvaged.

"My pa's dead," Johnny blurted out of the blue.

Grayson jerked his gaze to the boy. "Yes, lad, he
is."

"You reckon he'll stay dead this time?"

"Yes, I'm afraid this time he won't be returning."

Johnny nodded. "Lydia says he came outside to
try and stop the storm. You think he mighta done
that?"

So much hope was reflected in the boy's eyes that
Grayson couldn't tell him the truth. His father had
come outside to save the cotton, not his children.
"He might have tried to stop the storm."

"Then he was mighty brave, wasn't he?"

Grayson smiled warmly. "Mighty brave."

Johnny raced off toward the barn, no doubt needing a few moments alone to ponder the magnitude of
the loss he'd suffered yesterday.

Grayson crouched in the fields and stared at the
muddy mess. He felt as uprooted as some of the
plants lying about. A respectable period of mourning
was in order for Abbie. Otherwise tongues would

wag. But if they were to get married right away, he could claim his baby and the child would never know the disgrace of being called a bastard.

He closed his eyes. If Abbie would consent to marry him. Yesterday, storms had raged within as well as without. That Abbie cared about him, he did not doubt. But did she still love him?

A wet, smelly substance landed with a smack against his cheek. His eyes flew open as he brought the sticky mud away from his face. Another round hit him.

Anger burning through him, he surged to his feet. Abbie stood a short distance away, her hand coated with the thick matter, her chest heaving, her eyes blazing.

"The land," she spat. "The land always has to come first, doesn't it?"

"What are you talking about?"

"I went through hell yesterday, and this morning I wake up and find out you've come to check on the land."

He held out his hands. "Because you were *asleep*. You had no need of me while you were sleeping."

"You want the land? Then, by God, you can have it." She scooped up another handful of mud and slung it at him. Too stunned by her actions, he felt it splatter across the center of his chest.

"The land always came first with John. And it comes first with you, doesn't it?" She flung another handful of mud at him, but it fell short of its mark as she sank to the wet earth. "I want to be loved for *me*, not for the land."

He crossed the space separating them and dropped to his knees before her. "I do love you for you."

"When I asked, you didn't deny it. You wanted the land!"

He swallowed hard, trying to think of a way to explain. "Yes, I can't deny that, but you have to understand. In England, if a man possesses land, he can gain a measure of respectability that is often granted only to the titled. When we were traveling here and I saw the abundance of land, I wanted it as I had never wanted anything . . . until I met you. That you had land was an unexpected bounty. But I would have loved you without it . . . and I still would have wanted you for my wife."

"But would you have asked me to marry you?"

"As God is my witness . . . yes. My mistake, Abbie, was in allowing my friends to think it was the land I coveted, and not you. It was easier to reveal greed instead of my heart."

He wrapped his hand around her arm. "Give the land to Johnny or sell it. We'll become gypsies. I don't care. As long as I have you, I don't care."

"Where would you hang your hat?"

"On a wagon wheel?"

She wiped the tears from her face, smearing mud across her cheeks. "You mean it? You love me— even if I come without land?"

"With all my heart."

John's funeral was held three days later, after the rising waters had receded and the ground was not as wet. Abbie did not care what her neighbors thought as Grayson stood beside her and the children. And when her grief caused the painful ache in her chest and her tears flowed, she didn't care if tongues wagged when Grayson put his arms around her. He was her strength, her comfort.

After the memorial service, with Grayson's hand pressed to the small of her back, she stood beside John's grave and accepted condolences. A widow once. A widow twice. She hoped never to be a widow again.

When the last of friends and family left, she knelt beside the headstone and pressed a cottonseed into the soil. As she rose, Grayson slipped his arm around her. She glanced at the blue skies. "Those clouds remind me of cotton."

Grayson's arms tightened around her, and she knew no words needed to be spoken.

"When they told me that he had died in the war, I didn't cry. Not one tear. I married him at sixteen. We were husband and wife, but never friends. He was always so formidable, so strong that he frightened me. And when he came home, I realized he was just a man."

She gazed up at Grayson. "I think a husband and wife should be friends. You asked me once to marry you."

His hand crept down to cover her stomach. "And I shall ask again when your period of mourning is over."

"I mourned John once before, and I will probably mourn his passing until the day I die, but I love you,

Grayson Rhodes, and I don't want to wait a whole
year to be your wife."

He bestowed upon her a tender smile. "What are
you doing tomorrow?"

"I want to sleep in the barn, too," Micah announced in his froggy voice.

Grayson watched as his wife—his wife, by God;
his father would never believe it—hugged the lad
closely.

"You can sleep in the barn tomorrow night," she
said.

"How come not tonight?"

Abbie blushed a deep red. "Because Grayson and
I need time alone to get used to being married."

"Will he live in the house with us after it's built?"
Lydia asked.

Abbie smiled at her daughter. "Yes."

Lydia snapped her gaze to Grayson. "Will you
read to us every night?"

"Every night." He had already ordered several
books.

"We should have a tournament to celebrate you
getting hitched," Johnny said.

Grayson patted his shoulder "We will, lad. As
soon as it gets a bit drier."

"Come on," Elizabeth said. "Hug your ma and
Grayson so we can head home."

The children did as she bade before scrambling
into the back of Elizabeth's wagon with her daugh-
ters. Elizabeth embraced Abbie. "You sure you don't
want to come to my house, too?"

"I'm sure," Abbie said.

Elizabeth cast a narrowed glance at Grayson. "A wedding night in a barn. Well, I suppose it'll be something to tell your grandchildren."

"Indeed it will be," he assured her. Grayson had considered taking his new bride to a room at the saloon, but that seemed tawdry. So he had selected a place that had surprisingly been spared the hurricane's wrath—a place of fond memories: the loft in Abbie's barn.

With a great deal of complaining, Kit and Harry had hauled a proper bed and mattress up to the loft. Jessye had hung lacy curtains over the opening. With a blush, she'd confided that women liked lacy things and he might do well to remember that.

"Good God, you almost look respectable," Harry said.

Grayson smiled. In the end, both Kit and Harry had stood beside him as he'd exchanged vows with Abbie. It had somehow seemed right.

"I don't think I kissed the bride," Kit said, reaching for Abbie.

Grayson clamped a hand on his shoulder. "You kissed her."

"Are you sure?"

"Absolutely." It had been no small peck on the cheek either, but a full-fledged kiss on the mouth that had Grayson contemplating punching his friend.

"And she didn't leave you for me? Incredible." He winked at Abbie. "Be happy, Abbie, and don't make him give up all his disreputable ways."

Smiling, she slipped her arm through Grayson's.

"There are some I will insist he keep."

Kit laughed before shaking Grayson's hand. "We'll be leaving tomorrow."

A tightness settled in Grayson's chest that had nothing to do with the bindings that held his mending ribs in place. "Let me know if you have any luck gathering a herd together."

"We will. Give some thought to joining us when we get ready to take them north. It has to be easier than cotton."

"I will, but I think it unlikely that I'll go. Based on all the information you collected, it seems to be an occupation more suited to a man who has neither a wife nor children." He shifted his gaze to Abbie. "And now I have both."

Grayson would have liked to carry Abbie to the loft, but neither his mending ribs nor his arm would allow it. When the house was built and he was completely healed, he would carry her over the threshold and to their room, a room they would share for the remainder of their lives.

But for now, he had to content himself with following her up the ladder. By the time he climbed into the loft, she was standing by the opening, the moonlight filtering through and around the billowing lacy curtains, casting an ethereal glow around her.

"I think I fell in love with you here," he said quietly as he walked toward her. "When I saw you holding my book, touching it . . . I wanted you to touch me."

Reaching out, she trailed her fingers along his cheek

before curving her arm around his neck and stepping within his clumsy embrace. "I think I fell in love with you when I saw you give Micah his first shave." She angled her head thoughtfully. "Or maybe it was that first night you caught me bathing . . . and you put the towel just beyond my reach. It seemed like something naughty that a rogue would do. I was surprised you didn't stay and watch me stand up to grab it."

"I did."

Her eyes darkened, and her brow furrowed. "What?"

"I only walked far enough into the shadows so you couldn't see me. Then I waited. And watched. When you came out of the water, I thought I'd never seen anything as beautiful in my whole life." He began to loosen her buttons. "It was pure torture to stand there and not touch you." He eased her bodice open to reveal the gentle swells of her breasts. "Thank God, I will never have to *not* touch you again."

He lowered his mouth to the tantalizing flesh, cursing the splint that made his right hand awkward when he cradled her breast and skimmed his thumb over the already tautening nipple. She smelled of roses, cotton fields, children's milky kisses, and a woman's musky sensuality. He trailed his lips along the column of her throat, nipped her chin, and settled his mouth possessively over hers.

She was his, completely, absolutely. From this day forward. He had not expected the relief that swamped him when the minister spoke those words—when she repeated them. No one, by God, would take her from him again. No one.

She would be his until the day he died. He planned for that day to be a long time coming.

He felt her fingers working to loosen his buttons. He drew away, giving her the freedom to remove his clothes.

"I fear that I'm a bit hampered by my injuries," he said as he watched her lower his trousers.

She gave him a wicked smile. "You don't look hampered to me."

He laughed, richly, deeply. "Dear God, Abbie, I think you're more of a rogue than I am."

"I never knew being wicked could be fun until I met you." She gave him a gentle shove, and he dropped onto the bed, relishing the sensations as she removed the remainder of his clothes.

Then she moved away from him, drew the curtains aside until she was limned by the moonlight, and began to remove her own clothes.

Abbie watched the appreciation creep into her husband's eyes, heard his rapid breathing, and saw his uninjured hand clench around the sheets as he sat on the bed, his gaze fastened on her. She had thought independence was being without a man. Independence was being with the right man.

With Grayson she was an equal, a partner. Her strengths tempered his weaknesses and his tempered hers. She smiled inwardly. If she had any weaknesses.

"Come here, Abbie," he rasped when the last of her clothing had pooled at her feet.

She stepped between his spread thighs and cradled his head as he buried his face between the valley of her breasts. She dropped her head back as he trailed kisses along the curves of her flesh, moaning throatily as his tongue circled, then his mouth closed around her nipple to suckle gently.

He wrapped his arm around her, pressing her against him as he lowered himself to the bed, carrying her with him. Awkwardly, he scooted to the head of the bed, and it wasn't until she saw him grimace that she realized he was experiencing discomfort.

Straddling his hips, she pressed a hand to his chest, just above the bandages. "Grayson, we don't have to do this."

He chuckled low. "Yes, we do." He cradled her cheek with his uninjured hand. "I love you."

"Oh, Grayson." She lowered her mouth to his, thinking she would never tire of his saying the words, never grow weary of his wanting her. With him by her side, she would never be alone or feel lonely.

She raised up, meeting and holding his gaze, shadowed by the night.

She slid off him and scrambled off the bed. He rolled over. "Where are you going?"

Very carefully, she removed the lace curtains from the opening. "I know Jessye meant well, but I prefer the light to the darkness."

She returned to the bed, returned to him.

"She said women liked lacy things," he told her.

"They do, but if I have a choice between lace and you in the moonlight . . ." She smiled seductively. "I prefer you."

"Thank God."

His callused hands skimmed over her body. She would not trade his roughened touch for the softest of silks. He cradled her hips, lifting her. His fingers dug into her as she lowered herself, sheathing him to the hilt.

She heard him release a deep sigh that more closely resembled a groan as he momentarily closed his eyes, and she silently thanked the moon for being so generous with its light so she could see the passion in his eyes when he opened them.

While he kept his injured hand on her hip, he cradled her face with his other hand and drew her down, down to his mouth for a devastating kiss that spoke of love and impatience. She rocked against him and the kiss deepened, their tongues imitating their bodies.

She tore her mouth from his, gasping for breath, reveling in his harsh breathing. She felt the sensations unfurling until she felt like the blossoms of cotton unfolding in the night.

He cupped her breast, shaping, molding, taunting the erect nipple, sending pleasure cascading through her. Her body tightened until she felt like the swelling boll of cotton, waiting ... waiting ...

Then the heightened sensations peaked and burst forth like the exploding cotton, revealing the whitened glory of fulfillment. As her back arched, she heard Grayson's roar of triumph, felt his final deep penetrating thrust, and the tremors wracking his body that so perfectly matched those rippling through her.

She collapsed on top of him, listening to his harsh

breathing, feeling the rapid thudding of his heart beneath her cheek. His hands lay heavy on her shoulders.

Summer was behind them and a cool breeze whispered over their bodies, lighting upon the dew that covered their flesh, slick and warm. She shivered, and he tugged the blanket over her.

"Am I too heavy?" she asked lethargically, thinking that it would be a shame if she was because she didn't think she could move off him if her life depended on it.

"No." He sighed, sounding equally content and relaxed.

He skimmed his fingers over the ridges of her spine. Her eyes drifted closed. She thought that of all the things she loved about Grayson she might love best that he prolonged making love even after the culmination of passion—with gentle touches and soft strokes—as though he loathed the separation that occurred after the joining as much as she did.

"Abbie?"

"Mmmm?"

"I don't think I'm accustomed to being married yet."

With a great deal of effort, she lifted her head and smiled. "Then we'll just have to keep working on it."

"That, sweetheart, was not work. That was my pleasure."

"Mine, too," she whispered as she lowered her mouth to his, kissing him tenderly, planting the seeds for another harvest of passion.

Epilogue

October 22, 1865

To the Duke of Harrington

Dear Father,

You told me this was a land of opportunity. How right you were. My land is especially so.

Yes, if you can believe it, I am a landowner. Not a great estate by any means, but I consider myself the wealthiest of men.

I suppose I should mention that I got married as well. I have a wonderful wife and three children. Soon we shall have a fourth. I always fancied this child would be a daughter, but Abbie assures me it is a son.

I have learned to trust her judgment.

We have weathered many a storm, she and I, and grown stronger as a result. Although she assures me I am still a rogue at heart and loves me in spite of it, or perhaps because of it.

If you should ever have occasion to visit, rest assured, we shall provide you with a place, as Abbie would say, to hang your hat.

> *My fondest regards,*
> *Grayson*

> *December 15, 1865*

My dearest Grayson,

Reading your letter brought me intense joy—joy equal to that which I experienced the first time I held you in my arms.

You have succeeded where lesser men, including myself, would have failed. How proud I am that your mother graced me not only with her love but with you for a son.

I often wish that things might have been different, but obligations, you know—they are often a damnably hard burden to carry.

Hold your wife close for it is through the love of a woman that a man truly gains wealth, and through the love of his children that he gains immortality.

> *With my deepest love,*
> *Your father*

"Grayson?"

At the softness of his wife's voice, Grayson set his

father's letter aside. He knew it by heart anyway. He rose from the chair by the window, walked to the bed, and stretched out beside her. Spreading his hand over her stomach, he waited for the movement of his child.

"Do you think your father will ever come visit?" she asked, threading her fingers through his hair.

"Perhaps. I'd like for my father to see my land." He had used the money he'd given Westland to purchase the farm next to Abbie's when the owner had decided to move on.

"I've been thinking," she said.

He glanced up, meeting and holding her violet gaze, thinking how much he loved the depth of emotion they so often reflected.

She licked her lips. "I think you should go with Kit and Harry in the spring—when they take the cattle north."

"I have no idea how long they'll be gone. Could be months. I want to be here when the baby is born."

"But it'll be exciting—a new venture."

"Being with you is quite exciting enough, thank you."

"It's about to get more exciting."

He quirked a brow. "Oh?"

Nodding, she brought an apple out from beneath the blankets. Very slowly, very carefully, she twisted the stem until it snapped. Then she slipped it into her mouth.

His own mouth went dry, his heart pounding as he watched the hollows in her cheeks, the pursing and pouting of her lips. With a triumphant gleam in her eye, she pressed her fingers to her lips and withdrew the knotted stem.

His stomach tightened, his breath caught. "My God."

She gave him a deliciously sensual smile. "You should see what else I can do with my tongue."

He moved up, cradling her cheek. "Ah, sweetheart, I have a feeling it will be my pleasure."

"You are so incredibly wicked," she purred.

"Incredibly wicked."

The Avon Romance Superleaders,
where all your dreams can—
and do—come true.

What would it be like . . . to be swept off your feet by a handsome stranger . . . Or to be a princess for a day? What if your world was turned upside down by an English lord? Or if your one true love came back to you?

It's like a wonderful, romantic dream . . . Enter a glittering ballroom in Regency London, wearing a gossamer gown and dancing with the most scandalous rake of the ton . . . Find yourself an independent woman of the Wild West, pulled into the arms of a jean-clad cowboy who lives by his own set of rules . . .Have your every need fulfilled by handsome millionaire . . .

At Avon, each month we bring to you love stories written by some of romance's best dream-

spinners—Kathleen Eagle, Christina Dodd, Barbara Freethy, and Lorraine Heath. Following are sneak peeks of their latest Superleaders . . .

"Kathleen Eagle is a national treasure."
—Susan Elizabeth Phillips

**Available now from Avon Books
Kathleen Eagle's latest
romantic bestseller
*The Last True Cowboy***

Everyone knows a cowboy is as good as his word, but what if the words are "I love you?"

When Julia Weslin returns to the High Horse ranch, she knows she has finally found a place to call home. And there she meets K. C. Houston, a long, lean cowboy . . . a man who's never stayed in one place for very long. K C. promises to help Julia revive the cash-strapped ranch, and Julia knows he'll keep that promise. But even though they find strength— and passion—in each other's arms, Julia also knows that K. C. has never promised he'd stay forever.

"Readers who like *The Horse Whisperer* will love this romance from Eagle."
Publishers Weekly

THE LAST TRUE COWBOY
by Kathleen Eagle

*J*ulia *turned her face to K. C.'s neck, and he could* feel the warmth of her breath when she whispered, "Where are you staying tonight?"

"Haven't thought that far ahead."

"Where are you going from here?"

"South, maybe west." He slid his hand slowly from the small of her back up to the center, pressing her close so that he could feel the rise and fall of her chest against his. "But that's beyond tonight. Way beyond where I am right now."

She tipped her head back and looked up at him. Her face was dewy, and her eyes glistened. "What are you thinking about now?"

He smiled. "Don't have to think when I'm dancin'. Comes natural."

"Maybe you'd like what I'm thinking."

"Maybe you'd like what you're feeling if you'd just . . ." He taught her with his hips. She laughed, and her hips improved on his move. "There, that's it. Just dance with me."

"It's easier than I thought." She gave her head a sassy toss. "Past tense. I'm not thinking anymore."

"Attagirl."

Suddenly, she studied him hard, then smiled. "I think you *would* be easy to love."

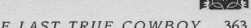

"You do, huh?" He smiled, too, but he was wondering what he'd said to bring her to that conclusion.

She slipped her arm around his neck and gave him a peck on the cheek. "And that you can do without. Good night, sweet cowboy."

He felt a little stung by her abrupt departure, by the motherly kiss that was about as welcome as a pat on the head, but when he saw how unsteadily she made her way toward the door, he followed her. He caught up with her just as she was stepping off the boardwalk. She turned the corner, and he wheeled around her, shoving his hands as far as they would go into the front pockets of his jeans as he matched her pace.

"Nobody's ever loved me and left me quite so fast before."

She laughed and linked her arm with his as though they'd been friends forever, and they strolled together. He figured she was headed for the little parking lot behind the bar, which was where he'd left his pickup. He decided that if she was heading home, he'd be doing the driving.

"You haven't told me your name."

"I assumed we had a tacit agreement to keep our names a mystery, since you're just passing through." She tipped her head back. "It's a pretty night, isn't it? Peaceful and still. No wind to blow you anywhere."

"It'll pick up tomorrow. Always does."

"And then you just go? South or west or wherever the road takes you?" She glanced askance, measuring him up for something. "Maybe I should hitch a ride. Would you take me with you?"

"Sure." He nodded toward the parking lot. "South or west? You choose."

"Right now? Choosing would take some thinking."

"True. We don't want that."

"So just take me with you." She tightened her grip on his arm. "Anywhere. This is a one-time-only offer, cowboy. I'll go with you anywhere."

"How about if I take you home?"

If you loved this excerpt from Kathleen Eagle's *The Last True Cowboy*, then you'll also love her newest hardcover, coming in August 1999 from Avon Books. Don't miss it!

Have you ever longed to be a princess for a day? To wear beautiful clothes, live in a palace, and have a handsome prince as your intended? Evangeline Scoffield gets to live that fantasy when a sensuous, virile man tells her that he is Danior and she is his runaway princess . . . his fiancée since childhood who he is bringing back to their homeland to marry. And as you read Christina Dodd's Runaway Princess, *you must decide if Evangeline is truly his bride . . . or the English orphan she claims she is . . .*

THE RUNAWAY PRINCESS
by Christina Dodd

*"***G***et your hands off of me."* She spoke with a fair imitation of calm.

"No, princess." He sounded very sure of himself, and as his grip tightened, her delicate glove escaped from his other hand.

Evangeline followed its descent with wide eyes. It landed on the toe of his black boot, an incongruous decoration on that serviceable leather. Then, slowly, her gaze traveled up his long legs, clad in black trousers. Up his torso, with its black jacket over a snowy white shirt. To his face.

No kindness softened the carved features. No flaw gave humanity to his godlike looks. He appeared to be an element of nature: inhuman, dangerous, harsh. Perhaps even . . . mad?

She had to do this.

Grabbing his wrist, she twisted. His fingers involuntarily opened, and she continued twisting until she stood next to him, his arm tucked, pale side up, beneath hers.

"I'd like to know where you've been to learn all that. If you hadn't hesitated . . ."

If she hadn't hesitated, she'd be free.

But she didn't say so. This man was, after all, mad. And she was a paltry orphan.

She remained still and the stranger relaxed slightly, looking her over as if he were a banker who'd been forced to foreclose on a hovel and found his new possession quite unprepossessing.

Fine. So she wasn't a beauty. The London dressmaker had clucked in disapproval at her coltish arms and legs, and the London hairdresser had refused to cut her long brown hair, citing distressing lack of curl. Her odd-colored eyes were faintly slanted, a heritage that would always be a mystery, and her chin tended to jut aggressively.

Only her skin had passed her personal test of nobility. So she might not be an enchantress, but she also wasn't this stranger's property, so he had no call to sneer like that. "Who are you?" she asked, this time in English.

His mouth, firm, full-lipped, and surrounded by a faint black beard, twisted in disgust. "You're playing

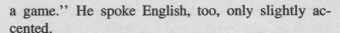

a game." He spoke English, too, only slightly accented.

"No . . ." Well, yes. The game of staying alive.

"You'll come back with me, whether you like it or not."

"Back?" *Where?*

He *towered* over her, and she had little experience with towering men. Actually, she had little experience with men at all. None had bothered to visit her eccentric guardian Leona, who viewed men as primitive, given to sweeping a woman away for the excitement of her mind and the pleasure of her body.

She started to inch toward the door, but without glancing at her he said, "If you move, I will have to give in to my baser instincts."

He didn't say what those instincts were; he didn't have to. Her imagination galloped on like a runaway horse.

She replied, "I think there's been a mistake. I am not who you think I am. That is, if who I surmise you think I am is really . . ."

He looked at her, and her voice trailed off.

"You dare deny you are Princess Ethelinda?"

If the truth weren't so pathetic, she could almost laugh. "I'm not any of the things Henri or the guests say I am. I'm only Miss Evangeline Scoffield of East Little Teignmouth, Cornwall."

Her declaration made no dent in his imperious stance, and he dismissed her claim without consideration. "What nonsense."

"There must be some superficial resemblance between us, and I'm flattered you think I'm a princess, but actually I'm a"—her laughter dried up—"nobody."

It was quite clear he didn't believe her.

Alex Carrigan, named one of the "Ten Most Eligible Bachelors," can command the best table at a restaurant, has the best looking model-of-the-moment on his arm . . . and always flies first class. But things are missing from his life, important things like a real home and a family. And when he meets Faith he soon discovers that the best things in life don't always come with a price tag . . .

In The Sweetest Thing, *Rita Award-winning author Barbara Freethy shows us that finding your one perfect love might take a lifetime, but that sometimes it's worth the wait . . .*

THE SWEETEST THING
by Barbara Freethy

"Well?"

Faith played with the medal that hung around her neck. She could see the amusement in his eyes, and it irritated the heck out of her. She felt like a blushing schoolgirl, and she was nothing of the kind.

"Maybe I should come back later."

"Maybe you shouldn't have come at all. In fact, why did you come?" Alex's stance was purely aggressive. "Did you come to help my grandfather search out his lost love? Because I don't get it. Why

369

would you take the time to bother? You're a busy woman. You have your own business. Your own life. Why do this? Unless . . ."

"Unless, what?"

"You're looking for an inheritance. If so, I hate to break it to you, but the old man hasn't got much more than that broken pot and a million stories to sell."

"How dare you! I have no interest in your grandfather's money."

"Then maybe it's me you're after. *San Francisco Magazine* called me one of the ten most eligible bachelors in the Bay Area."

"Bully for you. I didn't see the article, and if I had, I'd probably question their taste."

"Ooh, that hurts." Alex put a hand to his heart.

"I hope it does."

Faith tried to walk past him, but he caught her by the arm.

"Wait."

"Why? So you can insult me again?"

Alex let out a breath and shook his head. "You were in my dreams last night. I didn't like it."

His words startled her. When she looked into his eyes, she no longer saw dislike but fear. The emotion humbled him, made him far less arrogant, far more likeable.

"I can't stop thinking about you," he muttered. "What is it about you? You're not my type. Not at all."

"And you're not mine. That's why I haven't been thinking about you at all . . ." Her voice drifted away as she realized that wasn't true.

Grayson Rhodes is a maverick, the son of an English duke who refuses to live by society's rules. He leaves the stuffy drawing rooms of London behind to seek his fortune in a rough, rugged land called Texas. There, he discovers a place where a man is as good as his word, where you earn your fortune—not inherit it. And there he meets Abbie Westland . . . a woman whose fragile heart he dares not break.

In A Rogue In Texas by Rita Award-winning author Lorraine Heath, you'll meet a powerful, passionate man who rediscovers the promise of love . . .

A ROGUE IN TEXAS
by Lorraine Heath

*A*bigail stared at the man who had just made himself at home on her back porch. "It's scandalous for you to be out here while I'm bathing. You're . . . you're . . ." She couldn't think of a word bad enough to describe him or his behavior. In the moonlight, she saw him flash a grin.

"Disreputable?"

"You're no *gentleman*!"

"I never claimed to be. I've always thought of myself as a rogue."

She thrust out her hand. "Give me the towel."

"Finish your bath and I'll dry you off."

"No!" She cursed the tremble in her voice.

"What are you afraid of?" he asked quietly. "I won't ravish you. At least, not without your permission."

"You touched me!"

"That was an accident. Probably one of the most pleasurable accidents I've ever experienced."

Beneath the water, she clenched her hands. She was naked and vulnerable, and she could feel his gaze latched on to her, watching her, studying her.

"I never would have thought to take a bath outside, but it must be rather relaxing to have the hot water caressing your skin while the stars look down."

"It would be a sight more relaxing if you weren't here," she snapped.

He had the gall to laugh loudly, joyfully. "I'm not stopping you from washing. You're only a shadow in the night, Abbie."

Lord, she hated the way her name rolled off his tongue, soft and lyrical like a song she'd sing to put the babies to sleep.

She felt along the bottom of the tub until she found the soap she'd dropped when his hand had accidentally caressed her breast. The memory caused the heat of embarrassment to scald her cheeks. Her fingers closing around the soap, she brought it up, rubbing it back and forth across her breast, but she seemed unable to wash away the feel of his palm cradling her flesh . . .

If you liked these sneak peeks
at the Avon Romance Superleaders,
then don't miss the latest
Avon Superleader by Lisa Kleypas,
SOMEONE TO WATCH OVER ME,
her breathlessly awaited new
romantic bestseller . . .

What if you awakened in a stranger's bed, with no memory of your past? Your rescuer tells you he's Grant Morgan, that he was once your lover, and that you are Vivien Rose Duvall, a woman whose life has shocked Regency society to its core. Deep in your soul, you know he has you mistaken for someone else, but you have no proof . . . and he soon becomes your only hope to find out the truth.

In Someone to Watch Over Me, *Lisa Kleypas creates an unforgettable hero who is determined to rescue the one woman who has ever bewitched him . . .*

SOMEONE TO WATCH OVER ME
by Lisa Kleypas

Grant gathered Vivien in the mass of bedclothes and carefully pulled her into his arms. She gasped at the relief of it. He was so infinitely strong, holding her hard against him. Resting her head on his shoulder, she crushed her cheek against the linen of his shirt. Her vision was filled with details of him; the smooth, tanned skin, the silky-rough locks of dark brown hair . . .

"Who are you?" she whispered.

"Don't you remember?"

"No, I . . ." Thoughts and images eluded her efforts to capture them. She couldn't remember anything. There was blankness in every direction, a great confounding void.

He eased her head back, his warm fingers cupping around the back of her neck. A slight smile tipped the corners of his mouth. "I'm Grant Morgan."

"What h-happened to me?" She struggled to think. "I-I was in the water . . ."

"How did you end up in the river, Vivien?"

"Vivien?" she repeated in desperate confusion. 'Why did you call me that?"

"Don't you know your own name?" he asked quietly.

She shuddered with frightened sobs. "No . . . I don't know, I don't *know*. Help me," she whispered.

Long fingers slid gently over the side of her face. "It's all right. Don't be afraid."

And incredibly, she took comfort in his voice, his touch, his presence. His hands moved over her body, soothing her shaking limbs. Hazily, she wondered if this was what it was like when heavenly spirits ministered to the suffering. Yes . . . an angel's touch must be like this.

UNDER THE DESERT MOON, THERE'S NO PLACE TO HIDE

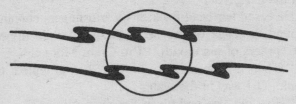

MOON MUSIC
by Faye Kellerman

"It's a credit to Kellerman's storytelling abilities
that long after she reveals 'who done it,'
readers will be frantically flipping pages
to find out how and why."
—*People Magazine*

ON SALE FROM AVON BOOKS
JULY 1999

DELECTABLE READING
AN ENTICING REBATE

SCOTTISH BRIDES
Christina Dodd,
Stephanie Laurens,
Julia Quinn, & Karen Ranney

Four of Avon's shining stars of romantic fiction create a luscious new anthology of utterly delightful wedding stories set in Scotland. To entice you to purchase a copy of this delicious collection, Avon is offering romance fans an exceptional rebate for purchasing SCOTTISH BRIDES (available in bookstores in June). Simply purchase a copy of the book, send in your proof-of-purchase (cash register receipt) along with the coupon below by December 31, 1999, and we'll send you a check for $2.00.

Void where prohibited by law.

Mail to:
Avon Books, Dept. BP, P.O. Box 767, Dresden, TN 38225

Name_____

Address_____

City_____

State/Zip_____